THE RAPE OF

St Clare is a tiny fishing village in Cornwall. A
Birmingham-based company, Pirana House
Investments, in partnership with the
Japanese, are looking for an obscure rural
location to develop their secret experiments
– extracting edible protein from fungus. They
are attracted to St Clare, where Lord St Clare
is selling his ancestral home. They pursue
negotiations under the guise of wishing to
develop the estate for tourism – but things go
awry as the private lives and amorous
machinations of the villagers become
inextricably tangled with the scheme to
develop the sleepy village. Perturbed that the
village will be destroyed, the
conservationists, led by the Rev. Owen
Borage, cause mayhem at the annual St Clare
festival. The Queen of the Feast is to be
chosen from among the unsullied maidens –
but a drugs raid and drunkenness on a large
scale ruin the chances of success – and put
an end to the plan for the wonder food
factory.

THE RAPE OF ST CLARE is riotous picaresque
satire in the comic tradition of Tom Sharpe.

The Rape of St Clare

Philip Trewinnard

NEW ENGLISH LIBRARY
Hodder and Stoughton

Copyright © 1986 by Philip Trewinnard

First published in Great Britain in 1986
by New English Library

NEL Paperback edition 1987

British Library C.I.P.

Trewinnard, Philip
   The rape of St. Clare.
   I. Title
   823'.914[F]   PR6070.R4/

ISBN 0 450 40940 6

Printed and bound in Great Britain for
Hodder and Stoughton Paperbacks, a
division of Hodder and Stoughton Ltd.,
Mill Road, Dunton Green, Sevenoaks,
Kent (Editorial Office: 47 Bedford
Square, London, WC1B 3DP) by
Cox & Wyman Ltd., Reading.

For A.M.W. Wherever.

Houl sooth, Tor leabm paravy an gwaynten.

(South sun, full belly, brings on pleasures of spring.)

Cornish proverb

PART ONE

MARCH

1

AFTERWARDS THEY would blame it all on Sharkley for coming up with such a daft scheme in the first place. Nevertheless, it had seemed like a good idea at the time. But then so had the *Titanic*.

Sharkley, however, would blame it all on the chubby young model in the advert for Powagrippa Supafirm 72-hour corselettes. But then *he* thought he was sick.

Sharkley had only just realised how sick he was. The disease had taken him totally by surprise at the tender age of thirty-five with the arrival of Ormskirk's new secretary, Maud.

Maud was fat, and there was no escaping the fact. She wobbled. Everywhere. From head to toe. And wore very short leather skirts, tight jumpers, black stockings, and eye make-up by the shovelful. And she aroused in Sharkley the most excruciating lust. Which terrified him, for he had never known true lust before, and he feared there might be something irreversibly degenerate about lusting after obese women.

(Ormskirk was also obese, as it happened. He was even *more* obese. But he did not wear short leather skirts, or black stockings, or shovelfuls of eye make-up. And Sharkley was definitely *not* stimulated by the sight of Ormskirk . . . Thank God. He could only cope with one perversion at a time.)

Maud had not remained Ormskirk's secretary for very long, however. Just long enough to sow the seeds of deviation in Sharkley's innocent breast and come to the

9

attention of the board of directors at Pirana House. Whereupon she had been transferred as fast as she could wobble, right up to the twenty-first floor, to wear short leather skirts and black stockings for Sir Wilfrid Macclesfield, chairman and chief executive. But the damage had been done. Maud had aroused in Sharkley a strange new turmoil of concupiscent desire, and he knew he could never look a plump wench straight in the thighs and ever feel quite the same again.

Why he should have fallen prey so suddenly to this monstrous deviation was a complete mystery to him. After all, he had been brought up in a decent class of council house, full of nice thin people. He had married and divorced a nice thin wife. He had stopped smoking. He had stopped buying South African apples as soon as the Pope had said it was bad for cricket. He had stopped wearing tight underpants as soon as Walsall Polytechnic had said it was bad for white mice. And he had stopped eating margarine as soon as the dairy industry had said it was bad for the dairy industry.

So what had he done to deserve this? Why, half-way through his thirty-sixth year, had he developed this insatiable longing for dumpy young trollops like Maud?

Anyway, he had, so that was that.

And there he was, sitting in a dentist's waiting-room in Edgbaston one dreary afternoon in March, pretending to be engrossed in an article in the *Woman's Mirror* whilst actually engrossed in the picture of a tubby little pudding bulging out of a Powagrippa Supafirm 72-hour corselette in the advertisement beneath, when the receptionist said:

'He's paying alimony to five wives. No wonder he's broke.'

Sharkley looked up. 'Who is?'

'Lord St Clare.'

'Who's he?'

She pointed at the *Woman's Mirror*.

'That bloke you're reading about.'

'Oh, *that* Lord St Clare.' Sharkley glanced at the top of the article.

It read: '*Frederick Charles Penryn Jago, 6th Baron St Clare, going bust in style . . .* '

'Five tubby wives, eh?' he mused. 'No wonder then.'

'*Last of a great Cornish estate up for grabs,*' he read.

And that was how the whole ghastly business began.

Leisure and Pleasure division was still very much the baby at Pirana House. It had been conceived in March, born in hope, and christened in a storm of Moët et Chandon. But one year on, nobody was at all sure whether they had an infant prodigy on their hands or a prime case for child euthanasia.

It had all started because the corporation had too much cash to invest. And the directors of Pirana House Investments plc of Birmingham, Europe's largest manufacturer of instant tasteless food, had decided that the company's image was boring. Which it was. And that profits from their notorious chain of Kwikbite and Speedisnak take-aways, chuck-aways and junk diners were flagging. Which they were. And that it seemed a shame to waste perfectly good money by investing it in British industry. Which anybody in Tokyo could have told them *years* ago.

So Sir Wilfrid Macclesfield OBE, chairman and chief executive, and all his wise boffins with their B.Sc.(Econ.)s, had put all their wise heads together, knocked back gallons of tax-deductible gin, and finally come to the conclusion that there was nothing in the United Kingdom that offered much real growth potential for the next few decades except unemployment. And with the prospect of six million permanently on the dole by the end of the century, they all agreed that it was their patriotic duty to Queen, country and shareholders to start marketing plenty of time-consuming things f r all those unoccupied people to waste their unemployment benefit on.

So Leisure and Pleasure division had been born, ensconced in some posh-looking offices on the sixteenth floor, and placed under the executive control of Geoffrey Ormskirk.

For the first six months or so, L and P had enjoyed considerable prestige at Pirana House. Its commercial adventurism seemed, to lesser mortals like typists and tea ladies, to be a revolutionary departure from the humdrum world of freeze-dried spaghetti Veronese, dehydrated pizzas, and Instamix Kwikfry hamburger powder. Ormskirk had been looked up to as the last of the nation's great merchant pioneers. And his brand new team of investment scouts, poached exclusively from reputable financial institutions like the First National Bank of Haiti, had been seen as intrepid young frontier fighters, blazing a trail that would lead Pirana House to the promised land.

As time went by, L and P had begun to show results. They had acquired a company that made tents, and hang-gliders, and microlight aircraft that kept crashing. They had invested in mountaineering gear, indoor ski slopes, and insurance policies for broken legs. And they'd bought a chain of DIY stores, hiring out power tools to enable the ordinary, average, incompetent handyman to damage his home beyond repair.

Meanwhile, public relations division had begun to send a hot-air balloon team around the country, gatecrashing major sporting events, in the faint hope that Joe Public might start associating Pirana House rather more with fun and fitness, and rather less with salmonella poisoning and summonses under the Public Health Act.

Yet it was all pretty tentative stuff. The odd fifty thousand pounds here, the odd fifty thousand there. And compared to the millions that Pirana House International were pumping into an Anglo-Yugoslav holiday complex on the Adriatic, it was miserably small beer indeed. And by the end of the first year of L and P's existence, His Phenomenal Significance, Sir Wilfrid Macclesfield, had come to the conclusion that L and P was deficient in three basic essentials: imagination, dedication, and balls.

The problem was Ormskirk, who, for all his two-and-a-quarter hundredweight of bluff and bluster, was secretly terrified that he might one day authorise the most spectacular financial cock-up in the world. Consequently, he refused to lend his illegible signature of approval to any investment scheme that his whizz kids put before him unless every possible hazard short of thermonuclear war had been eliminated.

It was for this reason that not one scheme from the fertile mind of Mervyn Sharkley had ever got further than the capacious wastepaper basket of Geoffrey Ormskirk. For Sharkley's high performance, formula one, financial brain was tuned to turn over on minimum budgets of seven figures, and the mere thought of that level of risk capital sent a *frisson* of feedback through Ormskirk's pacemaker.

Nevertheless, Ormskirk had high hopes of Mervyn Sharkley, and took no pleasure in scuppering every new idea that he came up with. For Mervyn was one of the most promising investment scouts on the L and P team. He was fresh from the ruins of a fund management outfit that had bedazzled the world one year, only to crash spectacularly the next, leaving millions of small investors utterly destitute, and all the directors' wives miraculously possessed of vast fortunes in Panamanian banks. Mervyn would go far, in Ormskirk's considered opinion. For the time being, however . . .

'Look, I hate to pour cold water on this latest idea of yours, Mervyn, old son,' he said. 'But chalet camps in Cornwall . . . ? That kind of thing went out with sugar rationing, and trolley buses and *Mrs Dale's Diary*.'

'Ah, but just consider,' said Sharkley, drawing his chair closer to Ormskirk's desk, 'the state of the nation. The British tourist industry could be on the threshold of a fantastic renaissance. The day of genuine, index-linked, mass poverty is with us at long last. And with all this unemployment, more and more ordinary working people are finding they can't afford to catch diarrhoea in Torremolinos or Corfu any more. So they're taking their holidays right here in Britain.'

'What's that got to do with Cornwall?' said Ormskirk.

'That county is an under-exploited Mecca of tourist potential.'

'Who says?'

'Everybody.'

'Who's everybody?'

'Everybody in Cornwall, for a start. And they should know. All it needs is the right kind of marketing.'

'And what *is* the right kind of marketing?'

'Ethnic.'

'Ethnic?' Ormskirk thought that had something to do with the West Indies.

'Yes, ethnic,' said Sharkley. 'In this age of synthetics, technology and automation, the ordinary working man feels depersonalised. He's craving for anything ethnic.'

'I see,' said Ormskirk, not seeing at all. 'And what is so ethnic about this Cornish fishing village of yours?'

Sharkley snapped open his attaché case and took out a scruffy little book that he had found in the vaults of the city library. It smelt of old age and rats' pee.

'May I read you something?'

'If you insist,' said Ormskirk unhappily. He didn't like books. They made him feel tired.

'I quote,' Sharkley said, 'from the 1905 edition of *Interesting Things To Do In Cornwall*. By Emily Beckwith-Brown. Chapter eight.' He cleared his throat and read aloud: '*Many parishes in Cornwall hold a feast day every year to commemorate the Celtic saint to whom their church is dedicated. Of all such feast days, I have never seen one more joyously celebrated than at St Clare, a fishing village in West Penwith not many miles from the Land's End, where there is a spring fayre, a wrestling tournament, and an annual contest of hurling between the east and west villagers. In the afternoon, a queen of feast is chosen from amongst the fairest maidens of the village and crowned with much festive pomp and ceremony, and a great banquet is held for everyone upon the common fields. Never in my travels through the Duchy have I come across a saint's feast more rapturously celebrated than at St Clare, where fisherman, tinner and farmer alike all lift their hearts in unison to greet the coming of spring.*'

Sharkley closed the book and looked at Ormskirk.

14

'Very interesting, I'm sure,' said Ormskirk, bored silly. 'But that was in 1900.'

'1905,' said Sharkley, as if it made any difference.

'That was before the First World War,' Ormskirk continued, with a fine grasp of historical perspective. 'A lot of things happened in those days.'

Which of course was perfectly true.

'But it's still going on, Geoff. Today. Only now they have it on spring bank holiday Monday. It's a major world event, all over the village.'

'Maybe,' said Ormskirk, unimpressed. 'But I don't see what that's got to do with us buying Lord St Clare's estate and plonking chalets all over it.'

'But it's history,' Sharkley protested. 'It's atavistic. It's the stuff of legend and folklore. It's ethnic. There's money in ethnic. With the right marketing and promotion we could make that village the biggest tourist attraction in the West Country.'

'Even if holidays in Cornwall *are* a growth industry, Mervyn,' Ormskirk observed coolly, 'spring bank holiday only comes once a year.'

'Well, use your imagination, Geoff. We'll make sure it comes once a *week*! We'll get it all organised on a sound commercial footing and get those yokels hurling and wrestling and crowning their feast queens right through the season. We'll have that village jam-packed with tourists from all over the world, celebrating spring bank holiday Monday every weekend from May to September! And Pirana House will have the biggest chalet camp in the country right there on site.'

Ormskirk stared out of his sixteenth-floor window and watched a distant DC8 ascend gracefully into the clouds above Coventry. He didn't like the thought of investing in places like Cornwall. It was full of countryside for one thing. Ormskirk didn't like countryside. He didn't trust it. It was full of sinister things one couldn't rely on. Like trees, and birds, and grass. He preferred the safety of civilisation. He liked to see a nice big reassuring factory. Or a blast furnace. Or the M6 with hundreds of shiny new cars whizzing along

15

between lane closures. He wasn't sure about this *ethnic* vogue either. It was all very well for Social Democrats, and muesli eaters, and people in yellow Citroëns with '*Nukes — no thanks*' stickers all over them. But was there really a reliable long-term profit in it?

'What else is Lord St Clare selling?' he asked, pensively scratching some of his chins.

'A terrace of eight fishermen's cottages with sitting tenants . . . '

'We'd have to boot that lot out, for a start.'

'A pub. And his old ancestral mansion, Tremorna Hall.'

'What do we want an ancestral mansion for?'

'We turn it into a highly exclusive, private hotel. Give it the full ethnic treatment, and charge foreigners the earth.'

'And this chalet camp?'

'It hasn't been built yet. It's still just the remains of a poultry farm that went bust, on fifty acres.'

'Planning consent?'

'He got outline permission and then ran out of gelt.'

'Who did?'

'This Lord St Clare.'

Ormskirk said *hmmmm* for about a quarter of a minute and stroked his chins again. It all sounded very dubious indeed.

'For Christ's sake, Geoff!' Sharkley exclaimed. 'It's good real estate, going for a song. We can only make a profit on it what*ever* happens.'

'Hmmmm,' said Ormskirk.

Sharkley began to wilt with frustration. You could offer Ormskirk a ten-pound note, free, gratis and for nothing, and it would still take him three weeks, two ulcers and one blockage of the coronary artery to decide whether or not he could lose on the deal.

'Just how desperate do you think he is to sell up?' Ormskirk wondered, cheered a little by the prospect of fleecing an incipient bankrupt.

'No idea.'

It occurred to Ormskirk that he'd never even heard the name before.

'Just who is this bloke, anyway? I take it he is a real lord, is he?'

'I suppose so,' Sharkley replied. 'Does it matter?'

'Of course it matters. There's profit in genuine aristocrats. We could market *him* as well.'

'Now *that's* a thought,' said Sharkley.

In fact, coming from a man with about as much imagination as a suet pudding, it was nothing short of a brainwave.

2

There is a rugged, narrow leg of land, about eighty miles long on a clear day, that sticks out of the bottom left-hand corner of Great Britain, defiantly separating the Atlantic Ocean and the English Channel with a barrier of granite, furze and pasties. Nobody is sure why, but it is called Cornwall.

The native inhabitants of this land are descendants of the ancient Celtic tribes who, in the course of five centuries before the birth of Christ, wandered off in all directions from the regions of the Lower Danube, as far as Asia Minor in the east and Ireland in the west, sharing with everyone they met along the way their unique love of civilisation, culture and extreme violence. They were extraordinary people, who did extraordinary things . . . like sacking Rome, and sacking Delphi, and settling in Redruth.

These Ancient Britons first wandered into Cornwall in about 600 BC, and despite the rain, they kept on coming in dribs and drabs for the next thousand years or so . . . Fleeing first the Romans, then the Angles, the Saxons, the Vikings, the Greater London Council, and all those other fun people who have helped to land Britain in the mess she's in today.

They were a poor, pagan people, saved from Satan and a horrible hereafter only by the goodly works of Welsh and Irish missionaries, who paddled ashore in the fifth and sixth centuries AD bearing the glad tidings about Jesus Christ, choral singing and Gaelic whiskey. In their wake they left many a pious Christian Cornishman, and many a village named after a Celtic saint. Hence St Ives, St Austell, St Columb . . . And if not last then most certainly least, that tiny hamlet on the craggy coast betwixt Penzance and Land's End: St Clare.

For centuries the people of St Clare remained isolated on that storm-scarred, south-western tip of England, scratching a subsistence from the soil, mining the tin and copper, or drifting and seining the shoals of pilchard around their shores. Many starved. A few prospered. And just one of them made a fortune: Matthew Saul Jago.

Matty Jago was a sailor and freebooting adventurer, the illiterate son of a fisherman, born in St Clare in about 1560. But such was the equality of opportunity in the days of Good Queen Bess that by the year 1592, when he commissioned the building of that fine Elizabethan mansion, Tremorna Hall, Matty Jago had amassed a vast fortune from smuggling, piracy and the pillaging of wrecked merchantmen that he was said to have lured onto rocks with false beacons.

This jolly fellow — himself taken prisoner by Turkish pirates off the Lizard in 1615 and never seen again — bequeathed sufficient wealth to keep his descendants in idleness and luxury for many centuries to come. And successive generations of the Jago family had applied themselves religiously to the responsibilities of their inheritance, tirelessly splashing up and down the muddy highways of West Cornwall in their carriages, keeping the peasantry in order and spreading syphilis.

It had come then as a terrible shock to the entire family when, in the year 1815, one of their number, one Colonel William Jago, had actually done something useful for a change (albeit by accident), and had achieved national fame thereby.

Colonel Will had bought himself a commission in the hussars, because he'd had nothing better to do at the time and fancied himself in the uniform. But soon after, to his horror, he had found himself dispatched to Belgium to fight the odious Bonaparte. And after various unsuccessful attempts to flog his commission at a bargain price to passing Flemish swineherds, he'd ended up on the battlefield at Waterloo, where he'd spent a thoroughly exhausting day, galloping around trying to keep out of everyone's way.

At a crucial moment in the battle, however, his horse — over which he'd never had the remotest semblance of control — had bolted . . . straight for the French lines. Yodelling with terror, Colonel Will had plunged clean through the thick of Napoleon's crack infantry corps, and straight out the other side, with his eyes firmly shut. And in doing so had precipitated a major British cavalry charge that had torn the French ranks to pieces.

In recognition of his outstanding valour and tactical genius, Colonel Will had been ennobled by the Prince Regent, and in later life had become a great favourite at court.

How it could be, then, after such selfless service to King and country by the first Lord St Clare, that within less than two hundred years the Jago family had been totally forgotten by a thankless nation, was a mystery . . . to anyone who still remembered them. Nevertheless, it was a fact — however unpalatable it may have been to those few remaining descendants of Matthew Saul Jago who had not yet parted company with their marbles or emigrated to the Falkland Islands, or both — that within less than one hundred and fifty years, a succession of congenital half-wits and dissolute prodigals had managed to dissipate the whole of that colossal fortune that their Elizabethan ancestor had worked so hard to plunder, and had left not so much as a footprint in the passage of British history in so doing.

And thus it had come to pass that Frederick Charles Penryn Jago, 6th Baron St Clare, oppressed by a burgeoning accumulation of debts, was facing the springtime of his fifty-third year with only the last few acres of a once great estate to his name, a FOR SALE sign at his gates, and a Mervyn Sharkley bashing on the front door.

Freddie did not much like the look of this Sharkley character at all. He arrived in the very latest Ford Something-or-other, with his jacket on a coat-hanger on the door pillar and Manuel's 'Music of the Mountains' on the cassette deck. He was a little fellow, with an expensive hair-do that didn't quite hide his bald patch. And he was littered with vulgar-looking gold bracelets, rings, tie-pins, necklaces, dog tags and anything else he could possibly engrave *Mervyn* on. He smiled up at Freddie (and Freddie was only five feet seven in trousers) through grey-tinted spectacles, and tore loose the Velcro from the wrist-tabs of his Niki Lauda driving gloves.

'Mervyn Sharkley,' he announced. 'Pirana House.'

He reached into the inside pocket of his jacket and produced several volumes of the very latest credit cards, a driving licence, a collection of Japanese writing implements, a coupon that knocked twenty pence off the price of his next litre of Domestos bleach, and finally a business card. He offered it to Freddie as if it were a collector's item.

Visiting businessmen from up-country were not always given the wholly deferential welcome which they seemed to expect of their less sophisticated counterparts west of the Tamar. (And to the people of St Clare, up-country meant anywhere east of Camborne.) Freddie, however, was a gentleman. Civilised, courteous and practically skint. And knowing full well that Pirana House was one of the richest temples of capitalism in the UK, and that this vulgar little acolyte of theirs had eternal financial salvation within his gift, he lavished upon Sharkley one hospitable cup of Maxwell House and two custard creams, and sped him down to the village in a warm Land Rover to show him what was up for sale.

It was possible to stroll around the whole of St Clare in less than an hour, but Sharkley wanted a map.

Freddie said there were no maps.

Sharkley said he had to have a map, it was necessary.

Freddie said it was not necessary. This was a village of nine hundred and sixty-two inhabitants, one main street and thirty-nine lanes. Nobody had ever got lost in St Clare, and anyone who *had* should have been shot.

But Sharkley still wanted a map. He said it was essential and blamed it on Ormskirk. He blamed everything on Ormskirk. So Freddie parked the Land Rover on East Quay, borrowed Sharkley's Japanese rolling-ball liquid pencil, and drew a sketch map on the back of a nice letter from Coutts bank reminding him he still owed them God's earth.

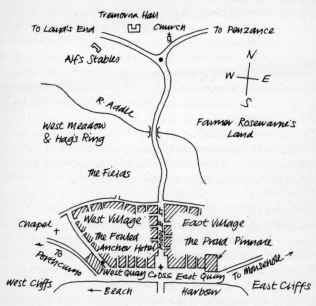

Freddie handed this precision-drawn cartographical gem to Sharkley and told him to present it to Ormskirk with his compliments.

Sharkley thanked him and said this would be enormously helpful. But as the place was so tiny, he wondered why it was divided into East village and West village.

Freddie explained that traditionally the fishing community had lived on the east side and the mining community on the west, and that in bygone days there had been a fierce and often violent rivalry betwixt the two.

Sharkley asked why.

Freddie said, because there *had*.

They climbed out of the Land Rover and walked across East Quay. Freddie pointed to a terrace of eight white-washed cottages at the foot of East Cliff. He said those were fishermen's cottages, and part of the Jago estate that was up for sale.

Sharkley said that was interesting and asked if they were in good condition.

Freddie said he hadn't got the faintest idea; and since the families who lived there only paid him about five bob a month in rent, he didn't actually give a monkey's.

He pointed across the quay to a rambling eighteenth-century building on the corner of the Mousehole road. That was part of the Jago estate too.

Sharkley chuckled and said, ho-ho, that looked like a right old tip of a barn.

Freddie did not chuckle. He said it was not a right old tip of a barn, it was the Proud Pinnace tavern, one of the most famous pubs in the world. It was full of smelly fishing nets and green glass floats, and packed to the eaves with grockles in the season.

Sharkley asked what a grockle was.

Freddie said that a grockle was a visitor from outside the county, usually a tourist, but could equally be a Sharkley.

Sharkley said that was interesting, and turned towards West Quay to survey the deserted strip of sandy beach and the sea-front cafés and souvenir shops, all closed and awaiting a lick of fresh paint before the approaching holiday season.

Two fishermen in oily sweaters and heavy rubber boots plodded past, giving Freddie a friendly nod.

One said, 'Right an?' And the other, ' 'Ow be doan, old mate?' And they walked on by.

'Tom Hoskin and Ben Curnow,' said Freddie. 'They're brothers-in-law. Tenants of mine in those cottages on East Cliff.'

'Friendly,' observed Sharkley, unimpressed. He was not at all convinced that the labouring classes calling their superiors *'old mate'* was a sign of a healthy society. This world was quite unpredictable enough as it was without people pissing over the sluicegates of social distinction.

But Freddie seemed to be on casual terms with almost everyone. They strolled along the narrow lanes that ran off either side of Middle Street, past endless terraces of eccentric, bulging shops, full of eccentric, bulging people wandering about their business. And Freddie said hello to everyone he saw, and even stopped to chat to one old harridan.

'Granny Polkinghorne,' he explained when she'd gone. 'The village pellar.'

'The what?'

'The witch.'

'Which what?'

Freddie said forget it.

Sharkley laughed. Freddie didn't.

Sharkley said this really was quite quite exquisite. Oozing in quaint, olde-worlde charm. Ormskirk would be tickled pink.

Freddie decided he didn't like Ormskirk.

He took Sharkley up Chapel Lane, waved to the lovely young widow Tremayne in her front garden as he passed, and stopped in front of the Methodist chapel.

'The building is theirs. But the land is part of the Jago estate. The rent isn't worth a Chinaman's fart but the minister, Micah Dredge, can be a powerful ally in this community . . . and a powerful enemy.'

'You mean,' said Sharkley, 'if one wanted to do something contentious here . . . like construct a chalet camp?'

That, said Freddie, was precisely what he meant. Because the local Anglican vicar, the Reverend Owen Borage, was a soppy conservationist, opposed to pretty well everything that could possibly be opposed. And relations between the Anglicans and the Methodists were unchristian at best.

Sharkley said that wouldn't worry him; he was a Catholic.

And Freddie never did quite work out what he meant by that.

*　　　*　　　*

Inland from the village there lay a fertile valley, divided by the winding lane that led to Tremorna Hall and the parish church, at the confluence of the roads to Penzance and Land's End. Most of the valley on the west side of that lane was part of the Jago estate. And most of the land to the east belonged to Tucker Rosewarne, the local farmer.

Half-way along the lane, the shallow waters of the river Addle flowed beneath an old humpback bridge, just wide enough to take the Western National omnibus that crossed it six times a day in the course of its unhurried shuttle between St Clare and Penzance.

And here, beside the bridge, Ned Gummoe — most ancient of swains, sages and soothsayers — was leaning upon a five-barred gate, puffing contentedly on a gnarled briar packed with smouldering black shag, and chatting to Socrates the bull.

The eternal mystery of spring. This was the text of Ned Gummoe's discourse to Socrates this fine March morning. Green shoots of cereals were already peeping through the furrowed soil in Rosewarne's fields. New-born lambs were gambolling on the hillsides. Swallows were back on Blakey's Ridge. And from the distant graveyard came the clink of shovel upon stony ground, as Eli Tonkin prepared a sacred resting place for old mother Hicks, dear soul, just now passed on. What, Ned wondered aloud, was the meaning to it all?

Socrates had his opinions on the matter but was keeping them to himself. In any case, he was more interested in the Land Rover that had just drawn up on the fields across the road.

Ned followed his solemn brown gaze. That was Lord Fred's Land Rover. And he had a stranger with him. Looked a bit Arabic to Ned. Darkish. In a suit. With a *waistcoat*. The only people who wore suits with waistcoats, in Ned's experience, were officials from the county council.

He observed the two men for a while before putting it to Socrates that no one in a waistcoat could be up to all good. And Socrates did not disagree. So Ned thought he'd better stroll over in that direction and accidentally overhear what they were talking about.

24

' 'Cos strangers do come, and strangers do gaw,' he told Socrates, recalling a jewel of Celtic wisdom passed on by his long-dead granddad. 'And that's how the Devil comes among us, you knaw.'

Socrates agreed in principle, but kept his peace.

The Fields, as they were known locally, comprised some thirty acres of open grassland that had belonged to the Jago family ever since Matthew the pirate's time. But they had been used as common recreation ground for over two hundred years. On the one side they were bordered by the road, and on the other by a bank of trees and a dry-stone wall that divided them from West Meadows.

West Meadows.– fifty acres of rough pasture that sloped gently up towards Blakey's Ridge, high above the valley — was where Freddie had planned to build his chalet camp.

'The perfect site,' he said to Sharkley. 'Natural landscaping. Short walk from the beach and the local shops. Horse riding on the doorstep . . . ' He pointed to what had once been his family's stables, on the far side of the meadows.

'Do they go with the estate too?' asked Sharkley.

'No. I sold those some years ago to Alf. Quite a thriving little business she's got there now.'

'And what are all those enormous stones?' Sharkley pointed to a rough circle of massive granite blocks lying half-buried in the middle of West Meadows.

'The Hag's Ring,' said Freddie. 'Some pagan thing. Like Stonehenge. It was hallowed ground to the Druids.'

'No kidding?' Sharkley was intrigued. 'Now that fascinates me. I'm really getting a taste for this ethnic lark.'

'Indeed?' said Freddie. He didn't want to be too rude to Sharkley — after all, the nasty little turd *was* holding out some semblance of a financial lifeline in his direction — but he was growing increasingly suspicious of Pirana House's intentions. 'Forgive my asking,' he went on, 'but one doesn't usually associate your company's name with *holiday* developments.'

'But one will,' Sharkley replied confidently. 'Pirana House is diversifying into the leisure and pleasure business in a big way. Pirana International have just gone in with a Yugoslav consortium to put up a thirty-million-dollar holiday complex on the Adriatic.'

'Thirty *how* much . . . ?' said Freddie, hastily reconsidering the ante on the Jago estate.

'Mind you, there's a big spin-off there for our mainstream fast-food catering side,' Sharkley added.

He broke off as an old rustic with a face like a bristly sultana tottered towards them. The ancient doffed a disgusting, sweat-stained hat in their direction.

'Keeping well, Mr Gummoe?' Freddie enquired.

'Aw ais,' Ned replied, with a toothless grin. 'Spry as a spring lamb, you.' .

He shuffled on by, then stopped and took a very long time to find a match and relight his pipe.

'Thirty million seems a hell of a lot for one holiday complex,' Freddie resumed.

'Well, it's going to be something pretty special,' said Sharkley. 'Sixteen-storey hotel and conference centre. Sports stadium, yachting marina, golf course, tennis courts, heliport, everything you can think of.'

Close by, Ned was listening incredulously to every word.

'The natives won't be any too pleased, mind you,' Sharkley continued. 'Because we'll have to flatten half the local village. But that's progress for you. And a lot of those peasant hovels out there aren't fit for habitation anyway.'

Flatten half the village . . . ? Ned choked on his pipe. *Sixty-storey hotel? Yachting stadium? Peasant hovels . . . ?* He waited, wide-eyed with anticipation, for the young Arab to say more. But at that point, the two men turned back towards the Land Rover and walked out of his hearing.

The natives won't be any too pleased . . . Ned could hardly believe his ears. Lord Fred selling out to the Arabs? He stumbled back onto the lane and set off towards the village at a brisk lurch to convey these devastating tidings to the patrons of the Proud Pinnace.

*　　　*　　　*

That afternoon, Lord Fred took Sharkley round Tremorna Hall.

Tremorna was one of the finest Elizabethan houses in the West Country. It was a handsome, granite-built mansion, three storeys high, and forming three sides of a square, with typically Elizabethan features — tall chimneys, high, mullioned windows with tiny, square lights and flattened-arch doorways.

Sharkley was enormously impressed. As soon as he walked into the place he was overwhelmed by the atmosphere and undeveloped potential of it all. It was full of oak-panelled rooms and creaking floorboards. There was a magnificent, one-hundred-foot long gallery on the first floor, hung with family portraits by artists with unpronounceable names. In the library downstairs, a real live prince had dropped dead at the harpsichord. The east wing was haunted by the ghost of a young lady in grey, and the whole place was riddled from top to bottom with smugglers' secret passages.

Outside, the house lay nestling in twelve acres of mature grounds, lovingly neglected for many years . . . Freddie being loath to interfere with the course of nature, especially when it involved paying wages or doing anything remotely like work. So what had once been flower gardens, landscaped terraces and flourishing orchards, had now begun to take on the appearance of a tropical rain forest, where Freddie's daughter, Miranda, was tenderly nurturing luxuriant beds of marijuana.

Nature, however, was no match for Sharkley. Chemical defoliants and bulldozers would soon obliterate all traces of plant-life, and in no time at all, Tremorna would be able to boast a beautiful, new, twelve-acre car park, with paved barbecue patios *en suite*, and super-de-luxe, concrete play areas for tiny tots.

Even Ormskirk would like this place, Sharkley reckoned. It groaned with atmosphere. It reeked of romance. You could *feel* history with every step you took. Seventeenth-century smugglers had hidden in those cellars. An eighteenth-century phantom walked those passages.

Nineteenth-century royalty had slept in those beds. And whole generations of loyal maidservants had yielded up their virginity to the ruling classes in those garrets. The house had everything that a cultured, discerning tourist could ever wish to find. Here was a forgotten corner of the nation, still wreathed in mystery, legend and downright lies.

'Tell me,' said Sharkley, over tea in the library, 'are there any medieval rights you still have? Like . . . flogging the locals, or chucking old biddies in the duck-pond?'

'Heavens, no,' said Freddie. 'I merely have an obligation, according to the letters patent of my title, to supply the Duke of Cornwall with one hundred puissant men-at-arms whenever he asks for them.'

'Get away . . . ?'

'Fortunately for me, the present incumbent hasn't been in touch yet.'

Puissant men-at-arms, thought Sharkley. The Yanks would love that kind of stuff.

'Why do you ask?' Freddie enquired, growing progressively irritated with this tiresome homunculus as the day wore on.

'Well, I wondered . . . Have you ever considered opening this house as a hotel?'

'As a . . . what?'

'A hotel?'

'An hotel?'

'Yes. A hotel.'

Freddie couldn't believe what he was hearing. 'An ho-*tel*! My *house*?'

'An exciting prospect, eh?' Sharkley went on enthusiastically. Having been born and raised in a council house in Solihull, he did not appreciate the finer sentiments of an aristocrat who was having to flog off his ancestral pile and all five centuries of family history that went with it. 'A highly exclusive little retreat for the most discerning class of paying guest.'

'Paying *what*?' said Freddie, horrified.

'Anything up to a hundred bucks a night.'

'A hundred bucks a . . . '

28

'Licence to print money. All you need is air conditioning, elevators, ace cuisine and a decent wine cellar.'

'Ace . . . Wine . . .' Freddie was apoplectic. 'I . . . I . . . I . . .'

'None of your *vin de pays* and share-the-sink lark,' chuckled Sharkley. 'Oh, no. Your flash spenders want all the mod cons, these days.'

'I have never heard of anything so . . . so . . . so . . .'

'With you *in situ*, playing host, and all those wealthy foreign punters, you could be turning over a quarter of a million a year.'

'With me in *where*?'

'*In situ.*'

'Tax exile, you mean? If you think I'm going to desert my country in my hour of need . . .'

'No, you don't go *any*where, that's the whole point. You stay right here. There are millions of foreigners who'd give an arm and a leg just to stay with a kosher English lord in his kosher baronial home.'

Sharkley's meaning suddenly became clear to Freddie. It burst in an instant, like a great, bright star-shell in the blackness of his financial night.

'With *my* company's finance,' Sharkley concluded, 'and *your* social status we could be tallking about a very profitable little partnership . . . if you get my drift.'

Freddie was staggered. Absolutely shattered. This was nothing better than prostitution. This was hawking one's birthright like a harlot at the court of King Midas. The very suggestion was quite breathtaking in its impudent audacity, stupendous vulgarity and sheer brilliance.

'My dear Sharkley,' said he, 'you'll be staying for dinner, of course . . . ?'

It was like a funeral parlour in the public bar of the Proud Pinnace that evening. Tom Hoskin walked in just after eight o'clock and found his brother-in-law, Ben Curnow, and all the regulars gathered grim-faced around the throne of Ned Gummoe, imparter of woe and scrounger of ale.

'Damnee,' Tom said to Jack Penna, the landlord, 'tes like the Rev'run Micah Dredge's Christmas party in 'ere tonight.' He turned to Ben and the others. 'What's up an, boys?'

'Graave news, Tom,' Ben announced. 'They'm builden on the Fields.'

'Builden . . . ? On the Fields? Who es?'

Ben turned to Ned Gummoe. 'You tell un, Ned. Tell un what ee 'eard.'

Ned had been bought more pints of beer that day than he'd managed to scrounge all year, and was scarcely able to tell his own name by this time. Tom waited for him to speak, but the glassy-eyed ancient just sat there sucking his toothless gums and gazing mournfully into an empty tankard.

'Well, p'raps another pint might juss jog your memory an, Ned?' Tom suggested.

A spark of anticipation glowed in Ned's eyes. He crooked a gnarled old finger at Tom and bade him sit close.

'Loord Fred's gone sold ees land, you,' he croaked. 'For thirty million pound. I 'eard maatey talken jusa this mornen, see. They'm knocken down half the village, and builden this hotel, wi' yachten stadiums and golf courts and . . . ' He tapped Tom angrily on the forearm. 'And maatey did call us *peasants*! *Peasants*! And said as our homes was *hovels*!'

'Hotel?' said Tom incredulously. 'On our Fields?'

'Sixty storeys high weren't un, Ned?' said Ben.

'Ais you, ais,' Ned replied. 'As the Loord es my witness.'

'Damnee, Ned, you'm drunk senseless,' Tom retorted. 'They can't knock half the village down, you daft old bugger. And they could buy the whole of Penzance for thirty million.'

'Sure as I'm a-setten en thees chair,' Ned insisted, all but falling out of it.

'Thear edden nothen wrong wi' Ned's ears,' said Dick Champion, the garage mechanic.

'It edden ees ears I'm a-worried of,' said Tom. 'Tes that great big empty space in between.'

'Thear's been talk of builden on that land for a long time

now, Tom,' Ben reminded him. 'Us did all fear this could happen some day.'

'Baaagh . . . pess'oles,' Tom scoffed. 'They'll have to hold a public enquiry. And then us'll juss toss a couple or two o' they lawyers into the harbour, same as usual, and that'll be the finish of un.'

'Peasants,' Ned was growling bitterly. 'Hovels. Dear life . . . callen us *peasants* . . . '

'Who was this bloke you did hear talken an, Ned?' Tom enquired.

Ned, even in this befuddled state, was well aware that there were still two hours of prime drinking time to go and that he was beginning to lose his grip on a captive audience. In any case, he was acutely suspicious of anyone with a strange accent and tinted glasses. So he replied, in a voice dark with foreboding, 'He was a *Arab*.'

That reduced the entire public bar to silence.

'Arab?' said Ben Curnow. This was a dramatic new twist to the tale.

'Arab,' Ned repeated sombrely.

'Arab, eh?' said Tom, wondering if this might not have been the very same man that he and Ben had seen talking to Lord St Clare on the quay that morning. 'And how did ee knaw maatey was a Arab an, Ned? Saw Eli Tonkin stick a parken ticket on ees camel, did ee?'

'I done my share in the Great War!' Ned retorted angrily, as if anyone had suggested that he hadn't. 'Me and Gen'ral Allenby . . . side by side . . . hammeren on the gaates of Palestine, us was. I do knaw a Arab when I see un.'

'Well now,' said Tom, shaking his head with admiration, 'be damned if I ever did hear of a man fight one war in so many places as you, Ned. Last summer I 'eard ee tellen visitors in this very pub you was a aviator in the Flying Corps and got wounded by Baron von Rickytick hisself. A week later you was tellen everywan in the Fouled Anchor how you did fight three years in the trenchies ovver to Vimy Ridge, and not a day's leave in all that time. And how many times have I 'eard ee tellen how you nearly got blawed to piecies in Mesopotamia?'

Ned contemplated the enormity of what Tom had just said, and nodded wistfully.

'Aw ais, you,' he said, holding out his empty tankard. 'Us did knaw how to fight a war in they days, all right. Proper job.'

Since the departure of his latest carnivorous, money-grabbing wife, Freddie and his daughter, Miranda, had had the whole of Tremorna Hall to themselves. They enjoyed a close, loving relationship but seldom saw each other. He spent most of the day in the west wing, she in the east, and they met in the middle for dinner each night.

So, with the addition of little Mervyn Sharkley, there were just three at table that evening.

'There are several different St Clares,' Freddie was saying, 'and ours isn't one of them.' He helped Sharkley to another goblet of Italian plonk.

'Ours is the patron saint of beauty, chastity and maiden-hood,' said Miranda, who looked as if she might have been on intimate terms with Dracula. She gave Sharkley a filthy smile. 'What a romantic old tart she must have been.'

'According to legend,' said Freddie, 'she was a holy sister, who was set upon by Saxon marauders. But she threw herself off a high cliff to protect her virtue. Whether she died *intacta* or not we shall never know, but they've been celebrating the rape of St Clare in this village for many hundreds of years. Over the centuries it has all become mixed in with the traditional Whitsun fair and the pagan rites of spring. But this is one of the last villages in the country which still puts on a decent thrash for its saint's day.'

'And this hurling thing still goes on, does it?' asked Sharkley.

'It most certainly does,' said Freddie. 'And hurling is an ancient Celtic sport, not a *thing*.'

'And what happens?'

'The men of East village take on the men of West village. Anyone who wants to take part can do so. There are usually about a hundred of them. And they play a sort of handball game, like touch rugby, through the village streets. The Easters' goal is the Proud Pinnace tavern, and the Westers' goal is the Fouled Anchor hotel. The game starts at noon when I *hove-up* the silver ball on Addle bridge. And the team which lands the ball in goal first are the winners. The losers buy the beer all round. And everyone gets legless. People flock here in their thousands to see it.'

'Interesting,' said Sharkley, wondering if they could make it violent enough for network television. 'And what about the queen of the feast competition?'

'The queen of the feast,' Freddie replied, 'is supposed to represent St Clare, and symbolise beauty, chastity and maidenhood. The contestants line up on the quay at three o'clock, and a queen is chosen by the captain of the winning hurling team. In theory, any girl from the parish can enter for the contest, as long as she's under eighteen and a good chaste maiden. But in practice they'd be a bit short of volunteers if they enforced that. So they accept pretty well anyone under twenty-nine who isn't in the family way or awaiting trial for soliciting.'

'And what does the winner get?'

'Nothing,' said Freddie. 'Just the honour. And a tin crown for a year. And her picture in *The Cornishman*. She's officially crowned at the village cross, and then driven to the Fields in a horse and cart at the head of a coronation procession. And there on the Fields we have a big fair. There are lots of sideshows and sporting what-have-yous, with music and dancing, and a barbecue feast in the evening.'

'Really ethnic,' said Sharkley, framing a mental collage of thousands of sloshed fishermen, plump, young virgins, and the most appalling debauchery.

'Our ancestors,' said Miranda, 'were always very generous patrons of the feast. We used to lay on these enormous alfresco banquets. The most riotous fun. Everyone was sick for months.'

'Nice,' said Sharkley. 'Very nice.' He didn't know who Alf Resco was, but he sounded like a very reputable Italian caterer. Probably something to do with Harrods.

'But nowadays,' she went on, 'Papa's so skint that we just give them a few sausages to chuck on the bonfire.'

She couldn't have been more than twenty-five, he reckoned. But she had the sort of husky voice that ageing actresses acquire after too much nicotine, gin and fortnightly rep. And she was what Dougal McCann, his chum from Fixed Assets, would have called *rude*. She had long, raven-black hair, green eyes and a wicked mouth. And he had a disturbing suspicion that beneath her silky black kaftan she was more than averagely chubby. It was difficult to tell because of the light . . . Or the lack of it. For that dining-room was a very dark chamber, and they were eating by candlelight, seated at some distance from one another, at a table that was long enough to launch a Vulcan bomber. This penumbral gloom did not seem to bother his lordship, who was obviously quite content to get plastered on filthy Italian plonk (Alf Resco's?) and spend the evening groping about on his plate in search of a comestible or two. But it bothered Sharkley, who could hardly see what he was doing.

'Well, Pirana House would be only too happy to continue the tradition of patronising the feast,' he assured Miranda, as if he had anything other than the stockholders' interests at heart.

'And how soon are we to be gobbled up?' she asked, in her husky baby-doll voice.

'That depends on my superiors. If they like my initial proposals they'll sanction a feasibility study. Some months at the very least.' Definitely chubby, he was thinking, if not positively dumpy. And he was beginning to find this uncomfortably stimulating.

'But why are you interested in the likes of *us*, dear Sharklet?' Miranda enquired, with the innocence of Lolita. 'We are just sleepy little babes in a wood that time has passed by. And you, I'm sure, are a wily wolf, wise to the wicked ways of the world outside.' She moistened her lips with the tip of her tongue and added, 'We've heard all about Solihull, you know.'

Sharkley was beginning to feel quite ill at ease. There was probably more to this girl than mere bed. There was something in her eyes and voice that smacked suspiciously of intelligence. And he didn't like too much of that in a woman.

'Well, that's precisely why I'm interested,' he replied. 'I like all these old ethnic customs and cultural traditions. And I think if we market them in the right sort of way we could really put St Clare on the map.'

'Market *what* exactly?' asked Miranda. She broke off a thick, white stalk of celery, slipped it between her lips and pushed it slowly into her mouth.

Sharkley mopped a little perspiration from his brow. 'Well, this hurling lark . . . and the coronation at the Cross . . . and choosing the queen from all the chubby little virgins . . . ' He could feel his face turning a fiery scarlet. 'I mean . . . well, you know what I mean.'

'I'm sure I don't,' said Miranda, refusing to take her eyes off him.

His face was ablaze with embarrassment. He shovelled a large quantity of Stilton inside it to keep himself quiet for a few minutes.

'If you're really interested in the hurling,' she went on, 'you should talk to Tom Hoskin. He leads the East village team. He lives in one of the harbour cottages you'll be buying when you gobble us up.'

'Gobble . . . ?' Sharkley managed a weak smile and began to sweat again. 'I hope you don't look on us as *cannibals*?'

'Well, being a meat-eater myself . . . ' She pushed the last of the celery stalk into her mouth and slowly crushed it to pulp.

Suddenly, Sharkley lost all control of his imagination. Mentally tearing off her silky kaftan, he found himself swamped with torrid fantasies of soft, plump flesh bulging out of taut, white lingerie. He struggled desperately to pull himself together. Normal people, he told himself, do not think like this. My mind is sick. Please, God, help me think of pure and decent things . . . like the Institute of Directors, or anti-union legislation. He tried in vain to think of something witty or intelligent to say to change the subject.

'So, what's your line of business, then?' he asked.

'I paint.'

'Decorator?'

'Artist.'

'Oh, pictures. What sort of pictures?'

She shrugged her shoulders, and long, spindly, silver things dangling from her ear-lobes began to tinkle like Tibetan sheep bells. 'Anything you fancy. Do you a handsome seascape for a mere fifty pounds.'

Sharkley was genuinely interested in that. He was genuinely interested in *any*thing if he thought he could make a buck out of it. Seascapes, landscapes. Ideal for the tourists. Pay Miranda fifty for an original, then run off five thousand repros at fifty pence each. Sign them all as a guaranteed limited edition of one hundred, and flog them to the chalet people for a fiver each, and twenty quid to the exclusive paying guests at Tremorna Hall.

'And I take a riding class at weekends,' Miranda added. 'With Alf.'

'Alf?'

'And we go for mad gallops across the cliffs sometimes, when we're in the mood.'

He thought she said *nude* at first, and began sweating again.

'Who's Alf? Alf Resco?'

'Alf Resco?' She burst out giggling. 'Dear Sharklet, you are too silly! Papa . . . you see, you were wrong. He *has* got a sense of humour after all.'

But Papa was three sheets in the wind by this time and wholly preoccupied with pleasant thoughts about the widow Tremayne.

Sharkley laughed too, to be polite, but couldn't see anything remotely funny in what he'd said.

'Alf isn't a *he*,' Miranda explained, flashing her teeth, her eyes, and about two dozen silver rings in the candlelight. 'Alf*reda* owns the riding stables. She's impossibly tall and frolicsome.'

The thought of all that flesh and overstretched Playtex, and now the impossibly tall Alf frolicking in the stables, was just too much for Sharkley. He felt a pressing need to get back to his hotel as quickly as possible and telephone someone normal . . . Like Ormskirk.

Beauty with chastity. The ideals of St Clare now began to commend themselves to Sharkley's weary soul. *Beauty with chastity . . . Beauty with chastity . . . Beauty with chastity . . .* He repeated these words over and over to himself as he drove back to the Fouled Anchor hotel that night. They had a soothing effect on his troubled mind. Like a Buddhist chant. They had a noble simplicity that appealed to his better nature. They elevated his thoughts to a higher plane of aesthetic consciousness. They cleansed his soul and washed away all that smutty filth.

    Beauty with chastity . . . Beauty with chastity . . . Beauty with chubbiness . . .

Night fell on St Clare.

    Somewhere in the granite ruins of a tinner's cottage an owl hooted. A fox trotted out across Farmer Rosewarne's fields in the moonlight, past the sleeping bulk of Socrates the bull.

    In her chamber in the haunted east wing of Tremorna Hall, the Honourable Miranda Jago retired to bed with her teddy bear, her Piglet, and her brand new, Grand-Massif, five-function vibrator.

    At the end of another dark passage, her father was sitting on the side of his bath tub, with his mind in the bed of the widow Tremayne and his testicles in a bowl of iced water.

    Not far away, at the Fouled Anchor hotel, little Mervyn Sharkley lay fast asleep, dreaming he was tempest-tossed upon a raging sea, and being sucked slowly into the slippery-soft, warm belly of a great white whale.

PART TWO

APRIL

1

ALTHOUGH FREDDIE ST CLARE did virtually nothing all
year round that required mental or physical effort, except
write his memoirs and commit adultery, he did occasionally
like to set off in the early morning and hack his way contemplatively around the twelve-acre weed forest that had once
been his garden, to ruminate upon the state of his affairs.
And in the course of recent ruminations he had come to the
conclusion that he was faced with three fundamentally
intractable problems. His house was falling down. He was
stony-broke. And he couldn't get the widow Tremayne into
bed.

But having been born into that stratum of society that the
Almighty, in His infinite wisdom, had ordained to be the
ruling class, Freddie was blessed with an innate sense of
priorities, and at the age of fifty-three felt that he could only
cope with one major crisis at a time. So he had decided to
concentrate entirely on bedding the widow Tremayne.

The widow Tremayne, however, did not appear to be
interested in men and sex . . . Or women and sex, for that
matter. Which was a mystery to Freddie. He couldn't
understand anybody who wasn't interested in sex. True,
her husband, Kenwyn, had been drowned at sea only the
previous summer, and a spell of inconsolable grief after such
a tragedy was only natural, seemly, and to be expected by
the neighbours. But Kenwyn had been dead and in his grave
for nine months, and still there was not so much as a breath
of salacious, idle gossip about her. And as heaven was his

judge, Freddie did all he could to keep a weather ear open for salacious, idle gossip.

It was quite possible, of course, that no fellow had dared to approach her yet. For most of the eligible bachelors in the village had known Kenwyn since childhood and would not have wanted to be seen wooing his young widow with indecent haste. But there was such a thing as indecent tardiness too.

A chap in Freddie's social position, however, had an entirely different problem: and that was, how to woo the widow Tremayne quietly and discreetly, without the entire village getting the right idea. With his reputation, he had only to tap on a woman's door after sundown and the whole of St Clare would be buzzing with gossip by the following morning.

For a time the problem had seemed insuperable. But then, having ruminated in the wilderness of his estate for many days and many nights, he suddenly fell victim to a rare attack of clear, incisive thinking and hit upon an ingenious plan. The simplicity of it astonished him. But then he was constantly being astonished by the simplicity of his own mind.

The key to it all was filth. The interior of Tremorna Hall was in a disgusting condition. (So was the exterior, as it happened, but that was neither here nor there.) For the grand days of housemaids and tweenies were long gone, and ever since Freddie's fifth man-eating wife had sued him for every last penny that the Inland Revenue hadn't already plundered off him in death duties, he and Miranda had lived in that house with a combined staff of two: old mother Hicks, the cleaner, and old mother Visick, the cook. Now old mother Hicks, bless her heart, had passed on and been swept up to that great broom cupboard in the sky, and everything in the house had begun to disappear beneath a remorseless accumulation of dust and grime.

This was not making the place any more attractive to prospective purchasers, and Freddie was finding his own efforts with Hoover and duster wondrously ineffectual. As for Miranda, he had long since given up hope that she would

42

ever do anything remotely useful about the house. An artist of considerable mediocrity, and noted for it in places as far away as the next village, she spent most of her time cultivating marijuana in the garden and bouncing in and out of bed with the working classes. Freddie took no great exception to the latter (he being one of the foremost exponents of the sport in that locality), but he would have preferred it had she chosen to devote her boundless energies to more worthwhile pursuits . . . such as bouncing in and out of wedlock with a rapid succession of dying millionaires.

It was at this moment of deepening domestic crisis in the world as we know it, that Freddie had been told by old mother Visick, the cook, that the widow Tremayne — with a teenage daughter still at school — was absolutely desperate for work. And being absolutely desperate for her body, he had immediately conceived the solution to his problems in one blinding flash of ingenuity. If she were to come to work at Tremorna, he would be able to woo her every day in the privacy and comfort of his own stately home. He would simply have to take great care not to put the sound of wedding bells into her impressionable ears . . . for one of the hazards of seducing local widows, in Freddie's experience, was that they were all itching to get their paws on the family overdraft.

So, through the good offices of old mother Visick, he had offered Sally Tremayne a job. And she had very promptly accepted it. But now, it appeared, she was having second thoughts, and wanted to discuss the matter further. So it was with some apprehension that Freddie was awaiting her arrival at Tremorna this fine April morning . . .

Spring was in the air, and it was quite probable that Sally would have set her mind on becoming the next Lady St Clare, anyway . . . The fifth or sixth since Freddie had succeeded to the title, she was not sure. (Nor was he, for that matter.) But the latest news about Pirana House had decided the issue, once and for all.

She had been thinking about marrying Lord Fred for

some time, but had had her doubts at first. For although he was unquestionably the most eligible bachelor in the area, it was reliably rumoured that he was almost bankrupt. And a highly desirable widow of thirty-six, with total assets of just eighty-one pounds in the Bristol and West Building Society, and a fifteen-year-old daughter to look after, occasionally had to think of ungodly things like money. And with so many local pillars of the community — like fisherman Tom Hoskin, and butcher Arthur Pascoe — now looking for a wife, she rightly felt spoilt for choice.

But the rumours had been confusing at first. It had always seemed to her, whatever any gossips said, that an Elizabethan manor, twelve cottages, a pub and half a valley had to be worth a sight more than her eighty-one pounds in the Bristol and West. Then *Woman's Mirror* had printed an article about his lordship *'going bust in style'*, and she had begun to have second thoughts. But *now* the village was vibrant with rumours about Arabs buying the estate for mass development. And during the past few weeks, an endless succession of surveyors, architects and Range-Rover owners had been tramping all over West Meadows in expensive green wellies, doing meaningful things with tape measures and pocket calculators.

So far, Lord Fred had refused to comment on the matter . . . either to the parish council, or to *The Cornishman*, or even to his next-door neighbour, the vicar. But as she was now — technically, at any rate — an employee at Tremorna Hall (and, if Lord Fred did but know it, a prospective mistress of the place) she felt that it was perfectly in order for her to ask his lordship, quite bluntly, just what precisely was going on. After all, if she was going to be fifty per cent of his entire domestic workforce, she had a right to know. Which was why she was pedalling powerfully up the drive to Tremorna, this fine April morning, on her rusty Hercules bicycle . . .

'*Going on*?' said Freddie, trying to look mystified. 'What ever do you mean, Mrs Tremayne? Nothing's going on.'

'Thear's rumours buzzen everywhere, like flies, my lord,'

she said, politely but firmly. 'And if I'm to be employed here, I have to know where I stand. Because thear's talk of you sellen out to the Arabs. And where will that leave me, I'm wonderen?'

Freddie was staggered. The brazen audacity of the wench. Fancy thinking about herself at a time like this . . . When he had a serious crisis on his hands, and was doing everything in his power to help her into his bed. How could she stand there — five feet seven in cycling shoes and permed blonde curls — with her hands on her hips, puffing out her 38C chest, and bluntly demand to know what was going on? He was shocked. So shocked that he told her. Precisely what was going on. Anything for a busy bed.

She was poleaxed. 'A ho . . . *tel*? This house? Tremorna? A hotel?'

'Ah, but only for the most select, exclusive kind of guests,' he assured her quickly. 'Like millionaires. And . . . millionaires.' He went on to outline Sharkley's scheme.

The mere thought of all these millionaires brought an instinctive glow of human affection to Sally's kind, intelligent face.

'Why, Lord St Clare,' she said ecstatically, 'that es a *won*derful idea!'

'I'm modestly proud of it myself,' Freddie confessed. 'But I can assure you that this will not mean selling out . . . To the Arabs or to anyone else. It will mean change, certainly. But I feel sure that my ancestors would have approved, under the circumstances.' He shrugged philosophically. 'All things must pass. He who doth not sow, also shall he not reap.' He didn't seriously believe that sort of twaddle, but the widow Tremayne was a devout Methodist and he thought it might impress her. 'It will mean a vast infusion of capital, the rebirth of Tremorna, and the revitalising of St Clare. And your place, I can assure you, will be right here, Mrs Tremayne, if you so wish it.'

'Oh, Lord St Clare,' she said effusively, 'I'm quite overcome. What would Lucy and I do without a strong, upright, noble gentleman like you comen to our aid in time of need?'

Freddie thought for one palpitating moment that she was going to throw her arms round him and kiss him. But money had that kind of effect on him too.

'My dear Mrs Tremayne,' he replied, 'think nothing of it. The very least I can do. The very least.'

He watched her pedal away down the drive, and then dashed upstairs for a quick lie-down to get over an acute attack of priapic desire before applying himself to the serious task of worrying about money.

2

That very same April sunshine was even then streaming through the windows of Penwith magistrates court, in the nearby town of Penzance, and falling in a pool of brilliant golden warmth upon the figure of Benjamin Michael Curnow, forty-one-year-old fisherman of St Clare, standing in the dock in his Sunday best.

'Mr Curnow,' said Mrs Felicity Hope-Bolitho JP, chairperson of the bench, 'can you explain to us *why* you bear this profound and virulent grudge against the French?'

Ben cleared his throat. '*Me*, ma'am?' His face assumed a look of bewildered innocence. 'Grudge? Why, I do hold no grudgies. Me and the Frenchies, us do get on handsome, you.'

'But we have just heard from Monsieur Ramon Grenoux, master of the motor yacht, *Musetta*, that you attempted to ram his dinghy with your crab-boat, the *Eudoria Lynn*, in St Clare's Bay. And that without the least provocation, you insulted his crew — in terms that I blush even to think of — and threatened them with violence. Skippering your vessel, all the while, in a manner likely to endanger life and property on the high sea.'

'Aw no,' Ben chuckled. 'I was only being playful. Thear weren't no danger.'

'Playful?' echoed Mrs Hope-Bolitho. 'According to Monsieur Grenoux, you obliged him to take evasive action on seven different occasions in less than thirty minutes.'

'Aw no, ma'am. Monsieur Grenouille's exaggeraten juss a didjan,' said Ben, giving the Breton skipper a friendly smile from the dock.

'Monsieur Grenoux,' emphasised Mrs Hope-Bolitho, with an apologetic glance at the Frenchman. 'Not Grenouille. Grenouille, as you know perfectly well, Mr Curnow, means frog.'

Ben looked amazed. 'Now es that so, ma'am? Well, I'll be . . .'

'That is the third time I've had to make the point this morning, Mr Curnow.'

'Aw, I do beg the benchie's pardon, ma'am. I won't call Monsieur Frog a frog again. I didden realise I was callen him a frog, mind, but now I do knaw . . .'

'Mr Curnow!' ·

'Your worship?'

'You repeatedly obliged the master of the Musetta to take emergency action to avoid a collision at sea, did you not?'

'Well, tes true, ma'am,' Ben confessed, 'that the Frenchies don't have the skill of the Cornish sailors. And poor maatey here kept getten hisself all of a pother to windward.'

'Whilst you sailed round and round his boat, pelting it with putrid fish and shark bait, and threatening to suspend Monsieur Grenouille from the mast-head by his . . .' Mrs Hope-Bolitho hesitated, looked down at her notes and swallowed hard. 'By his private parts,' she muttered quickly. 'Now is that your idea of being playful, Mr Curnow?'

'Er . . . Grenoux, beggen the benchie's pardon, ma'am,' said Ben helpfully. 'You did call un Grenouille. That do mean frog, see ma'am. You'm callen maatey a frog . . .'

'Mr Curnow, before I hold you in contempt of this court, is that or is that not your idea of being playful?'

'Well, see, thear's al'us misunnerstandens, edden thear?'

Ben reasoned. 'Cos they Frenchies don't speak the Queen's English, you.'

'Mr Curnow, I put it to you that pelting someone with putrid fish means much the same thing in *any* language.'

'Aw, I wuzzen pelten they wi' fishies, ma'am,' said Ben, deeply wounded. 'Why 'twas a gift. A gesture of good will to our Common Market friends, for their breakfuss.'

'At five o'clock in the afternoon? Just tell me why you have this apparently irrational disaffection for the French, Mr Curnow, please.'

'Never a word spawke in wrath,' Ben protested. 'Not a finger raised in anger.'

Mrs Hope-Bolitho referred to her papers. 'You have appeared before this court on no fewer than seven previous occasions, charged with all manner of aggressive and offensive behaviour towards French vessels and their crews. And only last year you were found guilty of boarding a Breton trawler in Newlyn harbour and pitching her master and two hands into the sea.'

'Aw ais, well that's different ma'am, beggen the benchie's pardon. See, that was Corpus Christi fair, and us had extenuaten circumstances.'

'And what were they, pray?'

'I was drunk, ma'am.'

Mr Nathan Gouldmann, defending, rose from his chair.

'If it please your worship, time presses and I should like to call upon the testimony of a totally independent, expert, technical adviser to show that it was impossible for my client in his humble tosher to do anything that could have endangered life aboard a powerful yacht like the *Musetta*.'

Mrs Hope-Bolitho sighed audibly and resigned herself to another fifteen minutes of wholly incomprehensible nautical argument.

'Oh, very well, Mr Gouldmann. Call your totally independent, expert witness.'

'I call Mr Thomas Hoskin,' said Nathan Gouldmann.

'Your go, Tom!' said a voice in the corridor outside.

*　　*　　*

Not many streets away, in a quiet, cobbled lane, the proprietor of Sindy's Boutique (mags, tapes, fun-wear and marital aids) was arguing with a highly dissatisfied customer.

'Well, I've sold dozens of these and I haven't had any complaints yet,' he grumbled, reassembling the few constituent parts of a Grand-Massif five-function vibrator. He switched it on again. 'What's the matter with it?'

'It doesn't vibrate,' Miranda replied crisply.

He listened to it. 'Well, it rumbles,' he said, as if that was any consolation.

'It does not rumble. It scarcely even murmurs.

He leant his ear to the shaft. 'I don't call that a murmur. I call that a distinct *rumble.*'

He looked rather like Mervyn Sharkley, she was thinking. A creep. But perhaps a little paler, balder and weedier.

'Look,' she said, 'I don't care if it rumbles, grumbles or hums a fandango. I expect a vibrator to vibrate. This does *not* vibrate.'

'It trembles . . . sort of,' the proprietor said, hoping for a compromise.

'It does *not* tremble. It barely even tingles. If I had wished to spend £9.99 on something that tingles I would have bought a £9.99 tingler. As it is I spent £9.99 on something that is supposed to *vibrate.*'

'Well, it isn't meant to jump up and down like a pneumatic drill, you know.'

'Do not presume to tell *me* what a vibrator is supposed to do,' Miranda retorted imperiously. 'I know a good vibration when I feel it. And that is *not* a good vibration. It is not even a *poor* vibration. In fact, it's about as vibrant as a stick of limp rhubarb.'

A postman walked in with the mid-morning mail.

'Two registered,' he announced, blithely unaware of what he was interrupting.

Miranda rounded on him. 'Feel this . . .

He obediently held out his hand, and she slapped the Grand-Massif, five-function vibrator into it. He recoiled in horror and gaped at it as if it were gelignite.

'Is that vibrating, or is it not?' she demanded.

'Izzer what?'

'Vibrating? Can you feel a vibration?'

The postman thought long and hard about it, then shook his head. 'Thear's a bit of a tingle, you. But I'd be tellen a lie if I said 'twas anythen more.'

'Thank you,' said Miranda. And triumphantly handed the vibrator back to the proprietor. 'You will either replace it, or refund my money . . . or I shall write to the editor of *The Cornishman.*'

With the greatest reluctance, the proprietor took another Grand-Massif from a drawer behind the counter, fitted it with batteries and switched it on. It burst into life and snarled aggressively in his hand.

'Satisfied?' he asked, passing it to Miranda.

'Now *that* is what I call a vibration,' she agreed. 'And next time I come in here don't try and fob me off with shoddy merchandise that has already been returned umpteen times by dissatisfied customers.'

'That is slander,' the proprietor warned her, returning the defective vibrator to the display cabinet so that he could fob it off again on the next unsuspecting customer.

Miranda said goodbye to the postman — who was just getting engrossed in that month's edition of *Latex News* — and marched briskly out of the shop. Outside, she found Tom Hoskin and Ben Curnow contemplating an inflatable, life-size nymph called Randetta, who had lost some air with the passing of time and was now languishing, sadly misshapen, on the floor of the shop window.

They were not in the least surprised to see Miranda emerging from Sindy's with a jumbo-size vibrator in her hand . . . And would not have been surprised if she'd had half the contents of the shop in her arms, to boot.

'Boys!' she exclaimed, thrusting her body between them. 'What a divine surprise. What are *you* doing here, drooling over droopy Randetta in your best Sunday suits?'

'Us es celebraten,' said Tom.

'I juss got a discharge,' Ben added proudly.

'So us es goan for a pint down the quay, you.'

'Are you sure that's wise?' Miranda asked Ben, assuming that he was talking about a venereal infection.

But Ben said that any smack in the eye for the French was worth celebrating, and insisted that she came too. And she certainly wasn't going to let someone else's urethritis interfere with her drinking life; so she set off down to the harbour with them. On the way, she gave a detailed account of her contretemps with the proprietor of Sindy's sex boutique, and proudly demonstrated the five functions of her new Grand-Massif vibrator as she did so — much to the bewilderment of the passing population of Penzance.

When they arrived at the pub, they found Ramon Grenoux, the skipper of the *Musetta*, drinking in the other bar with his crew.

'That's the bugger,' Ben growled, pointing him out to Miranda from the public bar. 'Damnee ef I ent got half a mind to go en thear and black ees glazers for un right now.'

Miranda took a good look at him. He was tall, slim and strongly built, with dark, gypsy looks. 'Naughty Ramon,' she said, moistening her lips. 'Whatever did he do to upset you so?'

'He's a Frenchie,' Ben replied, as if that covered a multitude of vice and crime. 'He's got a brand new fifty-footer. Charters her out. Fitted out like the *Queen Mary*, her es. Must be rich as bloody Croesus.'

'How frightfully vulgar,' said Miranda, and sped away to the loo to pile on more eye make-up.

When she came back she found that Ramon and his crew had left. She bought another round of beers to drown her disappointment.

Tom asked, 'How's that dad of yours getten on sellen ees estate, an?' . . . But casually, as if he hadn't even thought about it for the last few weeks.

'There's a company that's interested,' Miranda replied. 'Pirana House, the food people. They sent someone called Sharkley to see us last month. But we still haven't heard anything.'

'Rumour has it,' said Ben, 'that somewan was thinken of builden a hotel on the Fields.'

'On the *Fields*?' said Miranda incredulously. 'Never in a million years. They'd never get planning permission.'

'Exactly what I thoft all along,' said Tom. 'Tes juss a load of fish-wives' gossep, you.'

'What this Sharkley creep was talking about was a chalet camp on West Meadows, where the old battery farm used to be . . . like the one that Papa was planning before he ran out of loot and the vicar started creating. And he wants to turn Tremorna into a hotel for filthy rich foreigners, and jazz up all the *ethnic* things.'

'What does he mean by *ethnic*?' Ben enquired suspiciously.

'Oh, anything that's more than five years old and not made in Hong Kong,' said Miranda airily. 'The hurling, the Hag's Ring, the feast day . . . '

'Jazz un up?' said Tom. 'How's he goan to jazz un up?'

'He wants to make feast day a weekly event throughout the tourist season, to attract the visitors.'

'Here . . . ' Ben protested. 'He can't go round doan things like that with other folk's feasten days!'

'I'm sure he won't succeed,' said Miranda. 'But it's all in the air at the moment and dreadfully hush-hush. So promise me you won't breathe a syllable about it to anyone.'

'Aw ais, our lips es sealed,' Tom assured her solemnly. 'Tight as a virgin clam, my dear.'

So it was all round St Clare by nightfall.

3

Tom Hoskin and Ben Curnow lived in adjacent cottages at the foot of East Cliff. Tom's sister, Nancy, was Ben's wife. And that evening, with the kitchen windows wide open, Nancy's opinions on the top-secret Pirana House conspiracy could be heard half a mile away on the far side of West village. But that was nothing out of the ordinary . . . On a clear day, it was said, Nancy's opinions on most matters could be heard five miles away at Land's End. And on a *very* clear day well out into the Western Approaches.

'Ovver my dead body!' she thundered that evening. 'My dear heaven, there'll be no jazzen up our feast day and no chalet camps out to West Meadows neither! Us stopped un afore and us can stop un again!'

They had just finished tea, and all Ben wanted to do was put to sea and drop his crab and lobster pots. But every time he tried to get up, Nancy kept pushing him back behind the kitchen table.

'Well, I can't see how you'm goan to stop un,' he grumbled. 'That edden your land, missus, and progress es progress. You'm like King Canute, you are, tryen to stay the tide.'

He tried to get up again, but she bashed him over the head with a rolled-up *Western Morning News* and pushed him back in his place.

'How can you juss sit thear, Ben Curnow,' she demanded furiously, 'when thear's plots afoot right now to turn thes village into one great big, jazzed up hollerday camp?'

'Aw, hell an' come pain, missus . . . I do have to go lay me pots, or us all shall be starven djrectly.'

'And you, Tom Hoskin,' she said, rounding on her brother now. 'What have *you* got to say for yourself?'

Tom was trying to be inconspicuous in a corner. It was not easy in a cramped little kitchen for a man who was six feet tall and weighed fourteen stone; but he was making a valiant effort, anyway.

'Aw, I ent got no hard opinion on the matter, wan way or t'other, Nan,' he replied meekly. 'Like Ben says though, you can't stop progress.'

'Like Ben says . . . like Ben says . . . ' she scoffed. 'One day you'm goan to have a thought of your own. Then you'll drop dead wi' shock.'

Tom had not volunteered to listen to all this. He had been on his way out for the evening, leaving his own cottage next door, when Nancy had collared him and hauled him inside with a roar of, 'And what's all this I hear about another chalet camp out to West Meadows, an?' Whereupon he had been remanded in custody in the Curnows' kitchen, and had been getting an earful ever since. Their seventeen-year-old son, Danny, was also being held; but he was deeply immersed in the *Beano*.

Tom's big sister had always been a formidable character, and from an early age he had cherished the hope that one day she might marry Ben, the lad next door — for he had been a bit of a hard case in his youth and had brooked no lip from man or woman. In fact Ben had been Tom's only real hope that Nancy would ever be subdued and brought under some semblance of control. The hope had never been fulfilled, however. Ben had obligingly married her, but Nancy had crushed the poor sod into abject and unconditional surrender within a fortnight.

'Now look, missus,' said Ben soothingly, 'why don't ee wait till us do find out percisely what es a-goan on, instead of getten all of a pother ovver nothen?'

'Ais you,' Tom agreed. 'That's wisest, Nan. Stuff a sock in un till you do knaw what tes you'm blatheren about.'

He got up to go but Nancy blocked his way.

'And juss where do you think you'm off to, all dressed up like that?'

'I ent dressed up,' Tom replied, puzzled. 'I al'us wears me jacket and trousers of a evenen.'

'You've put a tie on and combed your hair,' she said suspiciously.

'Well? It edden any of your business whether I'm wearen a top hat and bathing trunks, izzer now?'

'Goan courten, I suppose?'

'None o' your bloody concern whear I'm goan to, woman. Now you step out me way. I do have important business to attend to djrectly.'

'With a pint glass in your right hand, I don't doubt.'

Tom pushed past her and made for the back door. Ben coughed politely. He never came between brother and sister. A fisherman's life was quite hazardous enough as it was.

'I'll walk down to the quay with ee an, Tom,' he announced. He turned to his son. 'You comen with me, Danny?'

Danny looked up from his *Beano*. 'No . . . Mum says I got to do the washen up, and then take her to the vicarage.'

'So he has,' said Nancy. 'Tes about time he did somethen useful to earn his keep.'

'Washen up dishies?' Ben scoffed. 'Why, you'm enough to turn a man into a fish-wife, missus. You'll have un wearen pinnifores afore long.'

He picked up his cap and coat and followed Tom out of the back door.

The secret truth was that Tom Hoskin was getting married. At the age of thirty-seven he had finally decided that it was high time he stopped playing fast and loose with scrubbers in Penzance, and started playing fast and loose with a good wife.

His bride-to-be was the very lovely Sally Tremayne, widow of his dear old mate, Kenwyn. But it was a very closely guarded secret. Not even Ben knew, and Ben was his oldest and most trusted friend. In fact, it was so secret that not even Sally herself knew yet.

There were one or two minor matters of detail to be ironed out first, of course. For a start, it was not easy trying to court the wife of one of your lifelong pals, even if he *was* nine months dead and buried. And Nancy would go berserk when she heard about it. The Hoskins and the Curnows had been of the Anglican faith for ages — certainly since the Reformation, and probably since before the time of Christ himself. Whereas the Tremaynes were devout Methodists. And Nancy would have sooner had a Druid for a sister-in-law than a Methodist.

And finally there was the matter of getting Sally's consent. But Tom was confident that that would be a mere technicality . . . They had known each other since they were toddlers, and although there were other eligible bachelors in the village, he had to admit to himself in all modesty that none of them had his handsome looks, or strength of arm, or sharpness of mind.

He realised there would have to be a little courting,

naturally — if only as a concession to propriety. And it had occurred to him that she might be just a little shy at first . . . afraid, perhaps, of spying eyes and gossiping tongues. So he'd been thinking that for their first date he might take her somewhere well away from the village. To the north coast perhaps . . . For, say, a Sunday afternoon picnic. He could borrow Ben's Minivan . . . if he could get rid of the smell of lobsters.

With these thoughts of love and courtship in mind, he was strolling through the village, this warm spring evening, intending to stray up Chapel Lane and call in at Sally's cottage — purely on the spur of the moment, since he happened to be passing at the time. But he was barely fifty yards from her front door when a car came down the lane from the other direction and pulled up outside her house. The driver got out, took a bunch of flowers from the back seat and walked up to Sally's door. It was Arthur Pascoe, the local butcher.

Tom ducked down behind a pillar box and peered round the side of it. After a moment, Sally came to the door and Pascoe disappeared into the cottage. The door closed.

Tom couldn't believe what he was seeing. *Pascoe*? Arthur John Pascoe, butcher of this parish . . . a *rival*? Since when? How long had this been going on? Secret lovers' meetings? How barefaced and underhand could people be? How low could any man stoop? Sneaking openly into a defenceless young widow's home under cover of broad daylight . . . secretly brandishing gifts of flowers for the whole of St Clare to see. How contemptible!

Tom felt the disgust welling up inside him, a pang of jealousy in his heart, and a strong hand on his shoulder. The shock of this latter almost gave him heart failure.

'Why, Tom Hoskin!' said Constable Hawkins, possessor of the strong hand. 'Whatever are ee doan of, crawlen about behind a postbox at this time of evenen?'

Tom staggered back against the wall, clutching his chest.

'Damnee, Percy Hawkins, you nearly gave I a heart attack then . . . Creepen up on a man like that.'

'But what are ee doan down thear, my 'andsome?'

56

'What do ee think I'm doan? I'm looken to see what time the lass post do go.'

'On your *knees*?' said Percy. 'My dear life, you do need your eyes testen. I thoft you musta been took queer and doubled up in pain.'

'Well, I'm grateful for your concern, Percy,' said Tom abrasively. 'But next time you want to surprise somewan, for Christ's sake let the poor bugger knaw in advance. Tes enough to put a good man en ees graave before ees time.' He straightened his tie and smoothed down his hair. 'Now if you don't mind, I do have important matters of business to attend to.'

'Aw ais, well if you'm busy I won't keep ee. Night an, awld maate . . . I hope your poor awld eyes get better soon.'

'Thank you, Percy, and good night.'

Tom walked briskly back towards East Quay. Pascoe . . . The unscrupulous bloody rat. This called for clear, rational thinking. So he made all speed for that renowned temple of intellect and culture: the public bar of the Proud Pinnace.

Emerging from the lanes of West village deep in contemplation, and crossing Middle Street with head bowed, he all but collided with a passing BSA 125cc motorcycle that was coughing its way towards Addle bridge in an advanced state of senility. Vaguely in control of this geriatric conveyance was his young nephew, Danny. And perched upon the pillion, with warlike countenance, was the indomitable Nancy, on her way to the vicarage for a monologue with the Reverend Owen Borage, on the subject of the latest commercial shenanigans of the wicked Baron von Fred.

As soon as he had dropped his mother off at the vicarage, Danny sped straight home, as slowly as his two bald tyres would carry him, to get on with all the washing up. And when he'd finished that he went upstairs to measure his muscles.

Not one solitary fraction of an inch of growth. He sank onto the edge of his bed in despair.

'*In just fourteen days*,' the advertisement had promised, '*the amazing new Dynothrust spring-grip exerciser will add pounds of rippling, power-packed muscle to YOUR body.'*

So, hiding behind a pair of sunglasses, Danny had gone all the way to Penzance and purchased his own amazing new Dynothrust exerciser for an amazing seventeen pounds ninety-five p., and had smuggled it home disguised as a brown-paper parcel.

Now, he had confidently believed, the world would never be quite the same again. No more would he be at the mercy of local gang boss, Samson Trevaskis, and his retinue of apprenticed psychopaths. No more would he have to sunbathe on the beach with all his clothes on, ashamed to show his puny body. No more would Lucy Tremayne ignore him as she passed him in the street.

So, every day he had religiously performed all thirty-six scientifically-designed Dynothrust exercises, as illustrated in the amazing new full-colour wall-chart. And every day he had measured his spindly limbs to chart the development of his amazing new power-packed body. And after seven months, it had shrunk by half an inch all over.

Danny looked at himself in the bedroom mirror and contemplated putting a tragically early end to it all.

He decided to give up searching for a muscle, and to count his pimples instead. There were sixteen today. That was three up on the previous week. They were about the only part of his body that were showing any real signs of growth potential. He was saving up to buy an amazing new acne cure that he had seen in an advert for trusses and incontinence pants in the Sunday newspaper. It was only £5.95p. But he still had some way to go. There was a recession on after all.

He decided to count his money, in the faint hope that it might add up to more than it had an hour ago. He emptied his wallet. But it still contained just seven one-pound notes, a signed card donating his body to medical research in the event of a tragically early death, three photographs of Lucy Tremayne in a bikini, and two Black Stallion contraceptive sheaths that he'd found on the beach the previous weekend and did not know what to do with.

He lay back on the bed. He was bored. Bored to distraction. He had no energy. No enthusiasm for anything. No job. No Lucy. Not even one power-packed, amazing, new arm.

He looked at the photographs of Lucy. He'd had to pay a pound each for them, after secret negotiations with one of her rival admirers, Buster Tonkin.

Danny had been madly and desperately in love with Lucy for ages. The trouble was that everyone in the world seemed to be in love with Lucy, and he was too shy to tell her how he felt . . . Or even give her a hint of it . . . Or even give her the slightest indication that he so much as liked her. In fact he hadn't actually spoken one kind or civil word to her in ages. He *wanted* to. He absolutely *yearned* to. He hardly ever stopped thinking about her . . . imagining them both out together, walking arm in arm along the beach at sunset, or galloping through the surf on white horses. But the harsh reality of *his* life was nothing like the one he saw every night in soft-focus TV commercials for shampoo or aftershave. Lucy never sprinted across the sands to throw herself into *his* power-packed arms. She never even noticed he was there. And on those few occasions when they came face to face, in a shop or on the bus, Danny invariably turned red and mumbled something incoherent or plain, downright rude.

And now that he'd left school the situation was even worse. For he no longer saw her every day. All he could do was hang about in the village after school hours, risking a bruising encounter with predatory anthropoids like Samson Trevaskis, in the hope that she might pass by.

This then was why, now that the warmer evenings had come round again, he had taken to going for exhilarating burn-ups on his Bantam 125, whizzing through the countryside at speeds of well over twenty miles per hour, and returning to St Clare down Porthcurno Hill . . . a route that happened to take him straight past the back garden of Lucy's cottage in Chapel Lane . . .

'Well, thear we are, my dear,' said Arthur Pascoe, having

just taken two hours to fit a new washer to Sally Tremayne's kitchen tap. He let the water splash freely into the sink for a moment, and then shut it off again with a deft flourish of the hand to demonstrate the efficacy of his workmanship.

Sally was most impressed. 'Proper job, Arthur. I never realised 'twould take so long, mind.'

'Depends whether you want the work botched or done properly,' Arthur replied.

'Tom told me 'twould only take him a couple of minutes.'

'Tom?'

'Tom Hoskin. He noticed it was drippen, last time he called.'

'Did he now?' Arthur put the wrench back into his toolbox. 'Calls often, does he?'

'If he's passen this way.'

'He's a kind man like that, es Tom,' said Arthur.

'Well, we do have somethen sort of special between us, you know.'

'Special?' Arthur froze.

'Him and Kenwyn being such close mates all those years.'

'Oh, I see, yes.' Arthur breathed again. For one nasty moment he'd thought his worst fears were coming true . . . that Tom Hoskin was after Sally too. That possibility had been bothering him for some time. Hoskin was just the kind of heartless bastard who *would* try and take up with a dead mate's widow.

The other thought that had been on his mind for some time was that Sally, being a sensitive woman, might be afraid of gossiping tongues in the village. And that she might be more receptive to his advances, therefore, if they were to start their courting elsewhere, well away from St Clare.

'I might take a drive over to Godrevy, this Sunday,' he said, as if it were an idle passing thought.

'That would be nice,' said Sally, anticipating what was next. 'Tes lovely over Godrevy.'

Encouraged by this, Arthur went on, 'Take a picnic, maybe, if tes sunny.'

'Good idea, Arthur. You'll enjoy that. Do ee a power of good.'

'Well, perhaps you might care to join me?' he suggested, as if this brainwave had only just occurred to him.

'*Me*, Arthur?' she said, feigning surprise. 'Why that *es* a kind thought. But I'm busy this Sunday . . . We've a Methodist fête out to Madron.'

'Ah, now did I say *this* Sunday?' said Arthur. 'Well, when I said *this* Sunday, of course, I meant this Sunday *week*.'

Sally had seen this coming a mile off. In recent months it had been patently obvious what all the local bachelors had in mind . . . although none of them until now had managed to pluck up the courage to do anything about it. Which was probably as well, because most of them would have been wasting their time. But, discounting Lord Fred — who was way ahead of the field and in a class of his own — there were just two eligible men in the village, as far as she was concerned. One was Arthur Pascoe and the other was Tom Hoskin. And it was not easy to choose between the two. Both were over six feet tall, swarthy, hirsute, and in their late thirties. Tom was unquestionably the better looking, with his powerful shoulders, hair of thick black ringlets, and steely blue eyes. Whereas Arthur was going bald and had a substantial pot belly. But then *he* had a thriving butcher's shop; whereas Tom was a fisherman, trapped in a dying industry.

However, she had no intention of getting entangled with either man until she had finished giving Lord Fred, at the very least, a good run for his money. So for the time being, picnics with Arthur were out of the question. But before she had a chance to decline Arthur's invitation a second time, her daughter, Lucy, came bounding downstairs from her bedroom.

Lucy knew perfectly well what all the unmarried men in the village were after — and many of the married ones, to boot — and she had no intention of letting Arthur Pascoe or anybody else step into her father's place.

'Good heavens . . . Still here, Mr Pascoe?' she said, her face aglow with malevolent innocence. 'We must have the best plumbing in Cornwall, the time you've spent on that tap.'

'Arthur's just asked us if we'd like to go for a picnic over to Godrevy, Sunday week,' said Sally gaily. 'Isn't that kind of him?'

'Now isn't that just?' Lucy agreed. 'We'll all three have a handsome time.'

Arthur beamed at her with treacle smile and cyanide eyes. Dear, adorable Lucy. Almost sweet sixteen. With her clear blue eyes, fine blonde hair, and all the personable characteristics of a weasel. If anyone was capable of coming between him and Sally it was that precocious little brat.

'But I'm sure Lucy would prefer to spend Sunday with her own friends,' he said modestly.

'Oh, that *es* thoughtful of you, Mr Pascoe,' said Lucy. 'I'll ask a couple of them along too then. Angela and Pam. You'll like Pam. Her's got green and purple hair. We shall all have a brave old time.'

'But tes too early for me to say yet, Arthur,' Sally said. 'I may have to go and see my sister in Helston that afternoon. But I'll let you know nearer the time, if that's all right with you.'

'You do that,' said Arthur, putting a cheerful face on it. All was by no means lost. He could drop a subtle hint or two, later in the week, that Lucy's presence would not be required. Or maybe the dear sweet child would fall off her bicycle in the next week or so, and break both legs . . .

It was dark now. Danny Curnow parked his motorbike higher up Porthcurno Hill and crept down the quiet, unlit road to the screen of cypress trees at the bottom of Sally's back garden. He peeped through the foliage and looked towards the kitchen window in the hope of catching a glimpse of his beloved Lucy.

She was sitting at the table. Butcher Pascoe was just leaving . . . whatever was *he* doing there so late? Still wearing his Supa Niterider crash helmet and pure PVC gauntlets, Danny was grovelling about on his hands and knees at the side of the road for some minutes, trying to get a better view of Lucy . . . When, suddenly, without a hint of warning, someone seized him by the shoulder and shone a powerful flashlight in his eyes.

Instinctively believing that he was under all-out attack by the Sam Trevaskis gang, he curled up into a ball and squealed defiantly, 'No, Sam! Please, Sam! Don't Sam!'

'Dear heaven, Danny,' said PC Hawkins. 'Whatever are ee playen at down thear, this time of night?'

Danny stopped writhing about in the gutter and blinked up at the solid figure behind the flashlight.

'Aw . . . evenen, Mr Hawkins,' he said. 'I was juss . . . goan for a stroll.'

'On your knees? In a crash helmet?'

Danny scrambled to his feet and took off his helmet.

'Ah, well . . . see, I come here on me bike.'

'You'm goan for a stroll on your bike, are ee?'

'Er, naw . . . I *was* goan for a stroll. Then I changed me mind, and come on me bike instead. And somethen fell out me pocket juss now, as I was riden down to the village. So I'm looken for un.'

'Whear's your bike to now, an?'

'About twenty yard back up the hill. Tes quite safe, all tuck in snug by the hedge.'

'Well damnee, lad,' said Percy Hawkins quite at a loss to understand this, 'if you've lost somethen riden *down* the hill, how come your bike es still twenty yard back *up* un?'

Why me? Danny was thinking. *Please, God . . . why me?*

'Tes me wallet,' he said, totally evading the point at issue. 'I think I've lost me wallet.' He began fumbling about in the long grass at the side of the road.

At that moment, Sally Tremayne appeared in her back garden. 'What's goan on out thear?' she called.

'Don't ee worry, Sally,' Percy called back. 'Tes only I, Percy Hawkins, and young Danny Curnow. Lost ees wallet out here on the road.'

Sally was instantly concerned. 'Never? Well, us'll give ee a hand looken for un then.' She called in through the kitchen window, 'Lucy . . . Come out here, please, and help us look for Danny Curnow's wallet.'

And to Danny's horror, Lucy came out; and she and her

63

mother clambered up onto the road with torches and began searching through the grass and brambles by the roadside.

'What's it look like, Danny?' Lucy asked.

The mere sound of her voice stunned him into cerebral inertia.

'What's what look like?'

'Your wallet. What are we looken for?'

He tried desperately to think. To think of *any*thing. To produce even one rational, coherent thought. Lucy was staring at him, waiting for an answer. He felt giddy. He was sweating, churning over inside, paralysed by her proximity.

'Well, come on,' she prompted him. 'What does it look like? Where did you drop it?'

He was trying so hard to speak he thought he was going to burst. And when at last a sound emerged, he bawled at her, 'If I knawed where I'd dropped the bugger, I woulden have lost un, would I?'

Lucy said quietly, 'No call to bite my head off, Danny. I was only asken.'

Danny died a million deaths inside.

Then a voice called through the darkness from further down the hill, 'What's goan up thear, an?'

It was Eli Tonkin, grave-digger and traffic warden, who had come out of his house to investigate the disturbance.

'Tes only Percy,' PC Hawkins shouted back. 'Us es looken for loss property.'

Ever anxious to assist his superiors in the local forces of law and order, Eli called back, 'Right an, Percy. U'll juss summon assistance and be with ee djrectly.'

He arrived on the scene a few minutes later with a posse of neighbours, just as Dick Champion was driving down Porthcurno Hill in his breakdown truck. He stopped and played his headlights onto the scene.

Attracted by the lights and the gathering throng, Peter Rowe the chemist walked up the hill from the village and was joined by John Lanyon, the tobacconist, and his three dogs . . . just as Farmer Rosewarne and his eldest son, Tristan, drove by in their pick-up truck and stopped to help.

By quarter past ten, when PC Hawkins officially called off

the search, two dozen people were fruitlessly poking about in the hedgerows and verges of Porthcurno Hill, looking for a wallet that Danny secretly believed was not even within half a mile of the place.

But his agony was not over yet. For Percy Hawkins, ever painstaking in the performance of his duties, took him straight back to the semi-detached cottage that was both home and police station for St Clare's sole resident constable, and made out a full lost-property report.

It was gone eleven o'clock by the time Danny arrived home. He crept up to his bedroom, feeling crushed by fate and sick with remorse for having screamed at Lucy. And yet still his agony was not spent . . . Only now did he realise that his wallet *was* missing, after all.

He searched everywhere for it, but in vain. He had definitely taken it out with him that evening, he was quite convinced of that. But it had fallen out of his pocket somewhere . . . while he was messing about on Porthcurno Hill perhaps?

So, lying out there now — possibly somewhere in the Tremayne's back garden — was a black plastic wallet with his name inside, plus all his wordly poverty, three photographs of Lucy in a bikini, and two Black Stallion contraceptive sheaths . . . Just waiting to be found and handed in to Lucy's mum . . . or *his* mum . . . or PC Hawkins . . . or to vice reporters from *The Cornishman* . . . or to dread gang boss, Sam Trevaskis . . .

Danny lay awake for a long time that night, contemplating suicide by death at a tragically early age, and composing his own, most moving obituary for the *Western Morning News*.

4

Profung-17 was to be the miracle food of the century. It would solve all the world's food problems at a stroke. Partly because it would be dirt cheap. And partly because it would put millions off eating for life. And Pirana House Investments plc were the proud inventors and joint manufacturers of this highly secret new comestible.

Profung-17 was the triumphant culmination of many years of costly and intricate research into the extraction of protein from fungus. Other companies had produced protein from fungus — and very good protein it was too — but no company in the world had produced anything so revolting, tasteless and ridiculously cheap as Profung-17.

Profung-17 was so named because it was the seventeenth attempt to produce anything that stood even an outside chance of being passed by the Ministry of Agriculture as fit for human consumption. And as the Pirana House Corporation were world leaders in manufacturing food that was only just fit for human consumption, it was no surprise to rival manufacturers of perfectly *good* fungus protein to learn that Pirana House were behind all the disgusting, cheap imitations.

Profung, from its very conception, had been the adopted brainchild of His Huge Sagaciousness, Sir Wilfrid Macclesfield, chairman and chief executive. (Indeed *all* his brainchildren were adopted, or kidnapped.) And he had watched with loving parental pride and total incomprehension over every phase of its development. Profung, he was convinced, would do for the name Macclesfield what the internal combustion engine had done for Henry Ford. So he had staked his reputation, his self-esteem and everybody else's money in the project.

But the path to victory had been long and tortuously hard. And for years too numerous to mention in front of the shareholders, Pirana House's boffins had been experimenting in top-secret, fast-breeder fungus laboratories to find a way of separating marketable quantities of protein from all kinds of putrid, rotting growths. They had scoured all Britain and Ireland in a search for suitable fungi to cultivate . . . From the banks of Scottish lochs, to the slag heaps of the Rhondda, to the depths of God knows how many old Guinness bottles. And after eight years of trial, error and total lack of success, Research and Development division had run out of funds and the institutional shareholders had run out of patience.

But it was at this fateful watershed in the history of Profung-17 that the Japanese had come speeding to the rescue. Akiro Toshimoto, president and supreme autocrat of the Toshimoto All-Nippon Chemicals and Trading Corporation, had been aware for some time of Soviet and Third World interest in the development of new, cheap, high-protein animal feeds. And he had also been aware for some time of the secret experiments with Profung. He knew about the latter — and in considerable scientific detail — because he received copies of precisely the same briefings that Sir Wilfrid Macclesfield received . . . Thanks to an enterprising young typist at Pirana House, who had recently taken to changing her expensive Japanese sports cars every six months and taking luxury holidays in the Far East several times a year. So Akiro Toshimoto understood rather better than His Colossal Perspicaciousness, Sir Wilf (for Sir Wilf couldn't follow all that technical claptrap that was dumped on his desk every week), that Pirana House was frustratingly close to a major success. And for that very good reason, a team of Toshimoto's wiliest negotiators had hurriedly equipped themselves with lavish budgets, new umbrellas, and irresistible inducements, and had leapt on the first available plane for Birmingham.

However, desperate though he was to see his costly brain-child survive and thrive, Sir Wilfrid Macclesfield was a man of honour, and he had regarded Toshimoto's offer of an Anglo-Japanese partnership as a simple question of principle . . . Or more precisely, *two* principles. The first being loyalty. Loyalty to Queen and country. For Profung was a wholly British enterprise. It had been conceived by British brains, developed with British technology, mismanaged with British ineptitude, and stymied by British penury. But the second principle was one of priorities. And principally speaking, any offer of five hundred million yen in cash had to take priority over minor considerations like Queen and country.

So almost overnight, Toshimoto Chemicals and Pirana

House Investments had become partners in the search for ways to extract protein from micro-organisms. And within just two years, this fruitful and happy marriage had produced that extraordinary miracle of food technology, Profung -17.

This was to be the first official tasting of Profung-17, and it was to be a highly secret affair. Special invitations had been secretly printed by a company (whose name was never revealed) in a secret town, hundreds of miles away from Research and Development's secret headquarters. It was so secret that the original invitations had made no reference whatever to the nature of the function. So they had had to be secretly reprinted.

At long last, the great day had arrived. And on a sunny spring morning, soon after Easter, dozens of cars packed with executives and boffins took to the leafy lanes of Warwickshire and converged on Pirana House's secret research establishment at Deepmire Grange.

Shortly before midday, the official tasting party of privileged executives from Birmingham and Tokyo began to assemble in the grand reception hall for the long-awaited ceremony. In the nearby kitchen, the chef was putting the final decorative touches to his two precious creations — the first of their kind in the world: the incredible new Fungusburger, and the curried Profung biriani.

Upstairs in the chief research director's private office, Sir Wilfrid Macclesfield was making the final adjustments to his toupee, rehearsing an impromptu speech, and knocking back another large gin.

At twelve o'clock his managing director, Humphrey Overstone, came to fetch him, and Sir Wilf set off down an entire flight of stairs totally unaided, followed by his vast retinue of tax advisers, doctors, and secretaries in short leather skirts. When he reached the bottom of the stairs he lurched straight into the wrong room and began a speech of thanks to absolutely nobody and had to be guided back into the grand reception hall.

Everyone stood and applauded as Sir Wilf entered the hall and walked along the red carpet to where an especially large chair had been placed like a throne upon a dais at the other end of the room. Sir Wilf deposited his expansive backside on the throne, and a dining table, covered in crisp white linen and laid with shining silver cutlery, was placed in position before him by liveried flunkeys.

Everybody sat down again, and a hush descended as Sir Wilf realised he'd left his speech of thanks in the other room. So Humphrey Overstone pressed the gold bell push, set in a polished marble slab (all specially made by Asprey of Bond Street for the occasion), and the doors to the hall were thrown wide open by more uniformed flunkeys in grey wigs and frock coats, and the chef made his grand entry, bearing a silver salver upon each hand. He walked up to the dais and humbly placed the salvers on the table before His Phenomenal Pre-eminence, Sir Wilf.

'The Fungusburger, Sir Wilfrid,' he grovelled. 'And the curried Profung biriani.'

Sir Wilf peered into one salver, then into the other, then back to the first, and finally turned to the chef.

'Which is which?'

'The Fungusburger,' the chef replied, indicating the thing between two halves of a rye-bread bun. And indicating the other filthy mess: 'The Profung biriani.'

With a brave smile, Sir Wilf picked up his silver knife and fork and sampled a first tentative mouthful of Fungus-burger. Everyone looked on in silence. The chef waited nervously.

Sir Wilf chewed the morsel slowly and cautiously. Then he hesitated and frowned, and chewed for a while longer. And gradually the frown began to disappear and gave way to a look of surprise and delight.

'Not bad,' he murmured.

He carved off a larger piece and chewed it contemplatively.

'Hmmm . . . Not bad at all.'

He polished off the rest of it in three huge mouthfuls.

'Gradely, lad,' he told the chef, spitting fried fungus all over him. 'First rate! Congratulations!'

The chef blushed with modest pride and satisfaction.

Sir Wilf started on the Profung biriani. Everyone looked on woodenly. The truth was it looked like something the dog had left behind. Sir Wilf tasted a first tentative forkful. Then another. And another. And a broad smile of appreciation began to spread across his face.

'This is quite *incredible*, Mr Chef . . . Beyond my wildest hopes and expectations!'

He gobbled down the rest of it and asked if there was more.

Humphrey Overstone pressed the gold bell push once more, the doors were thrown open, and a dozen busty, unemployed actresses in silver lamé catsuits paraded into the room, carrying salvers heaped high with Fungusburgers and Profung biriani.

A buzz of eager anticipation filled the room. All Japanese eyes were on the nearest plateful of steaming Profung. All English eyes were on the nearest catsuit of bulging actress.

Sir Wilf stood up and raised a hand for silence.

'Ladies and gentlemen,' he said, 'I'm only sorry that my very good friend and partner, Akiro Toshimoto, could not be with us here today, on this very special occasion. But at this very moment, I am happy to say, hermetically sealed containers packed with Fungusburgers and Profung biriani are on their way to Tokyo by air, for the official Japanese tasting ceremony.'

The Japanese delegation loyally applauded the prospect of that function.

'I can only add,' Sir Wilf continued, 'that this is one of the proudest moments in my life. We, as a team, have been striving for decades to achieve that ultimate goal in food manufacturing that has eluded this industry for so long. We alone have achieved what every food producer in the civilised world has been struggling to achieve for the past thirty years or more. We, and we alone, have finally developed the world's very first, one hundred per cent, guaranteed *tasteless* food. Ladies and gentlemen, I give you . . . *Profung-17*!'

And at that the entire hall broke into a storm of applause, and everyone began tucking in, wolfing down the filthy mess as fast as the Pirana Pussies could dish it out.

Jubilation reigned at Deepmire Grange. Profung-17 was obviously a miracle. Nothing less. It would be the beginning of an international revolution in eating habits. The bad old days of beefy steaks, piggy bacon and sheepy mutton were numbered. There was still a long way to go, but the day was fast approaching when the ordinary working folk of Britain, toiling in their millions each day to reach the nearest dole queue, could look forward to an unlimited supply of dirt-cheap, odourless, colourless, totally flavourless, indestructible, goodness-free, imitation food.

Small wonder then that the champagne and sake flowed late into the small hours in Birmingham and Tokyo that night.

By lunchtime the following day, the directors of Pirana House were busy waking up in strange beds all over Warwickshire, and phoning their wives to say they'd been delayed by fog at Orly. Those who were capable of reaching Birmingham without being breathalysed forgathered in the boardroom that afternoon over a relaxing case of Alka Seltzer to discuss important matters like Pirana Pussies and Profung-17, and to vote democratically in favour of everything that Sir Wilfrid proposed.

The boardroom, on the twenty-first floor of Pirana House, was a huge room, luxuriously carpeted in Pirana purple, dominated by a vast table of real simulated mahogany veneer, and hung with large portraits of extremely important people . . . like Sir Wilfrid Macclesfield. And his wife. And her husband.

'Gentlemen,' Sir Wilf began. 'After the successful low-volume production of Profung-17 at Deepmire Grange, it is proposed that we progress to selective consumer trials . . . both here, in our staff canteens, and out in the field.'

Sir Wilf turned to his managing director, Humphrey

Overstone, who nodded with total approval . . . Although he didn't have the foggiest idea which particular field Sir Wilf had in mind; but he presumed that it was some specific plot of land somewhere that nobody had yet told him about. He said, 'Hear hear,' and continued juggling with his gonads. The rest of the board duly nodded likewise, and carried on marking off their day's selections in *The Sporting Life*.

'It is proposed then,' Sir Wilf continued, 'that we concentrate all production from now on at just *one* of our three existing fungus nurseries, presently sited at Llanidloes in Wales, and at Mallaig in Scotland, and near Redruth in Cornwall. Scientific tests have shown that because of its extraordinary climate and subsoil, the south-western peninsula offers the most favourable conditions for the rapid propagation of our patent hybrid fungus, *Bellamorta Pirana*. And of our three existing pilot nurseries, it is a fact that Redruth has been cultivating ten times the quantity of fungus per square metre that Wales and Scotland have been producing.'

Overstone nodded again and said, 'Good, good.' Perhaps it was one of *these* fields that Sir Wilf had been referring to.

'Proposition one, then,' said Sir Wilfrid. 'We close down the pilot plants in Llanidloes and Mallaig and cease all production there. Whilst — proposition two — we intensify production at Redruth and increase the acreage under cultivation by acquiring additional agricultural land in that region. And proposition three, we keep the fast-breeder fermentation, filtration and processing plant on stream at Deepmire Grange, and maintain a twice weekly supply of fresh fungus by road from the Redruth nursery.'

He looked round the table. All heads were nodding. And some of them were still awake.

One particularly intelligent, good-looking, well-mannered, right thinking young director, who would go far in Sir Wilf's opinion, and who happened coincidentally to be his eldest son, Stanley, enquired, 'How much additional land are the R and D technicians asking us to acquire for fungus cultivation?'

'A very pertinent . . . wise . . . relevant . . . perceptive . . . question . . . ,' stumbled Sir Wilf, playing for time whilst he hunted through the pile of papers that his senior private secretary had painstakingly prepared for him that morning. 'And it just so happens,' he went on, alighting finally upon the relevant document, 'that I have the answer readily to hand. Speaking entirely from memory . . . ' He put on his spectacles and read, '*We shall require an area of between thirty and fifty acres, with local authority permission to erect between fifty and one hundred large aluminium breeding shelters*.' Sir Wilf looked up from his papers and added, 'Preferably away from the public eye, to attract the minimum of attention to the Profung-17 project. And preferably with a docile, reliable labour force in the vicinity, who will do all the back-breaking manual work for peanuts, and not bring any trade unions into it.' Sir Wilf removed his spectacles. 'The very cream of my investment scouts will be put onto this, to find a suitable location, as soon as I have your approval, gentlemen . . . '

Ormskirk had spent an exhausting morning booking his summer holiday. So the abrupt summons to the twenty-first floor came as an unpleasant shock. For Sir Wilf never sent for an executive in the middle of the day unless it meant trouble. And to be summoned at only a moment's notice probably meant that his recurrent nightmare had finally come true . . . There had been a really stupendous cock-up.

'Something's gone terribly wrong,' he bleated to his secretary as she straightened his tie and brushed his jacket. 'I know. I can tell.' He mopped his pink sweaty face with a handkerchief and passed his secretary her headscarf to dust his shoes with. 'I bet it's that indoor ski-slope at Accrington. It's fallen down or something. On top of thousands of tiny tots. I *knew* it was a lousy investment. Now half Accrington will be hammering at the turnstiles for their money back. Or trying to ski down a dead flat slalom. Oh, God . . . ' He got up and combed his hair in the reflection of an enormous, framed photograph of Sir Wilfrid on the wall. 'Perhaps it's caught fire?' He began to panic. 'Oh, Christ . . . the snow!

The snow's caught fire, I bet. All that friction. I *said* they shouldn't make snow out of combustible polyurethane . . .'

His secretary propelled him out of the office, and he trembled away to commandeer the nearest available lift.

By the time he arrived at the chairman's assistant deputy private secretary's office, his bowels were beginning to move. And by the time he reached the *senior* private secretary's office, seven ante-rooms further on, and was poised at the chairman's door, the whole of his lower digestive tract was in a state of rampant insurrection.

The senior private secretary entered first. After a moment, she emerged and told Ormskirk in a respectable whisper that he could go in now. Resisting the natural impulse to enter on hands and knees, Ormskirk clasped his fingers decisively in front of him to stop them trembling and crept into the all holy of holies, in the faint hope that Sir Wilf wouldn't notice him and might forget whatever it was he was going to sack him for.

Miles away, across a crowded Persian carpet that was worth almost as much as Ormskirk's five-bedroomed house in Edgbaston, sat God, surrounded by towering banks of visual display units, short-circuit cablevision screens, and videorecording monitors showing last night's episode of *Coronation Street*.

'Ah . . . Ormskirk!' boomed Sir Wilfrid. 'Sit.'

Ormskirk abruptly dropped into the nearest chair and awaited the next command.

'Margery,' Sir Wilf began sympathetically. 'How is she?'

Ormskirk didn't know anyone called Margery. But that didn't matter. 'Fine, sir, thank you. Thank you, sir, fine.' He wanted to say *my lord*, but managed to stop himself.

'What was it again?'

'Was . . . what, sir?' squeaked Ormskirk.

'The trouble.'

'The trouble . . . with . . . which, sir?'

'With Margery. Margery's trouble.'

Ormskirk shut his eyes and prayed. 'Margery *who*, sir?'

'Your wife, Margery.'

'My wife's name is Gladys, sir.'

'Ah-ha.' Sir Wilf looked puzzled. 'Are you sure?'

Ormskirk was bursting to go to the lavatory. 'Quite sure.'

'Divorced?'

'No, sir. No, my wife is definitely married.'

'Again . . . ?'

'No, just the once. To me. My wife's married to me. She always has been.'

'How long has this been going on?'

'Well . . . ever since our wedding, Sir Wilfrid.'

'I see.' Sir Wilf was not yet prepared to concede that Ormskirk might be right, but nor was he going to waste time pursuing a fruitless conversation. 'Then how is Gladys?'

'Very, very well, thank you, sir. Sends you and Lady Macclesfield her warmest personal respects . . . unpresumptuously, of course.'

Sir Wilf frowned. 'Did they have to amputate?'

'Amputate?' Ormskirk's voice hit a falsetto. He cleared his throat. 'Amputate what, sir?'

'The other leg.'

Ormskirk was hopelessly baffled. There was nothing wrong with his wife's legs. So far as he knew she had an entirely normal complement of legs. At least, she certainly had when he'd left home that morning. He shook his head. 'No, sir. There's nothing wrong with the other leg.' He cleared his throat again. 'Or the *other* leg, in point of fact.'

Sir Wilf's eyes narrowed. 'Must have got the wrong Margery. Perhaps I'm thinking of that chap Mukherjee from public relations . . . ?'

'A very understandable mistake, sir,' said Ormskirk graciously, as if the two names could possibly be confused by anyone other than a complete moron.

'Then to business,' continued Sir Wilf, briskly turning to a folder on his desk. 'I have here an investment report from Leisure and Pleasure division . . . '

'Accrington,' said Ormskirk quickly. 'Ridiculous idea in the first place. I fought tooth and nail against it . . . '

'This chalet camp scheme in St Clare . . . ' Sir Wilf went on, taking not a blind bit of notice of what anyone else was saying, as usual.

'All Sharkley's idea,' said Ormskirk loyally. 'Ludicrous. I fought tooth and nail to dissuade . . .'

'Who is this Mervyn Sharkley character?'

'A fool, Sir Wilfrid, a blind young fool. I'm entirely in agreement with you. I told him the idea was insane . . .'

'Fifty acres of agricultural land, with outline planning consent just expired for a large chalet camp. And a mansion nearby where we could house a considerable number of research technicians.'

'Research technicians?' said Ormskirk, puzzled.

He, of course, knew nothing whatever about the top-secret Profung-17 project. Sir Wilf hastily corrected his slip of the tongue.

'Or bus drivers, or window-cleaners, or any other sort of holidaymaker. It would appear from what Sharkley says in his report that permission to erect structures on these fifty acres might be easily obtained?'

'That could depend, sir, on the strength of local public opinion. There may be some opposition. They're very peculiar people the Cornish, you know.'

'I *do* know. My wife's family come from Cornwall.'

'Very peculiar-ly warm, friendly, wonderful people,' Ormskirk continued emphatically.

'Well, I like the look of this scheme,' Sir Wilf concluded. 'I like it very much.'

'Thank you, sir. It *is* a good scheme,' Ormskirk agreed. 'I liked it from the very first moment I suggested it to Sharkley.'

'But soft-pedal on that idea of turning Tremorna Hall into a hotel,' said Sir Wilf, reckoning that it would make excellent residential quarters for the technical and scientific staff. 'Don't let this Lord St Clare chap get the idea that we're definitely going ahead with it.'

'That *is* the weak part of the scheme,' Ormskirk agreed. 'That was young Sharkley's suggestion, actually . . . fatuous . . .'

'It's a very good idea, of course . . .'

'Oh, brilliant, unquestionably . . .'

'But in practice . . .' Sir Wilf smiled. 'You know . . .'

'Oh, undoubtedly.'

'A bit dubious.'

'Undoubtedly dubious.'

'So just keep Lord St Clare on a string for the time being, while we survey the area and sound out public opinion about a development on those fifty acres.'

'Precisely what I had in mind, sir,' said Ormskirk.

'Excellent.' The chairman nodded. 'That'll be all for the time being then.'

'Thank you, sir.' Ormskirk arose and crept backwards to the door.

'My regards to your wife,' said Sir Wilf benevolently. 'Whoever she is.'

'Thank you, sir,' said Ormskirk, bowing his way out. 'She'll be very touched.'

As soon as he was out of the door he sped off in search of the nearest lavatory.

Chalet camps in Cornwall? Sir Wilf was thinking, once Ormskirk had gone. How bloody stupid could those L and P investment boys get? *Chalet* camps? In *Cornwall*? That sort of thing had gone out of fashion with trolley buses, sugar rationing and *Mrs Dale's Diary* . . .

Sharkley had been having a ghastly time of it ever since his trip to Cornwall the previous month. The situation had been parlous enough before, but his encounter with the chubby Miranda Jago at Tremorna Hall had turned a disturbing situation into a potentially terrifying one. He had been having fantasies about her ever since. Disgusting fantasies. He had put up sterling resistance, but all to no avail. Every night as he climbed into bed in his non-iron, karate pyjamas, with rampant stag motif, he struggled to concentrate his mind on good, clean, wholesome things . . . Like brown bread, lemon barley water, and offshore funds. But as soon as he switched out the light, she would come creeping insidiously into his thoughts, peeling off that silky kaftan, like some snake-eyed Salome. And once more he'd be back on that familiar wrack of hot, sticky lust.

Not surprisingly, it had begun to affect his health . . . Because apart from the mental anguish, he was waking up completely knackered every morning. Even Ormskirk, who seldom perceived any deterioration in the health of his staff until at least a week after the funeral, had noticed that something was wrong and had enquired politely if he was well.

But Ormskirk was the very last person he could confide in. Ormskirk was so obese, it was rumoured he hadn't seen his testicles for ten years. He might have got entirely the wrong idea.

He turned for help instead to Dougal McCann, his pal from Fixed Assets. He had faith in Dougal. Dougal was a man of the world. He was a mine of information about all sorts of things that Sharkley didn't quite understand or believe in. And he was always talking about sex in one form or another, so it was not difficult to slip a new perversion into the conversation occasionally without drawing undue attention to oneself. And one night, over a few port and lemons at the Club Executif in downtown Birmingham, he said to Dougal:

'Here, there's this bloke I know who only goes for plump chicks. That's all that turns him on. You know, the podgy sort. All squoodgey and wobbly and chubby.'

'One of them, eh?' said Dougal ominously. 'A fat freak.'

'Funny, isn't it?' said Sharkley, with an airy laugh.

'No, it's not,' said Dougal. 'Not remotely funny. Thank God it's very rare.'

'Why? What do you mean?'

Dougal shook his head sympathetically. 'Poor sods. It's always just *chubby* girls at the start. But it gets them like a terrible drug. It hooks them. They start to need fatter and fatter girls as time goes by, to ease the craving. Until nothing less than a Michelin woman will do. It's harrowing to watch.'

'To watch . . . ?' Sharkley was seized with consternation.

'To watch a good man destroy himself, his career, and his family . . . Just because he's in the grip of a monstrous, incurable perversion. To watch him sinking deeper and

78

deeper into a quicksand of shame, depravity, and public humiliation.'

Sharkley tried to laugh. 'Oh, come off it, Dougal . . .'

But Dougal was unrelenting. 'If the specialists can diagnose it early enough, in its primary stage, they can treat it with drugs and psychotherapy. There are special clinics you can go to on the National Health. But in extreme cases it wrecks people's lives. Even drives men to suicide.'

'Phew . . .' Sharkley shook his head and smiled feebly. 'Well, thank God for being normal.' He downed his port and lemon and ordered a treble Scotch.

So it was with mixed feelings that he received the news in Geoffrey Ormskirk's office, the following afternoon.

'You're going back to St Clare, Mervyn.' Ormskirk was looking rather pleased with himself. 'I've got to be honest with you, Sir Wilf didn't think much of your scheme at first. But I had a natter with him this morning over a few cognacs up there on the twenty-first, and I managed to win him round. I had to fight, mind. Fight tooth and nail. But I stuck by you, Mervyn. And we've now got the amber light to advance one stage further.'

'I appreciate that, Geoff,' said Sharkley, believing every word of it. 'Appreciate that very much.'

'Think nothing of it, old son,' said Ormskirk generously. 'That's what working as a team is all about. Now what I'd like you to do is to sound out public opinion in the village and put in a bit of PR work while the surveyors and valuers get busy. And meantime keep Lord St Clare sweet . . . but soft-pedal on the idea of converting his gaff into a hotel.'

'Why?'

'Well . . .' Come to think of it Ormskirk didn't know why. So he played safe. 'Money.' That was as good a reason as any. 'Could cost us half a million to convert that house and grounds.'

'But it's a central part of the whole scheme, Geoff,' Sharkley protested. 'What can I tell Lord St Clare?'

'Tell him anything you like,' said Ormskirk, dodging the responsibility. 'Just don't make any promises.'

Far from feeling elated with the news that the twenty-first floor had finally given provisional assent to one of his very own investment schemes, Sharkley felt strangely depressed. So depressed that as he left Pirana House that evening and set off across the executive forecourt, with head bowed and eyes fixed morosely on the concrete at his feet, he almost walked under the wheels of a passing car.

But this was no ordinary car. This was an exclusive Rolls-Royce Silver Haze that had been hand-built for the Nizam of Chanderabad in 1932. It now bore the registration number WHM, for Wilfrid Herbert Macclesfield. And from the luxurious enormity of the aft quarters, behind mortar-proof glass panelling, Sir Wilf glared out at the offending Sharkley, who could so easily have been knocked down, seriously damaging the paintwork. He pressed a button, and a window opened with a respectful hush.

'Who the bloody hell are you?' he demanded.

'Mervyn Sharkley, Sir Wilfrid,' Sharkley replied, wondering how much his unemployment benefit would amount to these days. 'Leisure and Pleasure.'

'Well, damn lucky for you that my chauffeur is quick off the . . . ' He broke off in full flow. 'Did you say . . . *Sharkley*?'

'Yes, Sir Wilfrid.'

'Are you the silly bloody arse who drew up that plan for a chalet camp in Cornwall?'

'Yes, Sir Wilfrid.'

Sir Wilf sniffed and looked him up and down. 'Well, why didn't you say so before?' He lowered his voice. 'Going back down there to do a spot of PR, eh?'

'Yes, Sir Wilfrid.'

'Well done, lad. Ormskirk mayn't have told you but R and D might be sending a few boys down from the labs to do soil tests. So liaise.' It was one of Sir Wilf's favourite words. 'All right, Sharkley? Liaise.'

'Yes, Sir Wilfrid.' What exactly he was supposed to liaise about, however, Sir Wilf did not reveal.

'And one more thing . . . '

'Yes, Sir Wilfrid?'

The chairman's voice dropped to a confidential murmur. 'L and P division has not lived up to my personal expectations. I don't think that's much of a secret around Pirana House any more. If you can improve matters, Sharkley, you'll be doing your career prospects a power of good. Understand?'

'Yes, Sir Wilfrid.'

'Good.' He smiled. 'Well, it's nice to have had this informative little chat with you. I like my executives to speak their mind.'

'Yes, Sir Wilfrid.'

'Good night to you.' And the window shushed closed again.

'Good night, Sir Wilfrid.'

And the Silver Haze glided soundlessly out of the forecourt and straight through a crowd of old people on a zebra crossing.

Poor old Geoff, eh? thought Sharkley, driving home that evening. Up for the chop, by the sound of it. Now *there* was a turnabout in fortunes. Poor fella. With kids at public school, and a socking great mortgage, and millions of executives like him already on the dole. Ask not for whom the bell tolls, eh? Poor old Geoff. Could be gone by summer. Or even sooner.

He wondered if he'd be allowed to change the pot plants and choose his own secretary once he was installed in Ormskirk's place. And he thought suddenly of Maud. And of her high heels, and black stockings, and suspender belts, and tight leather mini-skirts, and fat thighs, and bulging waist, and . . .

In the midst of his agony, Dougal's words came crashing into his mind like a voice of doom: '*It's harrowing to watch a good man destroy himself, his career, and his family . . . just because he's in the grip . . .* '

Sharkley began to visualise the headlines in the national newspapers:

'MY LIFE OF SHAME' — PIRANA HOUSE INVESTMENT CHIEF QUITS IN DUMPY DOLLS VICE SCANDAL.

'MY LUST FOR CHUBBY CHICKS' — SIR MERVYN SHARKLEY, MANAGING DIRECTOR OF PIRANA HOUSE, EXPOSED IN HORROR SHOCK OUTRAGE.

LORD SHARKLEY OF SOLIHULL, CHAIRMAN OF PIRANA HOUSE, PRESIDENT OF WORLD BANK, CLOSE FRIEND OF ROYAL FAMILY, PLUMMETED FROM PUBLIC PEAKS BY PODGE PERVERSION . . .

PART THREE

MAY

1

THE REVEREND OWEN BORAGE had been vicar of St Clare-by-Addle for seven years. He did not look Cornish, but most people don't. And he did not sound Cornish. But then he came from Sidcup. And before moving to St Clare neither he nor his good wife, Constance, had been further west than Paignton on a wet weekend. Yet at no time during the past seven years had this deterred them from whipping up support in the locality for every conceivable kind of activity to help preserve the traditional olde worlde Cornwall that everyone had come to know and love and suspect had never really existed anyway.

The Borages had proven themselves to be indefatigable organisers. And like all democratically-minded leaders, they had a compulsive urge to form committees. And to dominate them. So St Clare was swamped with committees. Hundreds of them. All run by precisely the same people. In fact there were almost as many committees in the village as there were inhabitants. And to protect the interests of all these committees, the Reverend Owen Borage had founded the St Clare's Bay Community Association.

The distinguishing feature of the community association was that it was avowedly secular and non-denominational. For St Clare had a long and enviable record of appalling Christian discord between Anglicans and Methodists, and the community association had been designed to bridge this ever popular and much-loved gulf of bigotry and intolerance.

To which end, the vicar had determined that it should be controlled by a committee of totally disinterested, nonpartisan individuals who were above petty religious prejudice. And he had therefore had no hesitation in unanimously appointing himself chairman, and his wife secretary, and filling every other position of authority with devout practising Anglicans, conspicuous for their tendency to leave at least one pound sterling on the collection plate each Sunday.

The community association met once a month at the village hall, where everybody drank tea and ate sticky buns and discussed absolutely anything that anybody wanted to discuss, provided that the Reverend Owen Borage wanted to discuss it too. And amongst the myriad topics that the myriad committees regularly discussed was resistance . . . Resistance to everything except the *status quo*. But in particular, resistance to any sort of change, development or improvement in the locality that did not meet with the vicar's personal approval. And having discussed it over tea and sticky buns, they would spend the rest of the month lobbying councillors and members of parliament, and writing to the editor of the *Daily Telegraph*. None of whom ever took a blind bit of notice.

Precisely *why* the Reverend Owen Borage and his wife were so obsessed with protecting the Cornish heritage was a mystery to the inhabitants of St Clare, most of whom — unlike the vicar — were more concerned with such selfish trivialities as trying to earn a living. Nevertheless, the majority opinion, amongst those who cared sufficiently to voice one, was that as long as *somebody* fought to keep the traditions alive it didn't much matter who it was or whence he came.

Such however was not the majority opinion amongst Lord St Clare. (And Freddie was perfectly capable of holding any number of different opinions about anything at any one time.) For it was thanks to the virulent opposition of Mr Borage and his committees that it had taken two whole years for Freddie to secure outline planning consent for a chalet camp on West Meadows.

The Jagos and the Borages were, technically speaking, neighbours — in as much as the jungle surrounding Tremorna Hall did at one point share a length of granite wall with the jungle surrounding the vicarage. But relations between the two households had never been warmer than frosty, at best.

From his earliest days in St Clare, the vicar had felt slighted by his lordship. For Freddie had summarily refused to sit on any of his new committees (and there were *hundreds* to choose from) or to take the slightest interest in the community association. The fact that Freddie only attended church upon those few occasions when, by tradition, he was expected to read the lesson had not helped matters. And, just to put the tin hat on things, it had soon become evident to the vicar, after regular observations of Tremorna Hall through binoculars, that his lordship and the less than wholly honourable Miranda were indulging in all manner of unspeakable depravities . . . like enjoying themselves. *And* with members of the opposite sex, what was more. It had not yet become clear to the vicar exactly *what* was going on there, but it would eventually . . . just as soon as he could afford a more powerful pair of binoculars.

Nothing however had so incensed Mr Borage as the news that his lordship wished to erect one hundred and fifty wooden holiday chalets upon the ancient Druidic settlement of West Meadows. The vicar had produced an overwhelming couple of objections to this, neither of which had been disputable as a point of fact. The first was that it would involve change. And the second, that it would involve Freddie. On both counts therefore, the scheme had qualified for staunch resistance; and the vicar and his wife had immediately embarked upon a determined campaign of opposition, stirring up such a fug of uninformed hysteria throughout West Cornwall that it had taken Freddie twenty-two months and a QC to obtain planning permission.

To a large extent, the vicar's success in arousing local opposition had been due to various superstitions about the Hag's Ring. The Hag's Ring was a circle of huge rocks on the site of a Stone Age development dating back to about

2000 BC. Nobody had the faintest idea who had put them there, or when, or why. But the site was thought to have been of religious significance to the pagan Celts and their Druid priests at around the time of Christ, and it had been whispered down through the centuries that anyone who desecrated that hallowed ground would come to a nasty end. And there had been only two occasions in recorded history when anyone had seriously considered doing so. Once, in 1893, when the then Lord St Clare had given permission for the rocks to be broken up and used in the construction of the new harbour. And again in 1940, when some twerp from the War Office had shown up with a section of Royal Engineers, possessed of the inane notion of moving the entire Ring to Falmouth to serve as tank traps. On both occasions the curse of the Ring, which was greatly feared by some locals, had struck back with lethal rapidity. The unfortunate Lord St Clare had been killed the following day in a riding accident. And the twerp from the War Office had been killed the same night in the Plymouth blitz.

Now the Reverend Owen Borage, being a good Christian soul, did not believe in any of this twaddle about the curse of the Ring, or any other such fairy tales, but it was all power to his arm in the battle against Lord Fred's chalet camp. And on this occasion, for once, he was in full alliance with another influential protagonist in village affairs, Granny Polkinghorne, the local pellar (. . . or white witch).

Granny Polkinghorne, who was anything between eighty-seven and one hundred and twenty years old (according to whether one believed the official records or Ned Gummoe), lived alone in a cottage high up on Blakey's Ridge above West Meadows, with seven cats and a shed full of potent home-made wines and herbal medicines. She had nothing against Lord Fred, and no great affection for the Reverend Borage, but the desecration of the Hag's Ring was something that she felt compelled to denounce. After all, people came from as far away as Launceston to have their ring-worm and warts charmed away, and they expected the pellar to take a decent, upright, superstitious stance on matters like this. So, for sound commercial reasons she had deemed it politic to stick up for the Druids and predict all sorts of terrible ills were Lord Fred to go ahead and build on that sacred land.

Nevertheless, Lord Fred had still obtained planning consent, eventually, and everyone had had a quiet smirk at Granny Polkinghorne's expense. But within a week, Freddie had lost half a million pounds on the commodity markets and had been obliged to abandon the chalet camp scheme altogether. And it was that financial débâcle that had finally obliged him to put the last of his estate up for sale. So the only people to have emerged from the sorry tale with any credit were Granny Polkinghorne and the Druids. Even the vicar had been left to wonder at the pellar's powers of divination after that. But it had at least put an end to any further talk of building on West Meadows . . . Until Mervyn Sharkley, the diminutive Arab, had arrived on the scene . . .

The news of this latest shock horror chalet drama had taken St Clare by storm. And for some weeks now, in the face of Lord Fred's unrelenting refusal to comment publicly on the matter, it had been a subject of intense speculation and ill-informed rumour. Some stupid people had got it into their heads that Tremorna Hall was going to be pulled down, and a new hotel built on the site. A few *very* stupid people believed, further, that the new hotel was going to be built with the rocks from the Hag's Ring. And one daft old sod thought that Tremorna Hall was being pulled down, shovelled over to West Meadows, and rebuilt as a hotel on *top* of the Hag's Ring.

Most villagers, however, did not know *what* to think. Which was good news for the Reverend Owen Borage, who was only too happy, as always, to guide them along the path of wisdom and true righteousness. And having formed yet another new committee to co-ordinate a campaign against Lord Fred and Pirana House, he announced an extraordinary general meeting of the community association, to be held on the Third of May, and invited his lordship and the miniscule Sharkley to attend and speak, and put an end to all this rumour and speculation, once and for all . . .

The only extraordinary thing about the meeting was that practically the entire village turned up for it. For usually, only the vicar and his fan club bothered to attend the association's monthly gatherings. Tonight, however, even the public bar of the Proud Pinnace was deserted — a sure sign that, at the very least, the world was about to end or *Coronation Street* about to begin.

Tom Hoskin, for one, was delighted with the vicar's timely decision to convene this meeting. As a fisherman, he didn't give a stuff about chalet camps on West Meadows, but as Sally Tremayne's future husband he did value the opportunity to walk her home afterwards . . . Particularly now he knew that Arthur Pascoe was trying to muscle in on the action too. He had decided that it was high time he took decisive action. Which was why he was standing outside the village hall, just before eight o'clock, waiting for Sally to arrive. Inside, the place was packed to bursting.

Farmer Rosewarne's car approached, flattened three POLICE — NO PARKING signs, and pulled up outside the entrance to the hall, perfectly in line with the white markings that read '*parking strictly prohibited*'. As the only landowner of any significance in the area, Farmer Rosewarne was keeping a beady eye on the Jago estate, although it was largely useless for agriculture.

'Right an, Tucker?' Tom greeted him.

'Right an, Tom.'

'How's business an?'

'Aw, bad, bad . . . Never worse,' Rosewarne grumbled, easing himself out of his brand new Mercedes-Benz.

'Tes that Common Market,' said Tom.

'Aw, ais.' Rosewarne shook his head bitterly. 'Us shall all be in paupery djrectly.'

He barged his way inside the hall, just as Arthur Pascoe was barging his way out to see where Sally Tremayne had got to. And at that moment Sally herself came walking round the corner from Middle Street.

''Allo, Sally!' said Tom. 'Well, thear's a coincidence . . .'

'What es a coincidence then, Tom?' she asked.

'I was juss this minute thinken that I had to remember not to forget to ask ee somethen tonight.'

'And what's that?'

'Well . . . ' Tom took a deep breath. 'See, I was thinken of goan ovver to Lizard, Sunday.'

'Oh, that *will* be nice. You'll enjoy that.'

'And I was thinken you might fancy comen along too. Do ee a power of good, a drive out of a Sunday.'

'Well now that *es* a kind thought, Tom,' she said. 'But I can't say just now. I shall have to give ee an answer nearer Friday, if that's all right?'

'Aw, ais, you think about un,' said Tom, delighted not to get an outright refusal. 'Let us know when you'm good and ready now.'

He turned to open the door into the village hall, and only now realised that Arthur Pascoe was standing in the way.

'Right an, Art?' he said, with a blatantly false note of good cheer. 'Ow be doan, my 'andsome?'

Pascoe ignored him totally, bade Sally good evening, and stepped away from the door to let her enter. He then entered the hall right behind her and blocked the doorway so that Tom could not get in. Tom hammered furiously on the door, but the din was so great inside that no one could hear him.

At the far end of the hall, seated on a small stage about a foot above the commonality, the supreme praesidium of the community association, comprising the Reverend Owen Borage, his good wife Constance, and an entourage of elderly women in tweed suits, waited patiently for the stroke of eight o'clock.

Owen and Constance were practically indistinguishable. They were both sixty-one years of age, much the same height, and preferred wearing trousers. And with their white, wispy hair, and chalky complexions to match, they both looked as if they had just been hit with a bag of flour.

They were an untidy, absent-minded, maladroit couple and neither was blessed with perfect sight. Each possessed numerous pairs of round, wire-framed, National Health spectacles for various different purposes, and each frequently put on the other's spectacles by mistake. Since he was *long*-sighted and she was *near*-sighted their life together had been one of perpetual domestic chaos. Curious then that they should have had this irrepressible urge to organise everything and everybody, and an unshakable faith in their abilities so to do. However . . .

Drawing before him the official agenda for this extra-ordinary general mêlée, meticulously typed out by at least several committees, the vicar perceived that *two* contentious issues had been placed before the supreme praesidium for general debate. Apart from the burning question of the development on West Meadows, the sisters Alice and Dora Uglow, eighty-five and eighty-six years of age respectively, had complained that Socrates the bull had chased them off public rights of way across Farmer Rosewarne's land, and were pressing for the mighty beast to be penned up or gelded. After very little deliberation, the vicar decided to leave this matter until last.

As the clock of St Clare-by-Addle parish church struck eight, the vicar bashed his gavel smartly on the table to bring the hall to order. But no one took the slightest notice. In fact, such was the general hubbub, nobody heard him beyond the first couple of rows. These were occupied by his fan club, under the leadership of Nancy Curnow, who obligingly stood up to face the audience, filled her capacious lungs and bellowed '*Quieeeeet!*' for just long enough to stop every vessel within thirty miles of the Longships lighthouse.

Everyone in the hall fell silent . . . except Tom Hoskin, who was still trying to elbow his way into the room against the obdurate resistance of butcher Pascoe. Out of the silence, his voice could be heard growling, 'Shift yer bloody great arse, Pascoe, you silly bugger . . . '

'Are we quite gathered?' enquired the vicar, in a powdery, pale voice, the colour of his complexion.

'Aw yes, vicar,' Arthur Pascoe called out, pushing Tom back out of the door. 'All assembled now.'

A foul stench had reached the vicar's sensitive nostrils. Selecting a pair of spectacles from the assortment on the table, he surveyed the assembly through the filtering effects of old gravy splashes and thumbprints. His gaze alighted finally upon Ned Gummoe, whose gnarled briar was emitting clouds of grey-black smoke like the old steamship *Scillonian* putting out of Penzance harbour.

Ned came every month to the community association meetings. He usually arrived just in time for his free cup of tea and sticky bun, and left immediately afterwards upon urgent business.

'Thank you for not smoking, Mr Gummoe,' said the vicar tartly. 'There are signs everywhere in the hall.'

'Can't put her out now her's goan,' said Ned resolutely. 'Us'll have to let un die down natural in her own time, Rev'ran.'

'Aw, get on wi' un, vicar,' Dick Champion shouted from the back.

His cry was taken up by the irascible Methodist contingent packed into the rear of the hall.

'Order, order,' said the vicar, bashing his gavel on the table thrice more. 'We are gathered here tonight for an orderly and civilised discussion of grave matters. I must beseech you all to give every speaker a fair hearing. I call first upon Lord St Clare, who wishes to make a statement to the assembly.' He changed his spectacles again and peered round the hall. 'Lord St Clare . . . ?'

Freddie rose from his seat half way down the hall and walked purposefully towards the stage.

It was a little over a month since Danny Curnow had lost his wallet on Porthcurno Hill and sworn so furiously at Lucy Tremayne. And a thoroughly rotten month it had been. He still hadn't found his wallet. And as far as he knew no one else had found it either. And he still hadn't plucked up the courage to apologise to Lucy.

He had *tried* to apologise, dozens of times. He had ridden many miles on his BSA Bantam to various telephone boxes to call her. And on two occasions he had even got as far as dialling her number. But he'd lost his nerve and put the phone down while the pips were still beeping.

But now that a whole month had gone by, he had begun to hope that she might have forgotten the incident, and that as soon as he'd clocked up eight score draws on the football pools she might marry him . . . Or at least go out for a walk with him . . . Or at least glance at him occasionally.

But then he had had the horrendous misfortune to bump into her in Rundle's (fancy goods and post office). And she had cut him stone dead. She had refused even to acknowledge that he was in the shop. So that evening he decided to write a formal letter of apology.

The letter took him a long time — well over twenty minutes — and consumed several sheets of Woolworth's finest cream-laid notepaper, as successive revised drafts were tossed into the litter bin in a remorseless quest for perfection. But nothing is too much trouble for the woman one loves.

The hardest part was the beginning. He knew his own address all right, and a rough approximation of the date, but he came unstuck on the first line. '*Dear Lucy*' sounded too familiar. '*Dear Miss Tremayne*' sounded too formal. And '*Dear Miss Lucy Tremayne*' sounded like something out of *Gone With The Wind*.

He finally decided to call her nothing at all, and to leave the first line totally blank. Her name would be on the envelope, after all. So that was one literary crisis resolved.

The main body of the letter did not detain him long. After a first draft and three revised versions he arrived at:

'*I am very sorry I shouted at you on the night I lost my wallet outside your house in front of your mum and Mr Hawkins but I wasn't feeling so good see.*'

But bringing it to an end proved almost as difficult as

bringing it to a start. Real people, people who mattered, put *'yours faithfully'* or *'sincerely'*. But he wasn't important enough to write that. He certainly couldn't say *'love from'*, which was how he wrote to his Aunt Sylvia. He tried writing *'bye for now then'*, but it looked out of place. He thought about *'oh well, cheerio'* and *'well, I'll see you round'*, but they didn't seem right either. So he wrote the entire letter out yet again and allowed the natural flow of the prose to lead him to an instinctive conclusion.

' . . . *but I wasn't feeling so good see,'* he wrote. *'But now I'm not feeling so bad. I hope you're not feeling too bad either. And your mum. My mum isn't. Nor's my dad. So I'll just say all the best then, and better be going I suppose before I go on any longer. Yours, Danny.'*

He read it through. That didn't sound at all bad. *'Yours'* was brilliant. But just plain *'Danny'* didn't look right. So he added *'Curnow'*. But his writing was so bad that he thought she might not be able to decipher the word, so he printed his full name underneath in block capitals, like real people did. Having done that, he underlined it. Twice. And put *'Mr'* in front of it. And *'Esq'* after. That looked pretty impressive.

He read it through one last time. Well satisfied with his efforts, he decided to deliver it immediately by hand. As it was the night of the extraordinary general meeting, he was confident that Lucy and her mother would be at the village hall like everyone else, so there would be no risk of an embarrassing encounter on their doorstep. His motorbike was temporarily out of commission, because he couldn't afford to buy any petrol; but it was a fine May evening, and a walk of eight hundred yards or so did not seem too daunting a labour for the only woman in the world that he would ever adore.

Greatly cheered up by the thought of how delighted Lucy would be to receive his letter, he set off across East Quay in excellent spirits. There was a healthy smell of fresh seaweed on the breeze, a star sparkling in the sunset sky, and a gentle surf breaking on the beach. Life, he reflected philosophically, was a rich tapestry. Life was like the *Exchange and Mart* . . . crammed full of interesting things.

95

But then, half-way up Chapel Lane, he walked straight into dread gang-boss Samson Trevaskis and his fearsome mob. And in an instant, Daniel P. Curnow, philosopher and humanist, was transformed into Daniel P. Curnow, unashamed self-preservationist and fastest thing on thin legs.

Sam Trevaskis was easily several months older than Danny, and probably the most dangerous man in Cornwall. Instinct told Danny to turn and run like the clappers. But common sense told him to stop and think. So he did the sensible thing. And stopped and thought. And then turned and ran like the clappers. But another detachment of the Trevaskis gang had cut off his retreat. There was no escape. He skidded to an abrupt halt and took careful stock of the enemy's concentrations. There were four of them closing in from the south, and three — including Sam — from the direction of Lucy's cottage.

Danny gritted his teeth and struggled to remember some helpful hints from his *Steve de Rocca Manual of Self-defense*. But none sprang readily to mind. Why did people like Steve de Rocca (black-belt karate expert, and unchallenged controller of all United States' olive oil imports) make it all sound so easy?

> *Chapter 4. Street violence.*
> *Fifty fun ways to kill and maim . . .*
> *Walk up to gang of hoodlums and poke out all eyes with stiff fingers. Kick off kneecaps and knuckle-punch lethal pressure points A, B and C . . .*

Who was this Steve de Rocca, anyway? Had *he* ever come face to face with the Sam Trevaskis outfit? Why, Danny wondered, couldn't someone write a practical book on self-defence for normal, average weeds? . . . full of *sensible* suggestions like '*Bash opponent on head with amazing, new, Dynothrust spring-grip body-builder . . .*'

Danny took a careful look at the two lines of thugs closing in on him, and decided to exercise full force of amazing old science of self-preservation called rampant cowardice. Calculating that three were probably fewer in number than four, he ran for all he was worth up Chapel Lane towards the former, colliding at high speed with Samson Trevaskis and accidentally fetching him a resounding smack in the eye. Trevaskis was so surprised that he did nothing for a moment, but merely stood rubbing the injured area, saying, 'Cor, bugger me, that 'urt!' Danny apologised profusely, asked if he was all right, then turned and fled for his life.

The chase was brief, for Danny was no athlete. He tripped over his own feet, right outside the Tremaynes' cottage, and fell sprawling across the road. Trevaskis and his gang were on him in a second.

Danny didn't know what had hit him . . . and didn't wish to, either. He had no idea exactly what happened next. But one minute he was lying there in the road, defiantly shouting his total and unconditional surrender . . . And the next he was watching Lucy Tremayne belabouring Sam Trevaskis with her riding crop and chasing the whole gang away down Chapel Lane, screaming, 'Chicken livers!' and 'Yellow bellies!'

Danny sat up very shakily, staggered to his feet and dusted himself down. 'Well, that saw they buggers off all right,' he said to Lucy with a feeble grin. 'Proper job.'

' . . . So, to sum up this brief, clarifying statement,' Freddie St Clare was saying, after twenty minutes of totally confusing waffle, 'I repeat, there is *no* agreement as yet with Pirana House or with any other party. And that there is no possibility of anyone demolishing Tremorna Hall, or building on the Fields. The possible options of converting the hall into an hotel, and of constructing a few delightful chalets on West Meadows are currently under review. But no decisions will be made in the near future.'

Freddie paused for breath, smiled at the general assembly and gave the vicar a filthy look. He said, 'Thank you, ladies and gentlemen,' and walked back to his seat. As he did so, there was a spontaneous outburst of popular applause from Sally Tremayne, and much general murmuring in the main body of the hall.

The commotion was added to further by Tom Hoskin, who had finally managed to fight his way into the building and was now struggling to push butcher Pascoe back out. But he was being thwarted by a third substantial body still struggling to get *in*. This identified itself as Hermann H. Hermann of Des Moines, Iowa, and demanded to know what in the hell was going on.

Meanwhile, Alice and Dora Uglow were still tuning in their deaf-aids and had no idea what all the row was about. But assuming that their complaint against Socrates the bull was now under debate, they began shouting, 'Chain un up and geld un!' And kept on shouting it until Nancy Curnow got up and screamed in Alice's ear, 'Not yet, dear! Tezzen your turn yet! Your turn es comen up djrectly!'

In the midst of this bedlam, Mervyn Sharkley had been summoned to the stage by the Reverend Owen Borage to read out the genuine, sincere pack of lies that Pirana House's lawyers had painstakingly prepared for him. But he had hardly drawn breath to speak, when the main door at the back of the hall flew open and a violent gust of wind heralded the late arrival of Granny Polkinghorne.

People murmured with awe, 'The pellar . . . ooh, the pellar's 'ere, you . . . ' And Ned Gummoe suggested it might be a good time to adjourn for tea and sticky buns.

The tightly packed assembly made room for Granny Polkinghorne, as she walked slowly, tap-tap-tap with her walking stick, down the hall towards the stage. A respectful hush descended.

Sharkley did not like the look of this. This sort of thing didn't happen in Solihull. There was something very, very sinister going on here. And ethnic. And he wondered if it was marketable.

The wizened old harridan seemed to be making straight for him. She was wearing an ankle-length dress of coarse black wool, a loose black cape, and a black shawl over her head. Her face was very pale and shrivelled. She had a nose like an eagle's beak, and eyes the colour of slate.

She walked up to him and stared him in the eye.

'Knaw the awld waays,' she warned him, revealing the

few teeth she had left. 'The spirit of our fathers es with us always. Sleepen in the stones. Thear'll be no builden on West Meadows, mister. No wan shall desturb the spirits of the Ring. So go en peace.'

And so saying, she waved her stick slowly in front of his face, and with half-closed eyes she croaked a toneless incantation in the old tongue of the Western Celts:

> 'Che Dean Crêv, leb es war Tîr,
> Inthow grâ, gen skians fîr,
> ha'n Dew euthella, vedn-ri,
> peth ew gwella ull, rag whi.'*

Upon hearing this, many people in the hall shifted uneasily and whispered their anxieties for the fate of the little Arab. Some terrible spell had obviously been cast.

Sharkley blinked, stony-faced behind his tinted glasses, and broke out in a cold sweat.

Granny Polkinghorne walked slowly back down the hall, tap-tap-tap, and out into the night.

As soon as she had left, great agitation erupted in the hall.

'Mizzer Sheikh Lee's been ill-wished,' gasped Ned Gummoe. 'He won't last the night, Loord rest ees soul.' Ned believed totally in Granny Polkinghorne's powers. But then he also believed in piskies and knackers (the wee people who lived in the tin mines) and the ghost of King Arthur riding round Dozmare Pool on Bodmin Moor at night.

Charlie Penrose, fruit and vegetable merchant, standing in the throng at the back of the hall, wanted to know what the blazes that was all about. And Hermann H. Hermann of Des Moines, Iowa, who had forced his way inside by this time, said it sounded like Blackfoot Indian, and he just happened to be an authority on the language.

Sharkley was still waiting to speak. The Reverend Owen

---

* Thou strong man who on earth dost dwell/today with prudence act thou well/And God supreme for thee will do/what he thinks best is good for you.

William Gwavas, 1676-1741.
(Cornish writer and scholar)

Borage rose to his feet and bashed his gavel on the table for silence. But a commotion persisted at the back of the hall, where Tom Hoskin, who had succeeded in pushing Arthur Pascoe out onto the street in the wake of Granny Polkinghorne, was being hard-pressed to stop him forcing his way back in again. Nancy and the Owen Borage fan club turned round in their seats and made fierce shushing noises, like a lot of old tank engines.

When calm had been fully restored, the vicar selected another pair of spectacles and glared across at Mervyn Sharkley. 'Be ye guided by the wise old words of Mrs Polkinghorne,' he said, assuming the special godly voice he used for sermons. 'You shall not trample with impunity upon the heritage of the Cornish people. Or rest assured, as surely as our Lord chased the money-changers from the temple, so shall we chase you and your people back across the Tamar river, where you belong.' And with that he banged his fist passionately on the table, crushing three pairs of spectacles and knocking over his glass of water. The supreme praesidium of elders around him all applauded loudly, and Alice Uglow — who thought the debate had got around to Socrates at last — shouted, 'Send un to the abattoir, vicar!'

Then silence descended once more, as a lone figure emerged from the crowd at the back of the hall and addressed the reverend gentleman.

'Mr Borage,' said the widow Tremayne, 'when you first came here seven years ago from London, did the people of this village make you welcome?'

Silence.

The vicar, who was dripping in blood and water by this time, hesitated — because he didn't know where this was leading to — and finally said, 'Yes, of course. But of course. Most welcome.' He could hardly have said anything else under the circumstances.

'Well, that's because we do have a tradition of being hospitable people, Mr Borage,' Sally replied. 'And so tes a mystery to many of us how come an outsider like yourself es so stuck-up about grockles. This village edden *your* village,

100

my dear. This village was here hundreds of years before you or the Church of England was even dreamed of, and that's a fact. And it'll still be here long after you've been promoted and gone back up-country.'

The vicar fell back into his chair with shock. Not a soul moved. Even Tom Hoskin and butcher Pascoe had stopped scuffling for two minutes, riveted by the words of their prospective wife.

She looked round at all the faces turned towards her, and for a second her eyes met those of Nancy Curnow.

'I had a fine husband died to sea,' she continued, 'because he had to work twice the hours these days to make any kind of liven as a fisherman. Fishen's near finished here now. And thear edden no tin minen left to speak of. But then you woulden know what a *scat bal* was even if you fell down un, would ee, Mr Borage? All we have left es China clay and visitors. But you don't need *either*, Mr Borage . . . You do have a job for life. The Lord and the Church Commissioners will provide. But this village needs all the tourists it can get. Or most of us edden goan to survive. Then our children are goan to leave school, and move away from this village, and from this county, 'cos thear won't be nothen left to keep them here. Then the village will just grow old. And fade away. And die.'

Sally paused. You could have heard a mouse on tiptoe.

'Now I give ee fair warnen, Rev'ran,' she went on, anger rising, 'all that Lord St Clare's plans es goan to do es bring more visitors, more trade, and more jobs. If you stand in the way of that, thear es goan to be juss one man being chased back across the Tamar to where he belongs, and that's goan to be *you*, Mr Borage!' And she roared furiously, 'And *I'm* goan to be chasen ee!'

With that, the entire hall erupted into pandemonium. Nancy Curnow leapt to her feet and, screaming above the din, accused Sally of grossly insulting a holy man of the cloth.

Sally invited her to go and jump in the Addle.

Art Pascoe cautioned that that might cause a flood of ancient Biblical proportions.

Ben Curnow said he'd punch Pascoe in the mouth if he said that again.

'You and whose army?' demanded Dick Champion, the garage mechanic.

'*This* army!' bellowed Tom Hoskin, trying to wave a fist but finding his arms pinned to his sides by the pressure of the crowd.

Butcher Pascoe repeated his flood warning, were Nancy to inflict her bulk on the innocent waters of the Addle. So Ben, unable to raise his hands above waist height, angrily pushed him in the back in lieu of a punch in the mouth. Whereupon Dick Champion, similarly incapacitated by the crush, pushed Ben in the back, and Tom pushed Dick. The Reverend Micah Dredge, the Methodist minister, pushed his way in between the combatants to separate them, and got pushed back in return by Roger Holman, off-licensee, who pushed Caleb Trevaskis and Len Dunstan into the Pengelly brothers, Frank and Barry, in the process. Len and Caleb immediately turned round and pushed Nick Jenkins into Charlie Penrose, and the Pengelly brothers pushed Tristan Rosewarne, the farmer's son, into his younger brothers, Joshua and Luke . . .

Meanwhile, the Reverend Owen Borage was close to fainting from shock and several cut fingers, and was being nursed by his supreme praesidium and fan club, as a furious debate raged in the main body of the hall, and Ned Gummoe proposed that tea and sticky buns should be served immediately . . . a motion which he also seconded and passed unanimously.

With the hall now in total uproar, and hundreds of grown men furiously shoving each other in the back and hurling abuse in all directions, no one heard PC Hawkins and Special Constable Nancarrow screeching to a halt outside in their panda car. And no one noticed Lord Fred sneaking out of the fire exit with a sticky bun in his mouth, and little Mervyn Sharkléy close behind . . .

Danny Curnow was sitting in the Tremaynes' kitchen,

surrounded by swabs of cotton wool and Dettol.

'What hurts worst?' Lucy asked.

'Everything,' said Danny. He couldn't speak properly. His lips felt like footballs.

'You'm goan to look a funny colour tomorrow,' she warned him. 'Whatever did you do to upset Sam Trevaskis so?'

'Didden do nothen. I juss give un a bang in the eye.'

'Well, that edden bad for a start. What did you want to do a daft thing like that for?'

'It was an accident. Didden mean to do it.'

'Well, you'd better have an accident with someone your own size next time.'

'No one's my size,' said Danny hopelessly. 'Even you chased they all away, and you'm juss a girl.'

'Well, tes easier for me. Sam woulden hit a girl.'

But that was no consolation to Danny. He couldn't spend the rest of his life walking past Sam Trevaskis in a skirt. He suddenly felt overwhelmingly useless.

'Tes rotten being I. I ent good at *anythen*.'

She put a sticking plaster over a cut above his eye. He winced. She said sorry, and stroked his forehead. That gave Danny goose pimples all over.

'Oh, cheer up,' she said. 'Nobody's *that* useless. God gives everyone *some*thing. He gave Sam muscles. And me brains. And charm. And beauty. And He gave you . . . ' She couldn't think of anything offhand that God could have given Danny. 'Well . . . special sort of feelings, I expect,' she said mysteriously.

Danny was fascinated. 'Aw. What sort of feelens would they be, an?'

'I dunno. Maybe you'm a romantic, deep down.'

Danny blinked and thought about that. 'Mebbee I am. Deep down.'

Lucy began to warm to her new role as psychotherapist. 'I bet you'm the sort who writes love poems. In secret. And sings them to that guitar of yours.'

Danny hated to deny it. Particularly since Lucy seemed to like the idea. But the truth was that all he had ever got out of

103

his genuine Korean guitar and free play-in-an-hour tutor was a working knowledge of *Baa Baa Black Sheep* and agonisingly sore fingers.

'Now don't be bashful, Danny,' said Lucy. 'There's nothen wrong with being a poet.'

'Thear edden?'

'Heavens, no. It shows you have soul. And passion. And romance.'

'It does?'

'And girls love that in a man.'

'They do?' He was beginning to brighten up.

'Of course they do. I don't like boys who fight, anyway.'

'You don't?'

'They've got no manners. No brains. No culture.'

'They haven't?'

'You can't talk to them. Not seriously. Not a proper conversation . . . about your worries and problems.'

Danny couldn't imagine how anyone as clever, charming and beautiful as Lucy could have problems. 'You ent worried about anythen, are ee an, Lucy?'

'Well, no one's perfect,' she said modestly. 'Not even me. We've all got our little troubles.'

Danny inferred from this that he was being asked to offer counsel — and perhaps even a shoulder to cry on. (Doctors had not yet discovered where Danny's shoulders were, but that didn't stop him giving advice.)

'If ever you do want to talk about anythen in confidence,' he told her solemnly, 'don't hesertate to come to I. Lots of people probbly want to ask I advice but I do think they'm too shy to mention un, see.'

'I expect that's right,' said Lucy kindly. 'And I appreciate you offeren.'

'My pleasure,' said Danny. It suddenly began to dawn on him that he had hardly spoken two civil words to Lucy in as many years, and now here he was, seated in her kitchen, being patched up by her own tender hands, getting through tea and disinfectant by the pint, and being lovingly diagnosed as a romantic poet.

What a stroke of luck, he was thinking, getting bashed

104

up right outside the cottage just when Lucy was at home. Perhaps he could do a deal with Sam Trevaskis and fix up something like this every week?

'Now are you sure you're goan to be all right to walk home?' Lucy asked, when she'd finished tending his wounds.

'Aw, I dunnaw about that,' said Danny, suffering a sudden relapse at the prospect of being sent home so soon. 'I think I got a bit of concussion 'ere somewhere.' He wasn't sure what concussion was, but he rubbed his chest quite realistically.

'Then I'll phone your mum to come and fetch you,' Lucy said, always cool and decisive in an emergency.

'Aw, no, don't do that,' Danny replied hurriedly. He didn't want Nancy to know that Sam had just bashed him up. She would only give him another bashing for fighting in the street. And then his dad would bash him up for getting bashed up in the first place. 'They'm all at the meeten in the village hall, see.'

'Sure you'll be all right then?'

'Aw, ais. Tes the best thing for a bit of concussion, a good walk. Works un out of the system.'

She went outside with him and watched from the garden gate to make sure that he got as far as the bend in the street without collapsing or being ambushed by Sam Trevaskis.

Danny could scarcely believe this turnabout in his fortunes.

'*It shows you have soul. And passion. And romance. And girls love that in a man . . .*'

That night he put away his amazing new Dynothrust spring-grip body-builder, and his Steve de Rocca self-defence manual, and brought down from the bookshelf a very old, smelly tome that had lain there unopened and gathering dust ever since the day he had inherited it from the late great Granny Hoskin.

He clambered eagerly into bed, opened the book at the

title page, and read: '*A Treasury of Romantic Victorian Verse. Edited by Vernon Cripple M.A. (Oxon.)*'

So now the fat was well and truly in the fire. For the second time in two years, the prospect of a chalet camp on West Meadows had become a burning issue throughout St Clare. And once again the villagers were hopelessly divided. Some were passionately in favour. Some were passionately against. And the overwhelming majority were passionately undecided.

Against or in favour of *what*, precisely, no one was any too sure. But that had nothing to do with it. Any excuse to pit fisherman against tradesman, East villager against West, or church against chapel was OK by the worthy citizens of St Clare, and had been since time immemorial. In fact, in days of yore, whole squadrons of petrified cavalry had been dragged reluctantly down the Addle valley to intervene between warring tin miners and fishermen, battling it out on the village streets.

These popular outbreaks of mindless anarchy had seldom occurred for any good reason. On the contrary, they were the result of an accumulation of many centuries of complex personal grudges and blind prejudice, lovingly preserved and handed down from generation to generation. And every upright Christian man in St Clare cherished this historic legacy of civil strife bequeathed him by his forefathers.

As far as the chalet-camp issue was concerned, there were sound economic arguments on both sides, it was true. But naturally, these were considered wholly irrelevant. For nobody in his right mind wanted to see a perfectly complicated situation made any clearer by confusing the issue with facts.

As usual, the first person to take full advantage of the divisions amongst the villagers was the Reverend Owen Borage. He immediately organised an *ad hoc* resistance committee and called it the 'St Clare's Bay Preservation Front'. He then flooded the streets with his good wife,

Constance, to collect signatures for a petition, under the war cry: *'Stop the Rape of St Clare!'*

In response to this, Sally Tremayne (who in all honesty was after nothing more than justice, democracy, and what was left of Lord Fred's fortune) organised her own rival 'St Clare's Bay Development Front'. And with the aid of an extremely generous donation from anonymous well-wishers in Birmingham, she took to the village streets with her own petition, under the war cry: *'Fight for the Life of St Clare!'*

By the middle of May, practically everybody in the village had signed one petition or the other. With the notable exception of Ned Gummoe. And he had signed both. A number of times. Because he didn't often get a chance to practise his signature and he hated to let a good opportunity go to waste.

Motives for supporting one side or the other (or both, in Ned's case) were legion and frequently contradictory; for such was the way of things in St Clare. But as a general rule people tended to sign for the Reverend Owen Borage if they:

(1) Bore a grudge against Lord Fred

or (2) Were C of E

or (3) Did not approve of big conglomerates like Pirana House

or (4) Did not approve of little people like Mervyn Sharkley

or (5) Believed Granny Polkinghorne and all that claptrap about the Hag's Ring

or (6) Were scared stiff of Nancy Curnow.

And conversely, Sally Tremayne could more or less rely on the signatures of:

(1) All the local tradesmen

and (2) Everyone who thought the vicar should go back to Sidcup

and (3) Everyone who fancied her

and (4) Everyone who fancied Freddie

and (5) Everyone who fancied Miranda

and (6) Hermann H. Hermann of Des Moines, Iowa

All of which was extremely confusing to Mervyn Sharkley, who was only a little fellow, after all, and had somehow to report all this bewildering intelligence and interpret its meaning for the benefit of Sir Wilfrid Macclesfield and the board of Pirana House.

2

Spring had come at last to the great port of Yokohama, and the fluffy grey clouds of sulphur rain were plodding past the double-glazed windows of Akiro Toshimoto's air-conditioned suite, hundreds of feet above the Pacific Ocean. The docks were ringing with the glorious crash of exports being lowered into the bowels of hungry cargo ships. And through the open windows of the Toshimoto All-Nippon Chemical Works could be heard the sound of happy workers smashing the daylights out of their beloved president's image on the face of a thousand punch-bags.

It was eight o'clock in the morning, and Akiro Toshimoto IV, seventy-three-year-old president of the Toshimoto All-Nippon Chemicals and Trading Corporation, was already hard at work behind his desk, shadow boxing and inhaling deep lungfuls of recycled fresh air.

Seated before him at a large round table were three of his most reliably worried-looking advisers. Their spokesman was Takeo Subishi.

'Excellent news from England, Akiro-san,' Subishi spat, grim-faced. He held up the latest secretly encoded telex from Pirana House. 'Results of lab tests on soil taken from village of St Clare show perfect for cultivating fungus *Bellamorta Pirana!*'

The president remained very still. 'So,' he breathed.

The other two advisers dutifully looked even more depressed.

'And survey studies,' continued Subishi, harshly piling on the glad tidings, 'show that ancient hall Tremorna ideal for technicians' residence and mini-lab.'

'So,' breathed the solemn-faced president.

'And now awaiting only financial feasibility report from economic intelligence unit to be presented to meeting of Anglo-Japanese joint investment board on 26 May.'

'Excellent,' said Toshimoto miserably, holding out his presidential hand for the decoded telex translation.

Subishi arose and passed it to him. Toshimoto read it through very slowly. When he had finished he sat in contemplative silence for some time.

Then he said, 'Mystery, Takeo-san. What is *Druids*?'

'Hah,' breathed Subishi knowledgeably, '*Druids* is very, very old English priests. Grow mistletoe.'

The president stroked a hand over his venerable white hair. 'Why do very old Druids grow mistletoe?'

'Latest copy of *AA Guide to Britain* not explain,' Subishi replied. 'But English stand under mistletoe every winter and kiss.'

'So,' said the president blankly. As a lapsed Buddhist the mysteries of daft Western religious cults were totally beyond his comprehension, but he was prepared to believe anything of the British. 'And chalet camp in meadow is insult to very, very old Druids?'

Subishi nodded. 'There is opposition in local village.'

'So.' Toshimoto nodded and contemplated the telex for a while longer. 'Mystery, Takeo-san . . . *We* don't want to build chalet camp.'

'True, Akiro-san.'

'And very, very old Druids don't want chalet camp.'

'True, Akiro-san.'

'And nobody anywhere wants this chalet camp.'

'More or less true, Akiro-san.'

'So what is argument about?'

Subishi turned to one of his junior colleagues. 'Yoshio-san! Clarify please!'

'So!' screamed the underling, leaping to his feet. 'Is necessary first to win agreement of village for building pretty wooden chalets . . . before we can hope to win agreement of village for building twice as many ugly aluminium fungus shelters, Toshimoto-san.'

The other underling leapt to his feet. 'Village very slow to adjust to modern-day life, Toshimoto-san. Need to break bad news gently. One step at a time.'

'So.' The president nodded very slowly and reread the telex once more. 'Mystery, Takeo-san,' he said after a while. 'What is . . . *Rev. O. Borage?*'

'Priest,' Subishi replied. 'Leading opposition to chalet camp.'

'Hah.' Toshimoto nodded. 'Understand now. He is very, very old Druid?'

'Presume so,' agreed Subishi.

'O'Borage,' said Toshimoto thoughtfully. 'Is Irish name?'

'Sounds Irish, Akiro-san,' Subishi replied.

'Then all is now clear,' spat the president gratefully. 'But how powerful is this very, very old Irish Druid?'

'Not sure,' said Subishi. 'But Pirana House planning public relations campaign in village to win over local peasants.'

'Excellent,' Toshimoto replied, scowling with approval. He knew of villages in the remoter corners of Japan where very, very old priests were still in total control of everything; so he could easily envisage a medieval place like St Clare, and such a power as the mysterious Irish Druid, O'Borage, who spent the winter kissing everyone under mistletoe. 'Kindly inform Sir Wilfrid Macclesfield,' he instructed the first underling, 'of my great pleasure at having received his latest telex. And that I and my advisers hope to fly to England for Anglo-Japanese joint investment board meeting on 26 May. Would like also to see ancient Druid village of St Clare and all proposed realty investments during our brief stop in UK.'

3

What with Anglo-Japanese translation difficulties, and ham-fisted telex operators, and all the complicated secret encoding systems understood by only a handful of people at Pirana House and Toshimoto Heights, communications between Birmingham and Yokohama left something to be desired.

'Happy to inform you of my pleasant greatness,' Sir Wilfrid read aloud, *'to have telexed your new receipt. And that I my adversaries hope to fry in England on 26 May as joint meat for Anglo-Japanese investment board. Wish to see all St Clare's ancient Druids and pose in really brief vestments whilst halting UK.'*

Sir Wilfrid stopped, went back to the beginning and read it through again . . . For the fourth time. But it still didn't make any sense. Perhaps it was the Japanese sense of humour, he concluded. Yanks talked about 'busting asses'. Brits talked about 'giving the enemy a good hiding'. Japs obviously talked about 'frying' their opponents up as a 'joint of meat'. And to allude to the tired old Church of England reactionaries as ancient Druids showed a very keen and witty appreciation of Celtic culture. But what could possibly be meant by *posing in really brief vestments* was anybody's guess . . .

'Will there be any reply, sir?' his assistant deputy private secretary enquired, twenty minutes later.

'No. Just acknowledge receipt,' he said. 'And tell Geoffrey Ormskirk from L and P to come up and see me at two o'clock this afternoon.'

Ormskirk had been so petrified of missing an elevator and arriving late for his appointment with God that he'd set off from his own office on the sixteenth floor soon after half past one, and had been waiting outside Sir Wilf's door ever since.

But Sir Wilf had been avoidably detained at a business lunch at the headquarters of Warwickshire County Cricket Club. And it was getting on for half past three by the time he came crashing out of the lift onto the twenty-first floor, totally legless and propped up by a lot of very kind, sympathetic employees all gasping for promotion. They piloted him gently into his office, pursued by Ormskirk, and

111

abandoned him by his desk, reminding him as they left of their names and departments.

Sir Wilf could vaguely remember sending for Ormskirk, but hadn't got the faintest idea why. He collapsed behind his desk and tried to focus on something.

'Play cricket, Gerald?' he enquired gravely.

'Fantastic game, sir,' enthused Ormskirk, not knowing one end of a cricket ball from the other. He remembered something that Sir Wilf was frequently heard to say, and added, 'Nobody who puts leather to willow can be all bad.' Or was it the other way round?

Sir Wilf's eyes glazed over with affection.

'How true, how true. How very true and wise,' he mumbled, wondering where he'd heard that brilliantly perceptive axiom before.

Then he asked Ormskirk what he wanted. Ormskirk said *he* didn't want anything, it was Sir Wilf who had sent for *him* . . . Possibly about St Clare. Sir Wilf thought he was talking about a red-hot tip for the three o'clock at Lingfield Park and asked how she'd done.

'No,' said Ormskirk, 'St Clare, the village . . . in Cornwall.'

Cornwall rang a bell. God decided to call his senior private secretary for enlightenment. He asked Ormskirk if he knew how to work a telephone and told him to try and get through to the office next door. Which Ormskirk obligingly did. The secretary then reminded Sir Wilf of the strange telex from Japan.

'Oh yes, the Japs,' Sir Wilf remembered, slamming the phone down and missing the cradle by a considerable distance. 'Now look, Ormskirk, I've got some highly distinguished Nips coming here on the 26th of this month, and they want to visit St Clare. So I don't want any protest demonstrations against Pirana House while we're there. Now what are you doing to clobber that vicar, Porage, and his preservation front?'

'I'm setting in motion a two-pronged public relations counterattack,' Ormskirk replied, trying to make it sound impressive.

112

God nodded approvingly. 'Attack. That's the spirit. Attack. And *kill*.'

'Prong one will be a campaign in the local media — radio, TV, papers — to help exaggerate all the good things a chalet camp will do for the local traders, and to play down all the damage it'll do to the bed-and-breakfast business.'

God nodded again. 'Damage. That's the stuff, lad. Lots of *damage*. Keep going.'

'Prong two will involve Pirana House patronising the annual feast day celebrations at the end of the month. We can lay on free beer and pasties. Put up a cash prize of one hundred pounds for the queen of the feast contest. Send the Pirana House hot-air balloon team down there and give free rides. Make sure we get maximum TV and press publicity. And maybe stage an artistic re-enactment of the historic raping of St Clare in person.'

Sir Wilf looked horrified. 'Rape? Re-enactment of *rape*?'

'Tastefully, of course. To show how much we care about their cultural traditions.'

'How can you rape *taste*fully?'

'The point is she wasn't actually raped, sir,' Ormskirk explained. 'Legend says they only *tried* to rape her.'

Sir Wilf didn't understand what he was talking about.

'Who did?'

'The Saxons.'

'What . . . *all* of them?'

'Well, a few. Apparently.'

'Filthy German swines. Who told you this?'

'Lord St Clare . . . Told Sharkley.'

'And what happened to her?' Sir Wilf asked, trying to remember who Sharkley was and where he fitted into all this.

'She jumped off a cliff to save herself. And committed suicide.'

'The poor child,' said Sir Wilf, deeply shocked. 'She could have been killed. Was this in the papers? *I* didn't see it.'

'It all happened a very long time ago,' said Ormskirk soothingly.

'But hasn't anyone told the police, for heaven's sake?' Sir Wilf demanded, trying to remember who Ormskirk was.

4

Pinned to a blackboard in the crowded briefing-room of Penzance police station were three photographs of three different faces . . . all so grossly over-enlarged that they were completely indistinguishable. Detective Inspector Maxwell, of New Scotland Yard, tapped each picture in turn.

'The Chinese connection,' he announced. 'The Iranian connection . . . And the French connection.'

Above the three photographs were chalked the words *Operation Snowhawk*. Beneath them was pinned a map of the Channel coast from Cornwall to Essex.

The entire West Cornwall drug squad had been assembled in the briefing-room that morning — both in plain clothes — along with twenty-eight local village PCs in uniform, and a squad of Customs and Excise officers in sensible shoes.

Percy Hawkins, sole constable and chief of police for St Clare, was feeling very significant. He realised that he would never be permitted to know even the half of Operation Snowhawk (for these clandestine operations against narcotics smugglers were highly complex and secret affairs involving Interpol, the US Drugs Enforcement Agency, and vast numbers of tremendously serious people in grubby white mackintoshes). But no matter how humble a part he was called upon to play, Percy was proud to be a vital thread of Cornish sinew in the mighty arm of international law enforcement.

'Bank holiday, the weekend after next,' Detective Inspector Maxwell continued, 'will be an ideal time for smugglers. There'll be a lot of extra pleasure craft pottering about in the Channel, and they'll make good cover for larger yachts and cabin cruisers from the Continent who want to slip in and land contraband. I'd like all you police officers from coastal stations to enlist the eyes and ears of the local mariners that you know and trust, and to liaise with the Customs and Excise investigation officer seconded to your area . . . '

His name was Norman Strait. And he was one of the tremendously serious people in grubby white mackintoshes. He had an earnest young face, and was as keen as the March wind off Gwennap Head. But he'd spent most of the thirty-three years of his tremendously serious life in the London suburb of Raynes Park. And this, Percy suspected, could well prove to be the lad's undoing.

'I believe in working *with* the local community not against them,' Strait explained, as they set off for St Clare in Percy's panda car. 'I want your fishermen and sailors to get to know and trust me, and feel a part of our team.'

'Aw, ais?' said Percy, wondering if the poor fellow could swim. 'Well, you'm the man in charge, Mr Strait. So I'm sure you do know what tes you'm doan.'

But Percy was not at all sure. It probably would never have occurred to anyone born and raised in the London suburb of Raynes Park, but smuggling — the oldest form of free trade known to civilised man — had been an important cottage industry and a major stabilising factor in the Cornish economy for many hundreds of years. And in consequence there were few mortal sights less conducive to trust and co-operation amongst the local mariners than that of a Customs and Excise officer . . .

Tom Hoskin and Ben Curnow were down at the harbour, fitting a new oil pump to the clapped-out Perkins on Ben's crab-boat.

'Got a moment an, boys?' Percy Hawkins called down to them.

They abandoned the engine and clambered ashore.

'Ow be doan an, Percy?' said Tom, eyeing the young stranger in the grubby raincoat.

'Boys,' said Percy, 'I do juss want to innerduce ee to Mr Norman Strait here. A preventive officer . . . ' He hesitated and cleared his throat. 'Of the Customs and Excise.' Turning to Strait, he said, 'This es Mr Curnow and Mr Hoskin.'

'Cussoms and Excise?' Ben echoed. 'Well, well, well . . . '

PC Hawkins took a deep breath. 'Mr Strait would like your co-operation.'

'Aw, he would, would he?' Ben replied. He offered his hand to the stranger. 'Well, tes a honour to make your 'quaintance, old maate.'

Strait readily gave his hand in return. It was promptly crushed and left dripping in thick, black sump oil. He smiled and put it behind his back, where it dripped down his grubby white mac.

'If you see any private boats of alien registration,' he told Ben and Tom, in great earnest, 'particularly French or Dutch boats, or any boat behaving in a suspicious way, I'd appreciate it if you'd report it as quickly and discreetly as possible . . . to the coastguard, the police, or my operations centre in Penzance. For security reasons, you'll understand, I can't go into details.'

'Don't ee worry, old cock,' said Ben. 'Us'll board the bugger and clap they Frenchies in irons for ee, no problem.'

'No, no, don't *board* her!' Strait replied, panic stricken. 'For God's sake, don't let her *know* . . . '

'Tes only in jest, Mr Strait,' said PC Hawkins, calmly. 'Only a joke, see.'

Norman Strait, however, did not possess a sense of humour. He did not approve of jokes. Such indulgence was frowned upon by the Customs and Excise. Life was far too serious a matter for amusement.

'I'll give you a number,' he said, wiping his crushed and oil-soaked hand on a clean white handkerchief, 'to contact in Penzance if you can't reach Mr Hawkins.'

He stuffed the oily handkerchief into his mac pocket, took out a scrap of paper and wrote down the special number at the CID office in Penzance. He handed this to Tom, since Tom's hands looked cleaner.

'Proper job,' said Tom, who looked at it and passed it straight to Ben, who covered it in sump oil.

'Aw, ais,' Ben assured him. 'You do have my solemn promise that you'm goan to get the same kind of co-operation as my family has been giving the Cussoms and Excise for hunnerds and hunnerds of years. Edden that so, Tom?'

'Tes our solemn promise,' said Tom.

Strait was so delighted that he almost permitted himself the luxury of a smile. 'That's the stuff, lads,' he said proudly. And in the pleasure of the moment, foolishly offered his hand again to Ben without thinking.

Ben obligingly took it, crushed it, and left it dripping in thick, black sump oil once more.

'Thanks for the chat an, boys,' said PC Hawkins. 'Us best be moven on now to see a few more of the lads.'

He and Strait walked on along the quay.

Tom shook his head sympathetically. 'Poor sod. They shoulden send they preventive boys down these parts so young.'

Ben nodded sadly. 'Like a lamb to the slaughter.'

5

There were only five days to go before the spring bank holiday weekend, and all over St Clare shopkeepers were busy doubling their prices and oiling their cash registers. And despite the ructions over Pirana House and the chalet camp, everyone was eagerly preparing for the feast day celebrations. Every keen athlete was out practising for the hurling. Every keen beer drinker was out practising in the Proud Pinnace. And even comprehensively useless people like Danny Curnow were out gathering firewood or practising hiding from Sam Trevaskis.

There was an official feast day committee, naturally. There would *have* to have been . . . For if there hadn't been one, then the Reverend Owen Borage would most certainly have founded one. Or indeed several. But this was one committee over which — for reasons which were wholly beyond his comprehension — he did not have supreme, autocratic control.

Nevertheless, he had the next best thing: a reliable, loyal spy in the committee's midst. This spy happened to be his good wife, Constance. And since Pirana House, like everybody else, had been asked to inform the committee in advance what they proposed to contribute to the feast, the vicar had received early warning of their outrageous plans. And he had been shocked . . . Nay, mortified. Mortified to discover that a major British corporation with as appalling a reputation as Pirana House could still sink to yet lower depths of scurrility. Giving away five hundred gallons of beer and a thousand free pasties to the innocent and unsuspecting citizens of St Clare was bad enough . . . as blatant acts of bribery went. But how anyone could contemplate anything so sordid and mercenary as to offer a prize of one hundred nasty, new-fangled, shiny, golden, delicious pounds sterling to whomsoever won the queen-of-the-feast contest was beyond all understanding. Particularly when the money could have been far better spent on some decent, worthy cause . . . Such as the Reverend Owen Borage's new holiday fund for distressed clergymen. And as for the proposal to stage a real, live re-enactment of the rape of St Clare . . . in front of real, live women and children . . . with a real, live victim . . .

'We must notify the vice squad straightaway,' he told Constance, the minute she broke the news of this insidious conspiracy.

And he immediately telephoned the chief of police in person.

Percy Hawkins was at home, in the kitchen of his semi-detached cottage in Middle Street, defrosting the fridge and listening to the cricket scores on Radio 2.

The telephone rang. He picked it up and straightened his

tie. 'Police headquarters,' he announced gravely.

'Percy? It's Owen Borage.'

'Aw, good evenen, vicar.'

'I hope I'm not disturbing you . . . ?'

'No, no. I was juss winden up a few investigations before supper,' said Percy, finding a mouldy sprout under the fridge. 'I'm glad you called, matter of fact. I been meanen to have a word with you. I hear you'm plannen a mass protest on feast day against the development on West Meadows.'

'But entirely within the law, Percy.'

'Well, I do hope so. Because I've heard you and your preservation front es plannen to occupy the Addle bridge. And to hold a sit-down demonstration in the road.'

'Indeed we are. And all law-abiding citizens of this country are at liberty to protest peacefully on the streets.'

'Peaceful protest is wan thing, vicar,' said Percy. 'But the Addle bridge es part of the Queen's highway. And it es an offence to obstruct un. If you do want to hold a sit-down protest, you'm goan to have to do it standen up and on the move.'

'In that case,' said the vicar, 'I cannot be held responsible if the protesting masses of this village choose to move extremely slowly, and alternately one step forwards, one step back.'

'This edden a laughen matter,' said Percy. 'I do give ee fair warnen, if your people obstruct the Addle bridge, which es a vital artery of communication within the territory under my control, I shall not hesertate to do my duty. And I shall have the full force of Special Constable Nancarrow in reserve.'

'Percy, Percy,' said the vicar impatiently. 'This is no time for melodrama. I am ringing to discuss matters of the most flagrant depravity.'

'Depravity . . . ?' said Percy, hoping he'd heard correctly.

'Simulated rape.'

'What about it?' said Percy, searching the draining-board for a dictionary.

'Certain persons are conspiring in our midst to perform

119

public acts of simulated rape . . . right here in this village, before an audience of thousands.'

'Get away? Well, tes first I've heard of it.'

'We must act promptly, Percy. As pillars of this community we must take the lead. Now. There's no time to lose.'

'Fair enough,' said Percy agreeably. 'You can put I down for a couple of tickets, if tes in a good cause . . . '

6

Sharkley had been summoned back to Birmingham to report personally on the latest state of civil war in St Clare. And he had a special surprise awaiting him in the basement of Pirana House.

'This will really put the icing on the cake,' said Ormskirk, puffing and wheezing from the effort of stepping into the lift. 'Sir Wilf is going to *love* this. I tell you, he's got really excited about this chalet camp idea of mine.'

'*Mine*,' Sharkley reminded him.

'No call to get petty, Mervyn,' said Ormskirk, more in sorrow than anger. 'We're a *team*, remember. I've worked like a slave to make sure that Sir Wilf knows you're helping too.'

The lift came to a halt at basement level, and Ormskirk gasped his way out into the carpeted passageway beyond, and led Sharkley along to the gymnasium.

The new gymnasium at Pirana House had been provided by the management in a determined bid to reduce the abnormally high incidence of colds, flu and death amongst its religiously unfit employees. They had cribbed the idea from the Yokohama works of the Toshimoto Corporation, where many thousands of gleeful workers exercised daily to keep their extremities at the peak of brick-shattering condition. But the Pirana House gymnasium was used mostly by apathetic slobs, like Dougal McCann from Fixed Assets, who retreated thither from the overcrowded club-room next door, with their pints of Bass and healthy low-tar cigarettes, to ogle at the keen young secretaries doing their aerobics exercises. Sharkley seldom dared venture into the place for fear that the sight of a few plump typists bulging out of their shiny black, stretch-satin leotards might precipitate an acute attack of perversion.

To his profound relief, the only girl in there on this occasion was a very long, bony-looking thing with a flat chest and a flat bum.

'This is Noreen,' said Ormskirk, introducing her to Sharkley. 'Our ravishable St Clare. And these are our Saxon soldiers.' He indicated two dozen young men, variously attired in dancer's wear.

They then retired to the back of the gym and Ormskirk called down to Noreen, 'OK, St Clara, baby . . . take it away!'

'I wish you'd tell me what this is all about, Geoff,' Sharkley muttered.

'Just you wait and see,' said Ormskirk proudly.

Noreen crossed to a portable cassette recorder and pressed the play switch.

'Stravinsky,' Ormskirk murmured, as if he'd even heard of him before Noreen had brought the cassette along. 'A charming piece, called *The Right Offspring*.'

Probably Russian, thought Sharkley disparagingly, with a name like that.

Noreen began to dance.

'This is St Clare the virgin,' Ormskirk explained, 'skipping happily through the forests of Cornwall . . . '

'There aren't any forests in Cornwall,' said Sharkley.

' . . . unaware that hordes of filthy Saxons are lurking behind the next tin mine.'

'She wasn't Cornish, anyway. She was Irish, and died somewhere like Beachy Head.'

'Oh, all right,' said Ormskirk irritably. 'She's skipping happily through the forests of Beachy Head.'

The ballet continued and the men began to join in, gradually encircling the happy, skipping maiden, and brandishing rolled-up newspapers.

'The lustful Saxons close in,' hissed Ormskirk, 'straining at their chain mail with menacing intent. Helpless, she fights to defend her virtue . . . '

'They don't look very menacing to me,' said Sharkley. 'Or lustful. Look a bit poovey, actually.'

'This is ballet, Mervyn. It's art. True art. Don't be so bloody literal.'

'I'm just saying that her virginity couldn't be in safer hands, that's all.'

After about five minutes of menacing, lustful skipping, the Saxons chased St Clare onto a chair.

'The perilous cliff of death,' explained Ormskirk.

And from this vertiginous peak Noreen leapt, with a look of tortured despair, all the way down to the floor, where she threshed about for several minutes, taking an inordinate length of time to die.

Ormskirk burst into enthusiastic applause and shouted '*Bravo*!' and '*Encore*!' and elbowed Sharkley in the ribs. So Sharkley clapped too. Then Ormskirk walked back across the gym to give the dancers the benefit of his artistic advice on one or two fine points of choreography.

'I'm not saying it *isn't* a work of tasteful genius,' said Sharkley, when they got back to Ormskirk's office. 'But what's it all in aid of?'

Ormskirk was poleaxed. 'In aid of? For Christ's sake, Mervyn . . . That was a beautiful, moving re-enactment of the rape of St Clare. For feast day.'

'For . . . ?' Sharkley was stunned. '*Ballet*? For the feast of St Clare? You've got to be kidding. They don't want ballet in St Clare!'

'How do you know?' said Ormskirk, shocked by this negative, philistine reaction. 'They could be gasping for it. It's ethnic.'

'There's nothing ethnic about a load of woofters waving rolled-up newspapers at some bird jumping off a chair.'

'They'll be in manly armour, you twot. And that won't be a chair, it'll be a mossy promontory.'

'Geoffrey, Geoffrey, Geoffrey . . . ' said Sharkley, sinking patiently into Ormskirk's favourite resting chair, 'you don't understand. You don't *know* these people.'

Ormskirk understood perfectly. He'd seen countryside before. Lots of it. Mostly from the comfort and security of a car travelling at high speed on the nearest motorway, true . . . But it was still countryside none the less. He was shattered.

'How can you *say* such a thing, Mervyn? To your old Geoff. To the man who's fought tooth and nail, tooth and *nail*, to keep you in favour with the twenty-first floor . . . '

'Geoff, I'm sorry, but the feast of St Clare is not a bloody arts festival. The people down there do things their own way. They don't mind drinking our beer and eating our pasties, obviously, but *this* . . . this is getting absurd. They're sturdy, tough, working folk. Fishermen, farmers, labourers . . . '

'Just because they're ethnic morons doesn't mean they can't appreciate fine art.'

'Whose idea was this, anyway?'

'Mine,' Ormskirk replied aggressively. 'A stroke of sheer genius. It would have been a bit more glamorous but Sir Wilf specifically wants it to be tasteful.'

'But why does he want it *at all*?'

'Well, I'll tell Sir Wilf how you feel,' concluded Ormskirk, terribly hurt. 'He, of course, can see the brilliance behind the idea.'

'But we've got the hot-air balloon,' reasoned Sharkley. 'And free booze and pasties. And a hundred quid for the queen of the feast. And television coverage. What does Sir Wilf want ballet for?'

Ormskirk was so deeply wounded that he didn't know what to say to get his own back. He opened a filing cabinet full of Maltesers and consoled himself with a fistful. He decided not to offer Sharkley any.

'I happen to be privy to some extremely confidential information,' he said grandly. 'After luncheon at Warwickshire County Cricket Club last Monday week, Wilfrid let slip to me, as a confidant of long standing, that

123

the Japs might be coming in on this.'

'The *Japs*?' Sharkley was astounded.

'Oh, yes.' Ormskirk nodded soberly. 'The big one, Mervyn, old son. I haven't just started *any* old ordinary investment. I have started the *big* one.'

'But a million quid would see the whole deal through and still leave change for a night at the movies. What do the Japs want to get involved for?'

'I'm not at liberty to divulge that,' said Ormskirk, because he didn't have the foggiest idea. 'But the head of Toshi Motors of Japan is here for a top secret meeting with the investment board. And he wants to visit St Clare while he's over.'

Sharkley was not immediately impressed. 'And who are Toshi Motors, when they're at home?'

Ormskirk didn't have a clue. He looked grave.

'I'm not at liberty to divulge that either,' he replied mysteriously.

Many miles away, in the heart of leafy Warwickshire, a group of Pirana House research scientists were standing in the driveway of Deepmire Grange, admiring the technical perfection of the luxurious new Fujokawa limousines that had just brought the president of Toshimoto All-Nippon Chemicals from West Midlands airport.

Inside the great house itself, Akiro Toshimoto IV and Sir Wilfrid Macclesfield OBE, with a large retinue of executives, geniuses and karate experts, had just finished a mouth-wateringly flavourless luncheon of roast sirloin of Profung-17, French fried Profungs, and Profung sprouts sautéed in sauce Profungaise. Toshimoto had not tasted a thing, and was euphoric in his praise of the stuff.

Spitting entirely in Japanese, with a running translation by Takeo Subishi, he told his audience that international cuisine would never be the same again, and that now all the world could look forward to the day when tasty food would become a thing of the past.

Then Sir Wilf got up to make a speech, and bored the

pants off everyone for twenty minutes. And after that, he and Toshimoto and their most trusted aides retired upstairs to the chief research director's private suite to continue heaping praises upon each other and discuss plans for the official visit to St Clare.

On the wall of the chief research director's office, between a comprehensive table of specific gravities and the tear-out centrefold of Patti, *Pussy Parade*'s pull-of-the-month, was a large-scale road map of Cornwall.

'Bank holiday is the busiest time for travel in Britain,' explained Sir Wilf's head of public relations, directing his words principally at Takeo Subishi, who was going to translate all this for his president. (Although if truth were known, the wily Akiro-san understood every word of what was being said.) 'It's the one time that everyone wants to travel,' he continued. 'Therefore all public transport is cut to the minimum.'

Which seemed to Akiro Toshimoto like a typical product of Anglo-Saxon logic; but he retained his inscrutable look of benign non-comprehension.

'So every road is chock-a-block from dawn to midnight,' the head of PR went on. 'If president Toshimoto is agreeable, therefore, we suggest that the party should fly by Pirana House executive jet to St Mawgan airport, here at Newquay . . . ' He prodded the map, 'on Monday morning. And from there, limousines will whisk them the final forty miles to St Clare. A total journey time of about two hours.'

Subishi translated the gist of that for his president, and Toshimoto told Subishi it all sounded like a very pleasant day out and asked, as a matter of interest, what the joint investment board would be doing to promote the good name of Pirana House at this ancient village festival. Subishi referred this to the head of PR who told him all about the free beer, the pasties, the hot-air balloon, the one hundred pound cash prize, the television coverage, and the rape of dear old Fanny St Clare in person.

President Toshimoto looked decidedly unhappy at the mention of this last item. (And his face was seldom a picture of joy, at the best of times.) The idea of associating the Toshimoto Corporation with live sex shows and other products of Western decadence did not appeal one iota to his dignified Eastern code of morality.

Sir Wilf could see that all was not well and hastily intervened. 'I've not yet cleared that last little number with my executive in charge,' he explained to Subishi. 'Kindly assure the president that nothing distasteful or ignoble will be involved . . . '

Ormskirk was aghast. Sir Wilf didn't even want to see his masterwork in performance. He didn't even want to *discuss* it.

'Ballet?' he bawled at the distant figures of Ormskirk and Sharkley. 'Are you out of your tiny minds? *Ballet?*' He thumped his desk, and the surrounding banks of VDUs and video monitors wobbled and swayed in terror. 'Two thousand pounds . . . to send twenty-five Saxon ballet dancers to Cornwall . . . for one *day?*'

Ormskirk swallowed hard. 'Former *Royal* Ballet dancers,' he squeaked tamely.

'I've never heard of anything so bloody stupid in all my life!' Sir Wilf thundered.

'Bloody stupid,' echoed Ormskirk, glaring severely at Sharkley.

'Was this *your* idea, Sharkley?' Sir Wilf barked.

'No, Sir Wilfrid. But . . . '

'I might have guessed,' said Sir Wilf. 'Stupid arse.' He smiled at Ormskirk. 'Thank heavens you had the good sense to bring this to my attention in time, Godfrey.'

Ormskirk nodded gratefully and wiped the sweat off his face with the handkerchief he'd just borrowed from Sharkley's top pocket.

'Pay those ridiculous dancers off and get rid of them,' Sir Wilf commanded.

'Rabble,' agreed Ormskirk.

'What we have to do,' Sir Wilf went on, 'is . . . ' He stalled abruptly for lack of ideas. 'Is what?'

126

Ormskirk looked hopefully at Sharkley.

Sharkley said, 'Is counter the image of Pirana House as a pack of Saxon invaders out to ravish the defenceless St Clare. Which is the image that the Reverend Borage and his preservation front are trying to put across.'

'Precisely,' said Sir Wilf, thankful that someone had come up with a constructive suggestion. 'What I've been saying all along.'

'Something that will be a striking counter-image,' Sharkley continued. 'That will make a good television picture. And that will get the public message across with simplicity.'

'Exactly.'

'All we want are two knights on white horses, with *Pirana House* plastered across the front of their shining armour, and a comely maiden between them, looking safe and radiant with gratitude for their virile protection.'

'Splendid!' Sir Wilf beamed with satisfaction and looked at Ormskirk. 'Perfect.'

'Magic,' agreed Ormskirk.

'That is simple,' said Sir Wilf, 'and pure, and honest.'

'And tasteful,' agreed Ormskirk. He turned to Sharkley. 'So hire two sets of shining armour from a theatrical costumier, Mervyn, and get them down to St Clare by Red Star.'

'And hire two local horsemen from the village,' added Sir Wilf. 'And a good-looking lass to be our St Clare.'

'Miranda!' said Ormskirk, with a snap of his fingers. 'His Lordship's daughter. She rides, doesn't she? And you said she was a right cracker . . . ' He turned to Sharkley.

'Ideal,' Sir Wilf agreed. 'She's got a vested family interest in the deal, so we could rely on her.'

'Fair enough,' Sharkley concluded. 'I'll get on with it then.'

'You see,' said Sir Wilf, 'it's all perfectly simple. Why does this entire corporation always depend on *me* to come up with the ideas?'

'Genius will out,' said Ormskirk, never afraid to speak his mind in front of the chairman.

'Now the next thing I want to know,' Sir Wilf went on, 'is what kind of reception are we going to get on Monday? I've got some highly distinguished Japanese guests attending these feast day celebrations, and I don't want any violent demonstrations or rowdy scenes.'

Ormskirk looked at Sharkley with 'Nyeah, told you so,' written all over his face.

Sharkley said, 'The present state of battle is that about a quarter of the village are in favour, another quarter against, and the rest are undecided.'

'Well, that's not good at all,' Sir Wilf replied. 'Not good at all. That means that most of the village could be against us by Monday. There could be riots and all sorts.'

'No, I really don't believe that's likely,' said Sharkley. 'I've discussed this with Lord St Clare, and he's got a trump card up his sleeve.'

'Trump card?' Sir Wilf looked suspicious. 'What do you mean . . . a trump card?'

'Three-quarters of the ordinary folk of St Clare,' Sharkley explained, 'are . . . wait for it . . . Methodists.' A conspiratorial smirk drifted across his face. He waited for the full significance of that to sink in.

After a long pause for thought, Sir Wilf said, 'Ah-haaaaa . . . ' And nodded wisely and grinned at Ormskirk.

So Ormskirk grinned too, and winked knowingly, and sang, 'I seeeeeeeee . . . '

Then Sir Wilf looked bewildered. 'So bloody what?'

Ormskirk shrugged and stared hopefully at Sharkley.

7

The Reverend Micah Dredge lived above Porthcurno Hill, on West Cliff, in a cottage that was crammed with Great Western Railway memorabilia and that reeked permanently of Brasso. He was a widower, barrel-chested and balding, with bushy, mutton-chop sideburns and huge, dark eyes. Folk came from all over West Cornwall to St Clare's Bay chapel just to hear his rich, mahogany voice and fiery sermons. He was a local man, upright and plainspoken. He didn't drink, he didn't smoke, and he did his best not to think about the widow Tremayne at nights. And he had the rare distinction of being the only man in the world who could still recite the times of every train from Newquay to St Agnes and back, some twenty years after the line had been closed.

Relations between the Jago family and the Methodist church had always been reasonably good. Partly because relations between the Jago family and the Church of England had always been reasonably bad. And partly because the St Clare's Bay Wesleyan chapel had been built upon land that successive Lords St Clare had leased to the Methodists at a mere peppercorn rent.

But with the imminent possibility of the Jago estate being sold to city business interests from up-country, the Reverend Micah Dredge had grown increasingly apprehensive about the long-term future of the chapel. He was afraid that new landlords would only renew the ground lease at an extortionate rent, since prime building land in the centre of St Clare was worth a small fortune.

So it had come as no surprise at all to Lord Fred that Micah Dredge had, as yet, declined to influence his flock one way or the other in the raging debate over Pirana House and the chalet camp . . . Which was partly why half the village was still uncommitted to either side.

And by the same token, it came as no surprise to Micah Dredge when, as the threat of demonstrations against Pirana House on feast day loomed ever nearer, Lord Fred paid him a discreet visit one afternoon . . .

' . . . so,' Freddie concluded, 'what would you say to a figure of . . . twenty-five pounds?'

The minister's eyes widened. 'Twenty-five pounds?' he echoed incredulously. 'You would sell me the freehold title under that chapel for just . . . twenty-five pounds?'

'My dear old thing,' said Freddie, 'you've been paying

rent there for nearly two hundred years. It's the least that any decent, liberal-minded landlord could do.'

'Well, I confess I'm quite flabbergasted,' said Micah, having expected something like this for some time.

'But it would of course be contingent upon the sale of my estate to Pirana House,' Freddie added.

'Oh, but naturally,' said Micah, understanding precisely what he was getting at.

There followed a pregnant silence, broken only by the plodding *dic doc* of the booking office clock on Micah's wall . . . a clock that had once hung in Green Park station, Bath.

'What are the prospects of a successful sale, might I ask?' Micah enquired.

'That rather depends,' Freddie replied, 'on the amount of opposition in the village to a development on West Meadows.'

'Ah, indeed?' said Micah ingenuously.

'For example . . . Some highly distinguished gentlemen will be here on Monday to attend the feast. And obviously, any noisy demonstrations against Pirana House would strongly deter them from proceeding further.'

'Ah, yes, I do see.'

Silence again. Just the ponderous *dic doc* of the booking office clock.

'Then it is devoutly to be hoped,' said Micah, 'that there will be no sign of popular disaffection on the streets on feast Monday, is it not, Lord St Clare?'

'Indeed it is, Mr Dredge,' said Freddie, and smiled. 'For both our sakes . . . '

At this very time, not half a mile away, another spiritual force in the community, Rebecca Polkinghorne, the Penwith pellar, was being interviewed for BBC Television.

The Cornish pellars of old were said to have acquired their healing powers from a variety of sources. Some by having been born feet first into this world. Some merely by being the seventh son of a seventh son. And a very distinguished few by having rescued a stranded mermaid and returned her safely to the sea. (Instances of the latter had been pooh-poohed by sceptics down through the ages, but had been proven beyond doubt by the welter of hard, scientific evidence obtained from highly reliable authorities like Ned Gummoe. For many a time and oft, in his four-score years, had Ned seen mermaids stranded on the fore-shore of St Clare's Bay . . . Most commonly at night, when he was staggering home from the Proud Pinnace after closing time.)

Granny Polkinghorne, however, had inherited her powers — by some tortuous and illogical process of succession — from her long-dead ancestor, Yseult Polkinghorne, the Penwith witch (1752-96). And with them she had inherited Yseult's prophecies and accrued medical wisdom, recorded in Cornish and English by an eighteenth-century amanuensis, bound in leather, and passed down through the generations, like a family bible.

So when BBC Television dispatched a film crew from Plymouth to find out what all this Pirana House rumpus was about, their interviewer, Soozie Smiles, naturally sought out Granny Polkinghorne in the hope that she could provide a little mystical insight that would help shed further obscurity on an already incomprehensible situation.

Granny Polkinghorne lived in a wobbly-looking thatched cottage that had been tottering on the edge of Blakey's Ridge for several centuries. It was full of moulting cats and rickety old furniture. And this afternoon it was full of moulting cameramen and rickety old sound recordists.

Soozie Smiles was an effusive young current affairs reporter, and the nearest thing the BBC could get to a toothpaste commercial.

'Tell me, Granny,' she began as the camera rolled, 'what *is* this curse of the Hag's Ring? What has actually happened to people who've desecrated it in the past?'

'Aw, ais, well now . . . ' Granny P. eased back a little in her rocking chair to put some of her colourful bottles of

131

home-made medicine into shot . . . After all, this sort of free publicity could do wonders for a pellar's business. 'The year I was born they was starten to build the new stone harbour down to East Quay. And the company did ask the maister of Tremorna, Loord St Clare, if they could buy they rocks en the Hag's Ring . . . to use un for builden weth. And the third Loord St Clare did draw up a contrack to sell they to the harbour company for fefty guineas. But the day they was goan to sign ees contrack, he went riden out to West Meadows, and took a tumble from ees horse. And ees boot got stuck en ees sterrup now, see. And the horse took fright and boltied. And his loordshep got dragged all round West Meadows till ees head was all scat to lembs* on wan o' they very rocks. And he did die screamen, you . . . ' Granny P. paused and shook her head, and sucked air in through her teeth as if she had been there to witness the terrible event herself. She went on in a quiet, eerie voice, 'Ais, he did die screamen somethen dreadful, you. Folk said ees terrible cries could be heard clear three mile out to sea. And to this day thear es bloodstains on they rocks that the rain juss can't wash clean.'

'But people do say that's brown paint left by the army,' Soozie pointed out.

Granny P. frowned and shook her head. 'Some people will tell ee anythen, my dear. Don't believe all you do hear, now.'

'And what do you prophesy might happen,' said Soozie, 'were anyone to try and build these chalets on West Meadows?'

'I do never make proph'cies,' Granny P. replied. 'But I can tell ee this . . . Tes written in the awld tongue . . . '

'In the Cornish language?'

Granny P. nodded. 'In the awld tongue. In the hist'ries of Yseult Polkinghorne, the Penwith pellar, my great-great-great-great-grandma. When the devils do come and make fire and sacrilege upon the Ring, the heavens shall split. A great light shall bright the night. The wild beasts will rage.

* Broken in pieces.

132

And the ghost of awld Matthew Jago, maister mariner who was took captive by the Musselmen pirates off the Lezard Point in the year of our Loord, sexteen hunnerd and fefteen, shall be seen gallopen across West Headland once again.'

'Sorry, Sooze,' the sound recordist butted in. 'We've got aircraft interference somewhere.'

'Oh, soddit,' said Soozie irritably. 'Cut it.'

Granny P. leaned forward in her rocking chair and tapped Soozie on the knee. 'Here . . . ' she enquired hopefully. 'Does that mean I can have another go, my dear?'

8

Sally Tremayne had spent most of Wednesday pushing a tired vacuum cleaner round the east wing of Tremorna Hall. It was the most neglected part of the house, the dirtiest part of the house, and the haunted part of the house. And it was shared in a spirit of peace and harmony by the Lady in Grey and Miranda.

The Lady in Grey was a peripatetic creature and given to appearing in any room in the east wing at any time; but at least she was clean and tidy, which was more than could be said for Miranda.

Sally did not enjoy cleaning Miranda's room. It was about the size of Sally's cottage for a start, and dominated by a Jacobean four-poster bed, large enough to sleep at least half a dozen consenting adults in an emergency . . . And Miranda was always game for an emergency. The place was invariably in the most appalling mess. There were things lying everywhere . . . All over the floor, all over the furniture and even over the ceiling. All sorts of things. Things to wear, things to paint pictures with, and things it was probably better not to know about.

And on this particular afternoon, whilst Hoovering under Miranda's bed, Sally encountered the Grand-Massif five-function vibrator, and accidentally fetched it an almighty crack amidships, hammering it like a croquet ball out into the middle of the room, where it came to rest, buzzing like a demented hornet.

Sally had never seen anything like it in her life, but whatever it was, it looked very unpleasant and sounded none too healthy. She picked it up, very gingerly, and it promptly fell to bits in her hands . . . the base cap flying off like an auxiliary engine from a space capsule, and being pursued to earth by two plummeting torch batteries.

Precisely *what* she had broken, she had no idea. But since Miranda was out and not due back until dinner, she thought she had better report the accident to his lordship. And she immediately went downstairs to the drawing-room, where she found Freddie very busy having a rest.

Freddie had been very busy having a rest all day. Pretty well ever since he'd got out of bed that morning. But then he had a lot on his mind these days, preoccupied as he was with the future of the estate and the seduction of half his employees. (The other half being Mrs Visick, the cook. But she was seventy-eight and happily married.)

There was little more that Freddie felt he could do about the sale of the estate at this stage, but it seemed the time was abundantly ripe to do something about the widow Tremayne. Her extraordinary loyalty and devotion to his cause against the Reverend Borage had not escaped his notice. Nor had the fact that she had started Hoovering the house each day in diaphanous blouses and flimsy brassières. From which he inferred that she could possibly be trying to tell him something. And it occurred to him that a quiet afternoon somewhere well away from the constraints of the *status quo* at Tremorna might just do them both a power of good. So, having given the matter the dubious benefit of his undivided attention over lunch that Thursday afternoon, he had decided to put into effect Masterplan D.

Masterplan D was the natural heir to Masterplans A, B and C, all of which had been worked to death ages ago. But Masterplan D could only be used at certain times of the year. For it required the use of an isolated outpost of the

Jago empire: a small detached cottage some fifteen miles away, near the north-coast village of Zennor. It was let to holiday-makers for much of the year, but there were occasions during the off-season — and this was one such — when the place was empty.

The beauty of Masterplan D was that he could take Sally out there on some domestic pretext, to attend to a few essential chores — like culling the woodworm, or counting the windows —and then if the atmosphere felt conducive to a little hanky-panky . . .

On the other hand the *dis*advantage of Masterplan D was that he had used it dozens of times before, and half the village was wise to it.

So having given the matter yet more of his undivided attention over tea that Thursday afternoon, he had decided to start work immediately upon Masterplan E . . . And was doing exactly that when the object of his desires knocked on the drawing-room door and walked in.

'I'm sorry for disturben you, my lord,' she said. 'But I've just broken somethen.'

'Broken?'

She showed him the pieces. 'I don't think tes serious, but I can't put the batteries back in.'

Freddie stared at it in amazement. It looked like a vibrator. He examined it. It *was* a vibrator.

'I was goan to tell Miss Miranda,' Sally went on, 'but she's up to Truro.'

Freddie was astounded. Was this *another* hint? Surely to goodness, domestic servants didn't usually bring their defective dildoes to the governor for repair?

'I'm afraid I don't understand electricity,' he confessed apologetically. 'Anything more technical than a nail-file and I'm flummoxed. This sort of thing is much more Miranda's line of country. I'll mention it to her when she gets home.'

'I'd be very grateful if you would. I'm sorry about it but it was just . . .'

'Not at all, my dear Mrs Tremayne. Anything to oblige.' If this was a hint, Freddie was thinking, then maybe there was a didjan of mileage still to be got out of Masterplan D.

'Before you go, by the way . . . '

'Yes, my lord?'

He did wish she wouldn't moisten her lips and fiddle with her bra straps like that when he was trying to concentrate on being duplicitous. 'I was wondering if you were going to be busy on Sunday afternoon?'

'Busy? Sunday?'

'I have to motor out to Zennor . . . '

'Oh, I'd like that very much . . . '

' . . . to the cottage to . . . '

'Tes lovely out to Gurnard's Head . . . '

' . . . make an inventory of the . . . '

'We could take a picnic if tes fair . . . '

' . . . egg-cups. Picnic?'

'And we can always eat indoors if tes raining.'

Freddie couldn't believe what he was hearing.

'Splendid, Mrs Tremayne,' he said, blinking in amazement. 'Splendid. I knew I could lie on you . . . rely on you . . . in a crisis.'

Now all he had to do was borrow a tenner off Miranda to put some petrol in the Alvis.

Sally could hardly believe her luck. She sang all the way back to the village as she cycled home that evening. Now if *she* was going to be Lady St Clare, what would that make Lucy . . . ?

Sharkley arrived back in St Clare late that afternoon and invited himself to dinner at Tremorna Hall to discuss the latest developments in Pirana House thinking. He arrived in time for early cocktails (which was pretty well any time after breakfast in the Jago household) and presented Freddie with a case of Scotch, courtesy of Ormskirk. Freddie decided that he could like Ormskirk after all.

Sharkley was delighted to hear the good news that the support of the Reverend Micah Dredge was pretty well in the bag. But he could not for the life of him imagine what that large plastic phallus was doing on the sofa at Freddie's side. And since Freddie did not even appear to realise it was there, Sharkley was loath to draw attention to it. But he was so disconcerted by the size and sickly pink colour of it that he quite ran out of intelligent conversation.

Then Miranda arrived home in her fiery-red Austin-Healey 3000 and a temper to match, complaining in execrably foul terms that the police had just nicked her for doing a hundred and twenty miles an hour on the Redruth bypass. She helped herself generously to Ormskirk's Scotch and flopped into an armchair, ignoring Sharkley completely.

This upset little Sharkley because he had gone to a lot of trouble to be noticed by Miranda. He was wearing a lounge suit by Riccardi of Roma, shoes by Serge of Genève, hair by Jeremy of Solihull, and cologne by the bucketful.

Freddie said; 'Mindy dear, Mervyn is staying for supper.'

Miranda said, 'Who's dear Mervyn?'

'Sharkley.'

Sharkley smiled modestly and adjusted his tie by Armand of Paris.

But Miranda was staring at what looked unhappily like the pieces of her Grand-Massif five-function vibrator, lying on the sofa beside her father.

'I really do think you ought to say hello to Sharkley,' he prompted her.

'Hello Sharkley,' said Miranda.

'Hello Miranda,' said Sharkley.

'And what, pray,' said Miranda, still glaring at the pieces of her Grand-Massif vibrator, 'are *they* doing there?'

'They are a vibrator,' Freddie explained, equably enough. 'And they are broken.'

'But what are they doing *there*?'

'Appreciably little,' said Freddie. 'Sulking by the looks of them. Sally Tremayne wondered if you could put them back together again.'

'Did she indeed?'

'Indisputably so.'

'Charming. They are *my* vibrator.'

137

'Are they?'

'Yes they bloody well are!'

'Well, there's no need to be so possessive about it,' said Freddie calmly. 'She told me she'd broken it, so I assumed it must be hers.'

'And how did she break it, for heaven's sake?'

'How should I know? How does one usually break vibrators? Perhaps she borrowed it.'

'One does not *borrow* vibrators,' Miranda replied, disgusted. 'It's just not done.' She turned to Sharkley. 'Is it?'

'I wouldn't know,' he confessed weakly.

He was dreadfully shocked. He was not used to this sort of behaviour. He'd been born and raised in a respectable council house in Solihull, where he'd been too respectable even to break wind for the first seventeen years of his life. He hadn't even realised what menstruation was until he was twenty-four, and he'd preferred to pretend that it didn't really happen even then. He would have to discuss all this with Dougal McCann from Fixed Assets.

However, Miranda was in a better mood once she had bathed and changed and consumed the best part of a bottle of Ormskirk's complimentary whisky; and over dinner, Sharkley broached the matter of St Clare and the knights in shining armour.

As one who believed that there was no point in doing *anything* in life unless there was an evens chance of getting laid or being the centre of attention, Miranda thought it was quite a good idea, casting her as St Clare. And when Sharkley mentioned the two hundred pounds modelling fee, she thought the idea was positively brilliant.

'All you have to do,' said Sharkley, 'is to be on the quay at the start of the coronation parade, and ride with it up to the Fields, pose for a few publicity shots . . . and that's it, finished. Won't take more than half an hour.'

'And completely nude,' said Miranda ecstatically. 'Every camera in the village will be on *me*.'

'Not nude, sweetie,' said Freddie irritably. 'Nobody said anything about being in the nude.'

'Well . . . some saintly little numero then. Like a stretch-lace catsuit.'

Sharkley shuddered as fantasies of Miranda, naked inside a cocoon of skin-tight lace, reared up in his mind.

'The problem is going to be finding a couple of knights,' said Freddie. 'Mervyn has ordered the armour. Alf can supply the horses. But every single man in St Clare, except Micah Dredge, will be paralytic by the time the coronation parade begins.'

'How much are you paying each knight?' asked Miranda.

'Twenty-two pounds, plus VAT, bed and breakfast,' Sharkley replied, still hypnotised by the thought of all that flesh inside a stretch-lace catsuit.

'Knights in armour, silly Sharklet,' she said. 'Not nights at the Fouled Anchor.'

'Oh, I see.' He smiled stupidly. 'Fifty quid each.'

'No problem then,' said Miranda confidently. 'I'll talk to Alf. She knows people who'll do *any*thing for fifty quid. Even work.'

9

Sally had been trying to avoid Tom and Arthur all week. Because whenever they saw her these days they asked her out for a Sunday afternoon picnic. And after a dozen such invitations in only seven weeks, she was fast running out of reasonable excuses for turning them down.

The point was she did not want to upset either of them — leastways, not before feast Monday. Partly because she had to keep her marriage options open in case her efforts to become Lady St Clare came to grief. And more importantly, because she wanted to make sure that Lucy won the Queen of the Feast competition.

To be Queen of the Feast was a highly coveted honour,

and practically every young wench in St Clare under thirteen stone unladen weight was prepared to stop at nothing to win it. But the fact that Pirana House, that bounteous benefactor of culture, tradition and the Conservative Party, were offering a cash prize of one hundred pounds to this year's winner had added an extra dash of panic to the proceedings.

Now in any straight and fair beauty contest, Lucy Tremayne would probably have won without even trying. But nothing in St Clare was ever entirely straight or fair, if it could possibly be avoided. And jury nobbling was not unheard of . . . and not too difficult to accomplish; for it was a one-man jury.

Traditionally, the Queen of the Feast was chosen by the captain of the team that won the hurling — providing, of course, that he was still conscious after the victory celebrations. And this was where Sally had to be careful. The captain of East Village was Tom Hoskin. And the captain of West Village was Arthur Pascoe. So one of them was going to have the coveted crown and one hundred pounds within his gift on feast Monday afternoon . . . Which was why she could not afford to upset either man before then; and why, consequently, she had been trying to avoid them both.

Tom had this sneaking suspicion that Sally had been trying to avoid him all week. He was not sure what gave him that idea, but it was just a canny feeling that he had every time he saw her doing an abrupt about-turn on her bicycle for no apparent reason and pedalling away from him at high speed. And he had an even sneakier suspicion that it might have something to do with Arthur Pascoe, who probably kept asking her out for picnics on Sunday afternoons . . . because that was just the kind of sneaky, snide thing he *would* do.

So Tom made a special point of lying in wait behind the habour wall that Friday afternoon, to ambush Sally as she went on her shopping rounds . . .

*   *   *

Sally did her best to look delighted with this latest invitation to go on a Sunday afternoon picnic.

'Why, I'd love to, Tom, but I'm worken all afternoon,' she replied, thankful that she could tell him a genuine lie for once.

'Worken?' said Tom, taken aback. 'You'm worken on a Sunday? Whear?'

'Out to Zennor.'

'Zennor?' This was getting more suspicious by the second. 'Why, thear edden nothen out to Zennor, es thear?'

'Lord St Clare has a cottage on the cliffs.'

'What are ee doan out thear on a Sunday, an?'

'Just a bit of overtime. As a special favour. Cleanen the place up and that. Tes the start of the holiday season, see.'

'Aw, ais, so tes, so tes,' said Tom. 'Well, some other time an, my dear . . . '

'Some other time would be lovely, Tom. Proper job.'

So Tom bade her farewell and plodded off with cheerful wellies towards the Proud Pinnace.

So, he thought, as he stormed into the public bar, *that* was Pascoe's little game, eh? A nasty, backhanded, grubby, seedy, cowardly, cheap, dirty, filthy, sordid, warm, cosy, loving, passionate, sex-riddled assignation at Lord Fred's cottage . . . Well, three could play at that game.

One hundred yards away on West Quay, Arthur Pascoe was hiding beneath his new red Vauxhall estate with a telescope, pretending to look at the exhaust pipe but secretly watching every second of this encounter down by the harbour.

Deep down inside he was writhing and burning with jealousy. That sly slug, Hoskin, was capable of anything. He even had the cowardly audacity to arrange an accidental clandestine meeting in full view of the whole village. Secret meetings in public, eh? Hah! Just how stupid did they think he really was? Did they take him for a complete idiot? Did they seriously imagine he didn't realise they had no idea he'd found out they were unaware he'd spotted the obvious pretence that they didn't even know that he thought they suspected he'd discovered for a proven fact what he wasn't at all sure about? If so, they had another think coming.

And did they seriously think he even *cared*? Dear life! How petty. How childish. How very, *very* small-minded. Deep down inside he was writhing and burning with total indifference.

And to prove it he stood up like a man as Sally approached across West Quay, and asked her straight out if she fancied going for a picnic on Sunday.

'I'd love to, Arthur,' she replied, 'but I'm afraid I'm goan to be busy.'

Yes, he knew damn well she was going to be busy. Busy with that dog's mess, Hoskin.

'Busy?' he said, sounding surprised. 'On a bank hollerday Sunday? Well, whatever are you doan, my dear?'

'I'm goan out to Zennor, matter of fact.'

'Busy in *Zennor*?' The village of Zennor had a population of just over several and was difficult even to see, let alone be busy in. 'On a Sunday?'

'Lord St Clare has a cottage out thear.'

'Ah, so he has, so he has . . . ' And a right crafty little place for her and Hoskin to meet up for the afternoon.

'Tes just a few small jobs he needs doan. And 'twill mean a bit of extra cash for me, see.'

'I quite understand, my dear,' he assured her. 'Some other time, eh?'

'Some other time would be lovely, Arthur.'

And he bade her goodbye and set off back to his shop.

What *could* he have been doing, lying under his car with a telescope, she wondered?

So, thought Arthur, as he plunged his meat cleaver into a fresh carcass of prime Hoskin, *that* was the sordid little plan, eh? Well, maybe he'd just happen to take a drive out to

Zennor himself, come Sunday. Three could play at this game.

'Zennor? On a Sunday?' said Lucy, when she got home from school. 'What ever for?'

'Tes just a few little chores for Lord Fred.'

Lucy could smell a rat. Her mother still held firmly to traditional Methodist values and never worked on the seventh day. Besides, they were supposed to be going to see Auntie Meg in Helston. And apart from that, Lucy knew all the stories about Lord Fred, his cottage at Zennor, and the basic principles of Masterplan D.

'Well, I'll come out to Zennor too, ma,' she suggested over tea, 'and give you a helping hand.'

'No need to trouble, dear. Tes only didjy little jobs.'

'No trouble. The two of us can get them done all the quicker.'

'I shoulden bother, my love, tes only . . . '

'No bother, mum. We can take a walk out to Gurnard's Head after.'

'Don't put yourself out, my sweet. You stay here and get your clothes pressed and ready for feast day . . . '

'Won't be putten me out at all, ma. Plenty of time on Sunday evenen to . . . '

'*No*, Lucy!'

Silence.

Lucy detected a note of panic in her mother's voice.

'Why not, ma?'

'Because Lord Fred doesn't want . . . ' She couldn't think of any good reasons. She was beginning to lose patience. 'Look, just mind your own business, dear. Lord Fred and I have a lot to do on Sunday afternoon, and that's all there is to it. Don't keep goan on and on about it, all right?'

Lucy finished her tea in silence. Then she put on her coat and announced that she was going for a walk. And fixing her mother with a haunting, reproachful look, she added, 'Might take a stroll through the graveyard.' And away she went.

Sally was furious. Lucy was too clever by half. She had already cottoned on to the game with Tom and Arthur, and now it looked as if she was on to the game with Lord Fred as well. Lucy had made it quite plain that no one was going to take Kenwyn's place in that household, and she was crafty enough to know how to play on her mother's guilty feelings. All she had to do was assume that haunting, accusing look, and hint that she was going out to water the flowers on her father's grave, and Sally would feel racked with guilt for days . . . Which she strongly resented. Because at difficult times like these, when a young widow was honestly and sincerely trying to pull the wool over everyone's eyes, the very least a loving, Christian daughter could do was mind her own bloody business.

Danny Curnow had had a very busy week. He'd failed several interviews for a job as a deckchair attendant, had sent off a postal order for one pound fifty for a copy of *How To Write Poetry*, as advertised in the *Exchange and Mart*, and had done an enormous amount of washing-up.

Yet despite this punishing workload, he had still managed to find time to start writing several important poems. He hadn't actually managed to *finish* any of them . . . In fact, he hadn't managed to get beyond the first few lines. But then all true romantics had taken days — sometimes whole weeks — to complete their masterpieces.

It was not easy being a true romantic. After a careful study of his *Treasury of Romantic Victorian Verse*, and the learned foreword by the late great Vernon Cripple, M.A., he had come to the conclusion that there were several essential qualifications. Firstly, it seemed, one had to know something about Ancient Greece. Well, he had at least heard of Athens, so that was a start. Secondly, one had to be pretty destitute . . . Which he thought he was, or could be, given time and a fair chance. And thirdly, one had to fall in love with one's sister.

Now this was where Danny foresaw problems. Because, unlike Wordsworth or Byron, he was an only child. But still, all was not lost. His mother was only thirty-eight. If she were to hurry up and get pregnant again, he would still be in his prime by the time his little sister was legally old enough to start being incestuous.

One thing, however, was abundantly clear. To be a true romantic, one had to *love*, and to love agonisingly. And to suffer, to suffer ecstatically.

Deeply moved by the tragic nobility of this whole romantic condition, and much impressed by an engraving of Shelley legging it round the Alps in a floppy hat and flowing cape, Danny had rescued a wide-brimmed, black velvet bonnet from a pile of moth's food destined for the vicar's jumble sale, had pulled the sleeves of his duffel coat inside out, and thus attired had taken to roaming across the cliffs, commencing new sonnets to Lucy.

And it was in this profoundly romantic attitude that he was rambling over West Headland one warm Friday evening, when he stumbled — literally — upon the object of all his dreams, desires and devotions.

He was mesmerised by the sight of his own feet at the time, and struggling to think of a word to rhyme with *chapel*. As in, 'Lucy, my love, lives next to the . . . etc., etc.' *Grapple* had sprung instantly to mind. And *apple*. But he couldn't think how either of these words could be linked logically to the sentiments of that exquisitely tender opening line. And at this critical moment for the future of world poetry, he tripped over Lucy herself, who was lying almost hidden in the long grass, gazing contemplatively out in the direction of the Bay of Biscay.

Danny was so startled he almost jumped over the cliff with shock. 'Did I frighten ee, Lucy?' he asked, collapsing on the grass beside her.

'No,' she said. 'I saw you comen a mile off.'

'Aw. That's all right, an.'

She was staring at the horizon. He too stared at the horizon.

'What are ee looken at, Lucy?'

'Nothen special.' She sighed. 'Just thinken. How wide the seas are.'

Danny nodded solemnly. 'They are that.'

'Just think of it . . . That's the coast of Spain, right out there.'

Danny was amazed. 'Es it?' He stared at the horizon but couldn't see anything except an oil tanker. But he didn't want to look stupid, so he said, 'Aw, ais. So tes. Fancy that, an.' And after a silence he said, 'What are ee doan up here this time of evenen, Lucy?'

'Trying to find some peace and quiet. So I can think. What are *you* doan up here?'

'Me? Aw, nothen much. Juss finishen off a few sonnets.'

'Well, I won't keep you then, Danny.'

'What are ee thinken about, an?'

'None of your business,' she said quietly. 'Just leave me alone please.'

'Righto.' Danny didn't move. After another silence he said, 'Funny you should be thinken. *I* was juss thinken and all. About the famous ode by John Keats. "*Aw, what can ail thee, knight at arms*", her do go, "*Alone and palely loiteren*".' Pause. 'Interesten that, edden it?'

'But what's it got to do with anything?' Lucy replied.

He'd hoped she wouldn't ask. That was the only bit of poetry that he knew. He'd learnt it specially for her. He'd learnt several verses of it, in fact, but had forgotten them all again.

'Juss a thought,' he replied mysteriously.

'Oh, Danny,' she said, getting irritated now. 'Please go away and leave me alone.'

'Upset about somethen, are ee?'

'Just go away . . . *Please*.'

'Like I told ee t'other week,' Danny went on, undeterred, 'if you've got any troubles, you can al'us talk to I.'

This was too much for Lucy. 'Oh, for God's sake, Danny,' she said, springing to her feet, 'I just want to be left *alone*! Talk to you, you bonehead? I might as well talk to a vegetable. You'm so bloody stupid you don't even know you're the village idiot. Now leave me *alone*!'

And with that she marched furiously away across the headland.

Danny sat there, blowing about in the wind, for a long, long time, her cruel words echoing in his ears, slicing like razor slashes deep into his soul.

To love, and to love agonisingly. To suffer, to suffer ecstatically.

Spirits refreshed and buoyed up once more by the nobility of this hopelessly depressing thought, he abandoned all further work on his sonnets and began thinking up the invitation list for his own tragically early funeral.

He gazed miserably out to sea for a very long while. But he still couldn't make out the coast of Spain.

Lucy walked inland from West Headland towards Blakey's Ridge, and eventually came to Granny Polkinghorne's cottage, where she found the wise old pellar feeding the chickens in her garden.

Lucy was not sure whether she believed in the power of pellars or not. But Granny P. had once cured her of a mysterious skin disease, and ever since childhood Lucy had confided her troubles in the old woman and sought her advice.

Granny P. took her indoors, gave her a tot of rue and pennywort cordial and sat and listened to her tale of woe. It was not a very long tale of woe. And it was not really a very woeful tale of woe. But Granny P. listened in sympathetic silence, creaking backwards and forwards in her rocking chair, with Guinevere, the eldest of her seven cats, snoozing in her lap.

'Well, my dear life,' she said, when Lucy had finished, 'your mother es a young woman still. You can't expect her to stay a widdy-woman all her days now, can ee?'

'But she's playen with people's feelings, Gran,' said Lucy. 'It's so deceitful. She doesn't know if she wants Uncle Tom, or butcher Pascoe, or Lord Fred, or what she wants.'

'Well, would ee have her marry the first man her sees?'

'Of course I wouldn't.'

'Then would ee have her go putten ribbons in her hair,

and paint on her face, and dress herself up like a Christmas tree, and go dancen in Penzance every Friday night?'

'No, you know I wouldn't.'

'Then you do have to ask yourself what tes you *do* want, and what tes you don't. Because I do think you'm fretten 'cos you don't want to see another man in your dad's place. Now edden that so?'

Lucy didn't answer. Because it was true.

'But that's juss selfish of ee, Lucy vean,' Granny P. went on kindly. 'You don't want your mother to be lonely all her life now, surely? By the time her's middle-aged you'm goan to be wed and liven in your own home. And I do knaw what tes like to be a widdy-woman. They took my young man away to France. And he never come back. Same as they did take all the brave young boys of Cornwall. Thear wasn't hardly any left be th'end o' the Great War. So girls my age never wed again. And us been all our lives alone. Now you woulden wish that for your mama, Lucy, I'm sure. I knaw tes hard for ee to unnerstand. And you'm still missen your dad, Loord rest ees soul. But it all do seem so easy when you'm young, child. When you ent got to buy food, and pay rent, and provide for a pretty growen girl not sixteen years old . . .'

Lucy walked back down the winding bridle path from Blakey's Ridge to West Meadows. Granny P. didn't understand either. No one understood.

There was still another half hour of sunlight left in the evening, so she decided to take the long way home, along the Addle valley. And as she was walking down through the wooded slopes of West Meadows, she noticed a solitary figure perched high up on one of the great rocks in the Hag's Ring. It was Mervyn Sharkley.

She walked to the foot of the rock. 'You won't move it, Mr Sharkley,' she called up. 'It's been like this for thousands of years.'

'And what do you think will happen to me if I try?' he called back.

She clambered up the sloping face of the rock and sat down beside him.

'Dunno. Somethen terrible, I expect. It's because of the Druids, see. They used to sacrifice things on these stones. Or so people say.'

'And you believe all these fairy tales, do you?'

'Maybe I do. Maybe I don't.'

'Well, I'll tell you this much . . . I've just been looking at all these rocks, and *I* can't see the bloodstains of the third Baron St Clare.'

'That's because you're a non-believer,' said Lucy wisely.

Not too far away, from the safe vantage point of a five-barred gate, Ned Gummoe and Socrates the bull had been watching the diminutive Arab for the best part of half an hour. The little fellow had been trampling all over the sacred rocks of the Hag's Ring, with contemptuous disregard for the dreaded curse which had stricken all desecrators of that hallowed ground in times gone by.

'Maatey won't last the night, the way he's goan,' Ned muttered fearfully to Socrates.

Socrates blinked in agreement.

The distinction between Christians and pagans was not wholly clear to Ned, and divine retribution was much the same to him whether it was wrought through the good offices of the Druids, the Methodists or the wee piskies who lived at the bottom of his vegetable patch. So, ever concerned for the welfare of his fellow men, Ned raised his eyes to heaven and prayed aloud:

'Aw, Loord . . . Mizzer Sheikh Lee, the Arab, es given us five hunnerd gallons of ale and a thousand pasties on feast Monday. So whatever wickedness he es a doan of, ovver thear on the Hag's Ring, for Chrissake don't go strike the bugger dead till Tuesday, now will ee?'

And Socrates nodded amen to that.

10

Sharkley was awoken the following morning at the crack of dawn by the man in the room next door — one Hermann H. Hermann of Des Moines, Iowa — singing the first verse of *The Wild Rover*, over and over again, while he performed his ablutions and did his exercises.

Sharkley eventually dropped off to sleep again and awoke a second time at the crack of ten to eleven. Whereupon he arose, full of the joys of spring, and had a blazing row with the management because he was too late for breakfast.

He pointed out to the manageress that a hotel was supposed to exist primarily for the benefit of its patrons, and not the other way about. Although he conceded that in England hotels have traditionally existed for the sole benefit and convenience of their proprietors. And warning her that she would soon change her tune when Pirana House opened their luxurious new establishment at Tremorna Hall, he stormed off to the village to try and find something to eat.

Outside, he found the place teeming with visitors. Spring bank holiday had arrived, bringing with it hoards of tourists and other riff-raff that Sharkley didn't much like the look of. He could hardly move for people. The beach was packed with happy families, shivering bravely behind their wind-breaks. The lanes were swarming with people carrying bikinis and Ambre Solaire, fighting off pneumonia and browsing round the shops in search of roll-neck sweaters. And the harbour front was swarming with Eli Tonkin, part-time traffic warden, eagerly slapping parking tickets on every windscreen that came along.

Sharkley couldn't get near a café. Every one was crowded with grockles. So he tried the saloon bar of the Proud Pinnace. But that was crowded with grockles too. So he tried the public bar. And that was only crowded with Ned Gummoe, waiting for someone to buy him a pint.

'Good morning, Mr Gummoe,' said Sharkley. 'How are you keeping?'

'Aw, well, don't mind if I do,' said Ned, handing him his tankard. 'Juss a small pint mind, seean as you won't take no for an answer.' He scrutinised Sharkley's face for symptoms of terminal death following the trespass upon the Hag's Ring. 'An how are ee keepen, an, Mizzer Sheikh Lee? All right an, are ee?'

'Apart from a grumbling rumbling tummy,' Sharkley replied.

'Aw, injestion? Then you do want wan tot of Rebecca Polkinghorne's special cordjal, you. And a pint of Jack Penna's keg scrumpy cider. That'll shift anythen, and naw mistake.'

Sharkley explained with feeling that thanks to the absence of service in British hotels he had nothing to shift. And he ordered a pint of bitter for Ned, and a pint of keg scrumpy for himself.

'Ais, you,' said Ned gratefully, 'I do reckon you'm th'only wan as es goan to bring prosperity to this village, true enough. True as I do stand ere, my dear, I been trampen the streets of St Clare all these weeks tellen ever'wan as Pirany 'ouse was th'only chance us all got left. I been signen me name reg'lar as clockwork every day on the widdy Tremayne's petition, the Loord es my witness.'

Which was perfectly true. But then he'd also been signing his name every day on the Reverend Owen Borage's petition.

But Sharkley was not listening. He'd been distracted by a man sitting at the saloon bar, staring at him. He was a total stranger to Sharkley, and he was pretending to be reading a newspaper. But he was definitely, quite definitely, staring at him, Sharkley could sense it.

'Thear's a rumour goan round,' Ned was saying, 'that your bossies es comen down from up the country for feast day. That right, an?'

'That's right,' said Sharkley. 'They're flying in to St Mawgan in time for the hurling.'

'For the hurlen?' Ned was surprised that the Arabs were even interested in it. 'Do they unnerstand what tes about, an?'

'No,' said Sharkley. 'But nor do I, come to that.'

Jack Penna placed their two pints on the bar. Sharkley gave him a twenty-pound note. Ned thought it was a cheque.

'Well, I'll tell ee all about un, my 'andsome,' Ned volunteered, reckoning that this might see him in free beer until closing time. 'Here, Jack . . . lend us the hurlen ball a while, so I can explain the game to the sheikh 'ere.'

Jack Penna took the silver ball from its glass display case in the saloon bar and passed it to Ned.

Ned drew Sharkley away to a table in the corner and they sat down.

The stranger was still surreptitiously staring at Sharkley from behind his newspaper. He was beginning to make Sharkley feel uncomfortable. He was a very serious-looking person of about Sharkley's age. In a grubby white raincoat.

'Now this es the proper hurlen ball,' said Ned, passing it to Sharkley. It was a little bigger than a cricket ball. 'Tes made of maple. And plated wi' silver. And her's been en use for the hurlen en this parish since 1836. The ball afore that wa' lost to sea.'

'At sea?' said Sharkley, wondering if there were no limitations to this game at all.

'Ais. Her was kicked off the quay accidental like by Andrew Davey. Tinner 'e was be trade. So they did chuck the poor awld bugger en the sea after un.' Which Ned thought was hugely funny. 'But Davey could swim like a fishy, you. So it didden do un no harm. Well, then the Loord St Clare, Colonel Will, did give the village half a pound o' silver to plate thes new ball. Her was made by a smith on Market Jew Street, ovver to Penzance. And thear's some words engrave on un en th'awld tongue. Thear now see . . . '

He pointed to a legend engraved in the silver in Cornish: '*Bethoh dur ha wheag.*'

'It do mean "*Be bold and fair*",' said Ned.

'Do you speak Cornish?' asked Sharkley, wondering if he could market Ned too.

'Naw. I can count to five. And Mizzus Polkinghorne, her do knaw a prayer or two en un. But thear adden been no wan round 'ere spawke un proper sence hunnerd and fefty years or more.'

He paused to lubricate his throat and began to pack a fresh pipe of tobacco.

'No wan knaws when the hurlen started,' he went on. 'Her was played be the ancient Bretons all ovver the country once 'pon a time. They did come here from France, see. And if you do want to see anythen like the Cornish hurlen today, then go ovver to Bret'ny, where Frenchies live. They call un *soule*. And they do wrastle like us an' all. And some o' they do still speak th'awld tongue.

'Now our hurlen en St Clare al'us used to be on the Whitsun hollerday. Till the government up London buggered everything up. So now us has to 'ave un on spring bank hollerday. And tes al'us West village takes on East. Cos once 'pon a time, see, 'twas the miners took on the fishymen. Now us don't have no proper teams, and thear edden no rules. Any man who wants to join in es welcome . . . juss so long as 'e do live inside the parish bounds.' He took the ball back from Sharkley. 'On feast Monday, quarter to noonday, ever'wan es gathered by th' Addle bridge, and the ball es pass round the crowd for ever'wan to touch. 'Cos et grants they wan wish, see. Then, at the stroke of noon, be the parish church clock, Loord St Clare — ever'wan since the days of Colonel Will — takes the ball to start the hurlen proper. He cries: "*Hove-a! Hove-a! Hove-a!*" And he chucks the bugger up, tosses un high in th'air, and gets eeself out the way quicker 'an a jack rabbit. 'Cos when that ball do come down, you, every man on Addle bridge es goan to wrastle for un. And my gran'father use to tell I, when we was childern, that wan year thear was so many miners and fishymen on th'awld bridge — 'twas made o' wood in they days, see — her was scat en piecies and ever'wan pitched tumblen down into the river.'

Ned chuckled to himself and broke off for more refreshment. Sharkley noticed that the man in the grubby white mac was still watching him.

'So,' Ned resumed, 'the hurlen es started. Now if you'm a Wester you do have to try and run the ball through the village to your goal, which es the doorstep of the Fouled Anchor hotel. And the Easters have to run that ball to the step of the Pinnace, right here whear us es drinken. And the losers all buy the ale for the winners. Tes a gentlemanly sport, mind. Thear edden no rules but if you'm tackled, like in the rugby, you do drop the ball free or pass un on. And thear edden no special course or djrection that you do have to run. You'm allowed to splash all the way to goal through th'Addle river if you'm daft enough to try.'

Ned broke off again and drained his tankard.

Sharkley looked across to the saloon bar. The man in the grubby white mac was still there, but he was in conversation with Ben Curnow now.

Ben had entered the Proud Pinnace through the rear yard and the saloon; and on his way through to the public bar he chanced to see no lesser delight than the serious young face of Norman Strait, plain-clothes preventive officer, trying to spy inconspicuously on everyone.

'Well, well, well!' Ben shouted, so loudly that everyone in the saloon bar looked up to see what was going on. 'If it edden my old maate Mizzer Strait of the Cussoms and Excise.' He slapped the inconspicuous Strait affectionately upon the back. 'How be doan an, old cock? All right, are ee? I do hope you edden looken for smugglers en the Pinnace, 'cos us es all honest mariners en here, my dear.'

Strait flushed scarlet with embarrassment and began blowing his nose so that he could hide behind his handkerchief until the worst was over.

Everyone else in the bar went back to their own private conversations. And then Ben noticed Sharkley sitting in the public bar with Ned Gummoe. He nudged Strait and whispered:

'See maatey talken to old Ned in t'other bar thear . . .'

'I've been watching that one,' said Strait. 'Looks foreign.'

'Funny you say that. Rumour es goan round he's an Arab. And he's been behaven very suspicious.'

'In what way?'

'Aw, no, tes only rumour. I woulden want to spread gossep . . .'

'No, please feel free, Mr Curnow,' said Strait keenly.

'Well, I'm sure it woulden be . . .'

'It might be . . .'

'Well . . . tes whispered that he's been asken the times of the tides. And looken for a motor dinghy to hire. And signallen to sea.'

'Seriously?'

'Tes only what I hear murmured, mind.'

Strait stared at the dark, sinister-looking little foreigner again. The Iranian connection . . . ?

'I'll keep a close eye on that one,' he said to Ben. 'And please keep on reporting any scrap of information that comes your way.'

'I'll do that, my handsome. You can rely on I to do unto the Cussoms and Excise as they would you should do unto I.'

'That's the spirit,' said Strait proudly.

And Ben walked on through to the public bar, where he encountered Mervyn Sharkley getting up to buy two more pints.

'Could I . . .' Sharkley dropped his voice and drew Ben to one side, 'have a word in your shell-like ear, Mr Curnow?'

'Now I do hope you ent took no offence at what my missus been sayen about ee all round the village, Mr Sharkley?' said Ben. 'My Nancy didden mean no harm, callen ee a liddel worm . . .'

'No, it's not that, Mr Curnow . . .'

'And a greasy skunk . . .'

'Not that at all . . .'

'And an oily lying maggot . . .'

'No offence taken, Mr Curnow . . .'

'Aw, well, that's all right an,' said Ben, with a sigh of relief. 'Phew. You had I scared for a moment, 'cos I'm a peace-loven fellow, see . . .'

'Mr Curnow, please, I just wanted to ask you . . . '

'Well, a pint of best bitter then, Mr Sharkley, thank you kindly. Most civil of ee, my old maate.'

'You're very welcome,' said Sharkley, nodding to Jack Penna to pour Ben a pint. 'But what I wanted to ask you was . . . that man in the white mac you were just talking to . . . '

'Strait?' said Ben, dropping his voice to a confidential murmur. 'Norman Strait?'

'Is that his name?'

'Ais. He do come from up London way, but he's been down 'ere a while now. Why? Been looken at ee a bit . . . peculiar an, has 'e?'

'He has, actually,' said Sharkley. 'Funny you should say that. He keeps staring at me from behind his newspaper.'

Ben nodded sympathetically. 'That so, ezzer? Well, truth to tell, my flower, he es a bit peculiar.'

'Peculiar?'

'Likes to call isself Norma. And hangs round men's toilets . . . If you do get my meaning?'

'You're joking?'

'I wish I was,' said Ben solemnly. 'He's a very sad case, es poor young Norman Strait. Comes down 'ere to St Clare looken, see.'

'Looking? For . . . ? You mean . . . ?' Sharkley couldn't steel himself to say it.

Ben nodded. 'Afraid so. Us don't get much of that down here in Cornwall, mind. In fact . . . I don't think us have 'ad a case of un since before the last war. So he gets lonely, see. But don't ee go getten all of a pother now. He's harmless. He juss can't help eeself. Best thing es . . . if he do start followen ee round . . . '

'Yes . . . ?'

'Juss say to un: ''Bugger off, Norma.'' And give un a good clip round the ear'ole. He won't mind. He's used to it. No call to scat ees brains out, mind. Juss a good bang in the eye or a smack in the mouth. It do sound a bit barbaric, I know, my handsome. But thear es times when us do have to be cruel to be kind. And he'll appreciate you taken the trouble, I promise ee.'

Sharkley nodded gratefully. 'I'll bear that in mind, Mr Curnow. Thank you very much for warning me.'

'Any time, my friend,' said Ben, reaching for his pint. 'You'm al'us welcome to my advice.'

Sharkley bought a pint of bitter for Ned and another pint of Jack Penna's tasty but distinctly tame keg cider for himself, and returned to the ancient teller of lore and fable.

'So,' Sharkley resumed, 'somebody lands the ball in his team's goal, and then what happens?'

'Ever'wan starts drinken,' said Ned. 'And they do keep on drinken till half pass two. All East and West Quay es pack solid wi' people now, villagers and visitors alike. And thear's a big, oppen space en the middle whear all the village girls form a circle, all en thear ribbons and bows and pretty dressies. And the captain of the winnen team leads ees boys out, singen and dancen round the girls. And the special song do go: "*Whear es our queen this saint's day feast? Our chaste and beauteous maiden.*" Thear es a bit more to un that that, mind, but ever'wan's gone and forgot what tes. Any'ow, they'm all so drunk benow they'm singen anythen as do come into thear heads. And whoever captained the winnen team, tes ees right to choose the new queen. And soon as her's been chose, her es put aboard the royal carriage, which es Farmer Rosewarne's awld cart, all paint up bright, weth ees awld Clydesdale, Lysander, en the shafts. And from thear the queen es tooken up the village Cross and crowned weth a silver crown by Loord St Clare, all dress up en ees furry robes. Thear edden really no silver en the crown, see, but that don't matter, do un? And when her's been crowned her gets back in Rosewarne's cart, and sets off at the front of a grand procession, right up Middle Street and out to the Fields, whear the fair es starten up proper now.'

And that, as Sharkley understood it, was where Ormskirk wanted the chaste and lovely St Clare to be seen riding safely between her two knights in shining armour, smiling warmly at the television cameras, to reassure the world that her honour was safe in Pirana House's strong, protective hands . . .

* * *

And that was how Miranda Jago understood it too. But at that moment, not a mile away across the Addle valley, in the tack-room of the local riding stables, she and Alfreda Mitchell were faced with an acute manpower crisis.

The problem was that two sets of chain mail, with breast-plates and optional extras, had arrived by rail from London, but they could think of nobody to put inside them. There was a severe shortage of likely knights errant in that locality. Out of all the competent riders they could think of, not one was tall enough, imposing enough, and likely to remain sober enough, long enough, to play such a technically demanding role.

So Alf, who was five feet eleven in her riding boots, had nobly volunteered to try on a suit of chain mail herself . . . There was fifty pounds in this, cash in hand, after all.

However, one suit of armour had obviously been tailor-made for a midget. And the other would have swamped a Titan.

'Is it the new me?' she wondered, hopelessly engulfed in a colossal sack of silver-painted string mesh, like a Michelin man with a puncture.

'Lost in the mail . . . ?' suggested Miranda.

'Ha bloody ha-ha.'

'Try the breast-plate, petal. And the sword. They might scrunch everything together.'

She buckled on the breast-plate. It did not scrunch every-thing together. It did not scrunch *any*thing together. It just flapped about like a shed door in a gale. The leather belt would have gone twice round a Japanese Sumo wrestler, and the sword trailed ignominiously along the tack-room floor in most unwarlike fashion.

'Try the helmet,' said Miranda, as if that could possibly have improved things.

There was a hood of chain mail and a large tin can, like an old fashioned coal scoop, to go on top. They consumed Alf's head entirely and would have consumed half her torso too if her shoulders had not got in the way.

'This is bloody ridiculous,' she protested from dark, tinny depths. 'I can't ride a horse like this.'

'It does need a tuck or two,' Miranda agreed.

In the meantime, out in the stable yard, a number of little people (smaller even than Mervyn Sharkley, but bigger than the little people who lived at the bottom of Ned Gummoe's vegetable patch) were just scrambling onto their ponies in preparation for the junior riding club's Saturday morning hack, when a little yellow car came screaming in from the lane at high speed and skidded to a halt outside the tack-room door. Anxious ponies started bucking with fright.

Alf shuffled to the door as quickly as her suit of chain mail would permit. A tall, bronzed, Latin-looking man got out of the car.

'What the hell do you think you're playing at?' Alf demanded furiously, removing the coal scoop from her head.

'*Pardon, monsieur* . . . ' The man began, plainly disconcerted to find himself addressing a heap of silver string.

Miranda recognised this handsome stranger at once. It was Ramon Grenoux, master of the *Musetta*, with whom Ben Curnow had done battle at sea the previous month.

'He's French,' she murmured to Alf.

'That much is obvious,' said Alf witheringly. '*Voici* a stables!' she told Ramon. 'Full of *chevaux*. Not Le Mans. You just terrified the ponies!'

Ramon clasped his hands in abject apology. 'Many many sorries, monsieur. Is not my car . . . I rent only zis morning.'

Mollified somewhat at having been addressed twice as *monsieur* in so short a space of time, Alf smoothed down her short back and sides as if they'd been blown into a frenzy of Gordian knots by the slipstream of the car, and said imperiously, 'Well, kindly test your brakes elsewhere, another time. Now what can I do for you?'

'I was 'oping to af 'orse,' said Ramon, still worried about Alf's appearance. 'Today . . . tomorrow, maybe, yes?'

'No chance,' Alf replied. 'We're booked solid. It's bank holiday. Feast weekend.' From her point of view, this was just another odious example of the archetypal macho, Latin male: vain, hairy, and obsessed with his cock.

And from Miranda's point of view, this was a promising

159

example of the archetypal French matelot: horny, virile, and — with any luck — obsessed with his cock. And there was a definite shortage of those in West Cornwall.

'A knight in shining armour!' she exclaimed to Alf. And to Ramon: 'How long are you here for, *mon admiral*?'

'We af emergency. Our steering af broke. We are at Penzance, yes? My engineer af gone to buy at the shop of Falmouth some new fings.'

'*Bien.* I have a proposition.'

'*Bien, j'accepte,*' said Ramon. 'We make maybe a party on our boat zis night, yes? We af much fun. You may join us . . . wis also some girlfriends, yes?'

'We may, we may,' said Miranda. 'But *écoutes, mon brave* . . .'

'And your 'usband?' he enquired, glancing at Alf.

'Well, really!' Alf protested, rather flattered.

'We're just good friends,' Miranda assured him. 'But listen to *moi*, saucy Pierrot . . . when do you set sail? How long will you be here on the shores of us?'

Ramon shrugged his shoulders. 'Eef my engineer make a good fix . . . until one week per'aps.'

'*Parfait*!' declared Miranda. 'How would you like to earn fifty crisp oncers and get your boat-race on the BBC?'

The Frenchman grinned, utterly mystified. 'What is . . . *oncers*?'

'Don't worry about a thing,' Miranda said, towing him swiftly into the tack-room. 'Just step into this vacant jump suit of old grey string . . .'

By one o'clock that afternoon, Mervyn Sharkley considered himself to be something of an authority on Cornish hurling. He had bought Ned his third tankard of best bitter, and was himself on his fourth pint of Jack Penna's tasty but distinctly tame keg cider. And he now knew all sorts of arcane things, like the difference between hurling to goal and hurling to country.

That fellow Strait was still there, too, pretending not to be watching him from the other bar.

By one-thirty Ned was ready for another half of bitter to top up his tankard, and Sharkley was knocking back his fifth pint of Jack Penna's tasty but distinctly tame keg cider. And he now knew the difference between a piskey, a knacker and a spriggan.

And that poof Strait was still gawping at him.

By two o'clock Ned had had his fill, and Sharkley was on his seventh pint of Jan Pecka's tinky but distastely tame egg tiger, and no longer knew the difference between a piskey, a knacker and a spriggan. Or an aardvark, or a tea cup, or West Bromwich on early closing day.

And he could no longer see Norman Strait in the other bar. In fact he could no longer see *anything* in the other bar.

By closing time, at half past two, he didn't even know his own name.

With both legs attempting to proceed in different directions at the same time, he made some sort of erratic progress through the saloon bar in a brave and desperate quest for the gents. In doing so, he careered about all over the place, like a man on the deck of a storm-tossed ship, crashing into every stool and table that was in his path and many more that were not.

When he finally reached the toilets, he failed to make it through the doorway at the first three attempts, and at the fourth collided head-on with somebody who was coming out . . . A man in a grubby, white raincoat. The force of the collision sent him flying backwards, and he would have fallen flat on his back had Norman Strait not been quick enough to catch him. But having in mind Ben Curnow's warning earlier on, Sharkley took this to be some sort of deviant sexual advance. So he assured Strait that what he was about to do he was doing only out of pure kindness, and then tried to bash him in the eye, but missed and hit the brick wall behind.

He then passed out completely and was delivered to the tradesmen's entrance of the Fouled Anchor hotel on the back of Charlie Penrose's pick-up truck, where he lay spread-eagled over half a hundredweight of swedes, assuring the sky that sometimes one had to be kind to be cruel.

161

Sharkley was as yet only at the gates of that terrible purgatory that awaits all who get plastered on scrumpy. For the next hour or so he lay mildly delirious on the bed in his room, burbling on about squoodgey typists in Powagrippa, 72-hour, stretch-lace catsuits. And seated on the chair at his bedside, Norman Strait — who was keeping an open mind about the possibility of this tiny pervert having Iranian connections — was faithfully copying down every syllable of his gibberings in an official, black, Customs and Excise notebook.

This continued until mid-afternoon . . . By which time Sharkley was babbling on about Noreen being ravished by Saxons with rolled-up newspapers. At this point, Norman Strait concluded that this was no longer a case for the Customs and Excise, and went back to his hotel in Penzance.

Sharkley was now alone, gazing up at the foggy ceiling and trying to fathom out the solution to a number of extremely pertinent puzzles . . . like where he was, what he was doing there, and why. By five o'clock the world was spinning with terrible velocity and all he wanted to do was chuck up or go to sleep. But for some time he was unable to do either. And by six o'clock the full force of seven pints of Jack Penna's tasty but distinctly tame keg cider was beginning to hit him, and all he wanted to do then was die . . . Whilst in the room next door, one Hermann H. Hermann of Des Moines, Iowa, was changing for dinner and singing ad nauseum the only lines he knew of an old Irish ballad:

'*Roll out a hogshead of the old potheen, Kathleen, mavourneen, and we'll all be drunk for a year . . .*'

Constance Borage, the vicar's wife, was out on Porthcurno Hill early that evening with her daft spaniel, Brian. And she was delighted to see that the widow Tremayne's cat was out mousing in the hedgerows.

Brian liked chasing cats. Because he was so daft he thought they were just a different breed of dog. And whenever he managed to corner one he rolled over on his back and wagged his tail and tried to purr.

'Look . . . Pretty pussy, Brian!' whispered Constance, pointing gleefully at the widow Tremayne's ginger tom. 'Go chase! Go chase!'

But Brian was so stupid he just turned round and looked in the opposite direction.

'Chase pussy!' Constance hissed angrily. 'Bite nasty pussy!' And she stamped her foot and dragged Brian round by the scruff of the neck to face the right direction.

But by this time the widow Tremayne's cat had seen the danger and was dashing for the safety of his own garden.

Brian took off in ecstatic pursuit, ears flapping up and down like old rags. Straight into a clump of nettles.

'Stupid dog,' Constance called after him. 'Come here.'

But Brian had discovered something far more interesting than the widow Tremayne's tomcat. And after much enthusiastic yapping and pawing and scraping, he emerged from the nettles with something clenched between his jaws. He dropped it proudly at Constance's feet and wagged his tail and waited for her to throw it for him. He thought it was a ball. It was not a ball. It was a wallet. A man's wallet.

The Reverend Owen Borage was upstairs in his study, focusing his 8 × 30 field glasses on the distant east wing of Tremorna Hall, where Miranda Jago was stripping off to take a bath. The knock on his study door almost gave him heart seizure.

'Are you busy, Owen?' Constance called to him from the landing outside.

'Just . . . finishing . . . off . . . this . . . letter . . . ,' he called back, tiptoeing over to the desk with huge strides, and just managing to hide the field glasses in his wastepaper basket as Constance walked in.

'What letter, dear?' she enquired, seeing nothing at all upon his desk but that day's copy of the *Western Morning News*.

'This letter in the paper,' replied the vicar, with an agility of mind that astonished even him. He opened the *News* and pointed to a letter to the editor on the subject of declining Methodist congregations in Cornwall. 'I thought I would bring it to the attention of the bishop.'

'How thoughtful,' said Constance fondly. She held out the wallet. 'But now see what *I* have found.'

He tried on several different pairs of spectacles before finding any that were of the slightest assistance.

'A wallet,' he observed perceptively.

'Young Daniel Curnow's. I found it on Porthcurno Hill while I was trying to stop Brian chasing Mrs Tremayne's cat.'

The vicar took it. It was made of genuine black plastic. Inside, he found the name *Danny P. Curnow*, seven one-pound notes, three colour photographs of a girl in the tiniest suggestion of a bikini, and two . . .

'Oh, good grief . . . !' he gasped.

Constance, who had never seen a contraceptive in her life, and had prayed regularly as a young woman that she never would, was under the misapprehension that *Black Stallion* was a brand of foil-wrapped bubble gum. But the photographs were self-explanatory and she shared her husband's sense of outrage.

'Lucy Tremayne,' said the vicar, mortified.

'Almost . . . *naked*,' whispered Constance, unable to say the word out loud.

'With absolutely nothing on beneath the bikini,' shuddered the vicar, amazed at how well developed she was at such a young age. 'Leave these with me, Constance. I shall see young Daniel tomorrow and get to the root of this wickedness.'

Constance agreed, willingly and gratefully. Owen was so wise and strong. She gave thanks to heaven each night that she had married a man of such goodness, compassion and humility, and had not ended up with one of those pathetic inadequates who enjoyed alcohol or wanted to sleep in the same bed.

She was about to leave and let him resume his labours in

peace, when she noticed that he'd left his binoculars in the wastepaper basket. This did not surprise her unduly, for he was an absent-minded man and she was always finding funny little things that he'd left in the wrong place . . . such as a pair of spectacles in the airing cupboard, or a dishcloth in the fridge, or her old suspender belts in the bottom drawer of his desk.

'Owen,' she said, 'your binoculars are in the rubbish basket.'

'So they are,' he replied crisply. 'How very observant of you, Constance.'

He fished them out. She smiled sweetly and left the room. He waited until her footsteps had reached the hall downstairs and then crept back to the window and trained his binoculars on Miranda's bedroom once more. But there was no sign of her. Gone. Probably in the bath by now. He cursed her for undressing in such ungodly haste, and returned to his desk to have a really good look at those disgusting photographs of Lucy Tremayne.

11

Daniel P. Curnow, romantic and sonneteer, was sitting in the fourth pew back from the pulpit, trying to think of a word that rhymed with *pasties*. As in, '*Lucy, my love, do cook 'andsome . . .*' etc., etc. Beside him sat his mother, Nancy, concentrating on every syllable of what the vicar was saying. And beside her, her husband, Ben, with head devoutly bowed, eyes devoutly closed, and a rhythmic buzz emanating from his adenoids, dreaming devoutly of the Proud Pinnace and the first pint of the day.

'I publish the banns of marriage,' said the vicar, 'between Jane Mary Hunkin, spinster of this parish, and Henry Michael Pierce, bachelor of the parish of St Tudy. All ye who know cause or just impediment why these two should not be joined together in holy matrimony, ye are to declare it. This is for the second time of asking.'

'Well, her's a slattern for a start,' Nancy muttered, and nudged her husband.

Ben awoke with a jerk, straightened his tie and went back to sleep again.

'The Lantern of Light committee against vice,' the vicar continued, 'will meet on June 4th at Miss Bosvigo's house, to consider ways of stamping out bingo at the Marazion old people's home, and closing down the family planning advice centre.'

Danny couldn't understand why the vicar was staring at *him*. And in that strangely meaningful way. It was a very penetrating, accusing stare . . . even through all the porridge and whitewash on his spectacles. Family planning . . . ? What was the significance of that? *He* wasn't planning a family.

'The St Clare's Bay Preservation Front,' the vicar went on, 'will forgather at noon tomorrow, the Feast of St Clare, at the Addle bridge, with banners, under the direction of the steering committee. The protest march will go ahead as planned, during the coronation parade at three o'clock. And the sit-down occupation of the bridge will be done standing up, in deference to the wishes of the police.'

'If Percy Hawkins tries to stop *I* sitten down,' Nancy whispered defiantly, 'I shall pitch un en the river, and naw mistake.'

'And now the hymn, six hundred and eighty-eight,' the vicar concluded, glaring at Danny once more. '*From the depths of sin and failure* . . .'

As the congregation filed out of the church it was the vicar's custom to stand outside and say goodbye to his flock. Members of the local Conservative Association and all those who put bank notes or cheques into the collection received a special handshake, smile and words of benison. Loyal committee workers and fan club members merely got the smile and words of benison. And ordinary mortals just got a friendly nod.

But Danny got pulled to one side and was told, peremptorily, to wait.

After everyone had left the church, the vicar said to him, 'My wife has found your wallet, Daniel.'

'Aw, proper job,' said Danny, thinking initially only of the seven pounds.

'All the contents therein would appear to be none the worse for their exposure to the elements. But that,' he added cryptically, 'remains to be seen.'

All the contents . . . The implication hit Danny like a sledgehammer.

'If you would like to come to the vicarage at three o'clock this afternoon,' the vicar concluded, 'we can make sure that everything is exactly as you lost it.'

Danny walked out of the church-yard with leaden tread, contemplating a tragically early end to it all as soon as suicidally possible.

Sally Tremayne had been in a state of nervous anticipation all morning and was barely listening to a word the Reverend Micah Dredge was saying. All she could think of was the afternoon, the cottage at Zennor, and Lord Fred.

Lucy was not listening either. 'I feel a bit peculiar, ma,' she said, rubbing her tummy.

'No you don't,' said Sally cheerfully. 'Tes juss a quick passen twinge.' This was no time for Lucy to be ill . . . with Lord Fred warming up in the Alvis, and her maternal conscience in the state it was in already.

But elsewhere in the chapel, all eyes and ears were on the minister, who was in full cry and building up to an angry climax.

'But there are voices in our midst today,' he warned them, 'that are raised against all change, all progress . . . Like the dinosaurs of old, who could not adapt . . . The dodoes . . . The pterodactyls. And consider what happened to *them*, brethren and sisters, and to all their kind!' And he dealt the side of the pulpit an almighty blow with his fist. 'Gone! Vanished! Extinct! Just fossils beneath the dust where the march of progress has tramped on by!'

There was considerable stirring amongst the congregation.

'But what about West Meadows an, praicher?' called out Eli Tonkin, much agitated and confused.

'Why, brethren . . . ' Micah Dredge leaned forward across the pulpit. 'Don't you want jobs? Don't you want work?'

'Ais, course us do,' Frank Pengelly, the plumber, called out.

'Then ask yourselves,' continued the minister, 'who would build those chalets on West Meadows? Why, *you*, the bricklayers, the carpenters, the electricians, the plumbers! And whose womenfolk would keep them clean and in good order? And in whose shops would all those thousands of new visitors spend their money?'

A general murmur of approval rippled through the congregation.

'Tes true,' said Caleb Trevaskis to everyone around him. 'Tes true, every word!'

'Ais, you,' agreed Ned Gummoe. 'Praise be the Loord!'

'Praise be to un,' croaked Granny Holman.

'Praise be the Loord!' shouted others all around.

'Got a pain,' whispered Lucy.

'No you haven't,' whispered Sally.

'Feel all peculiar and hot . . . '

'No you don't. Tes lovely and cool in here, dear.'

'But!' bellowed the Reverend Micah Dredge, scaring Granny Holman half to death. 'The Devil works in insidious ways!'

'So he does,' growled Noah Rundle. 'He does that, praicher.'

'He is always among us, brothers and sisters!'

'Al'us among us,' agreed Caleb Trevaskis, taxi driver and funeral director. 'Praise be the Loord.'

'He is even *now*,' thundered Micah Dredge, pointing straight towards the vicarage, 'plotting a dark and sinister course . . . to choke this tiny infant, *progress*, in its very cradle!'

'Praise be the Loord!' shouted Alice Uglow, who was still tuning in her deaf-aid and had only just worked out what Ned Gummoe had been shouting about a minute earlier.

'Praise be to un,' croaked Granny Holman.

'I tell you this, brethren, sisters . . . ' Micah Dredge went on.

'Ais, you do tell us, praicher,' said old Noah Rundle.

' . . . Those who march against the path of progress are treading on the hopes of every living soul in this village!'

'Every liven soul,' echoed Granny Holman.

'Trampling . . . !' raged the minister, 'on *your* jobs, my brothers and sisters! On *your* futures! And on the future of your children!'

This was all too much for Dick Champion, the garage mechanic, who now rose to his feet, scarlet with passion. 'Well, thear edden no wan goan to trample on *I*!' he roared. 'Noor on my childern neither!'

His wife, Mary, pulled him back into the pew, reminding him that they had no children yet, and apologising to the congregation all around.

'Naw, you scat to un, Dickon!' Ned called out. 'Us'll have they dineysaurs and terrydackles, and scat thear heads ope, proper job, you!'

Percy Hawkins turned round in his pew and told Ned to shush. But Ned was almost wetting himself with fervour.

'Shall *we* be dinosaurs?' boomed Micah Dredge. 'Shall *we* stand by and let our village fossilise? Shall we assist the forces of Satanic darkness at our feast day tomorrow . . . with their marches, and their banners, and their occupation of the Addle bridge? Shall we? *Shall* we?'

Dick Champion leapt up again and pointed threateningly at Constable Hawkins. 'You juss put a stop to that march tomorrer, Percy Hawkins, in the name of the Loord! Or else us es goan to stop un for ee!'

There was a loud and angry chorus of support for Dick. And even from the silent majority came mutterings of approval.

Micah Dredge held up his arms for calm. 'Peace . . . ! Peace . . . ! Peace . . . !' he pleaded, confident now that the seeds of discord had been sown and would burgeon forth in abundance. 'Let us all proceed in Christian harmony and brotherhood, bearing forth the banner of progress, assured of the righteousness of our cause.'

Amen, agreed the congregation with one accord.

It was a very short walk from the chapel to the Tremaynes' cottage. Lucy tottered into the kitchen as soon as she got home, and collapsed in a chair with a look of agony on her face.

'Why, whatever es wrong, dear?' said Sally, with a nervous eye on the clock. She was due to meet Lord Fred at Tremorna Hall at two o'clock.

'Got this awful pain,' groaned Lucy. 'And I feel really peculiar.'

'Because you didden have any breakfast, that's why.' She switched the kettle on to prepare that great British remedy for all ills from flat feet to brain failure. 'I'll make some tea. You'll be right as rain in no time.'

'I feel all hot and sick.'

Sally put her hand to the girl's brow. 'Feels normal enough. What sort of pain es it?'

'All over my tummy.'

'Well, perhaps you'm just starten . . . '

'Tes much worse than that,' said Lucy. 'Definitely isn't that.'

'My dear life, child, you do look all right. But I'd better take your temperature, in case . . . '

She went upstairs to the bathroom to fetch the thermometer. Lucy hurriedly got up, tipped some cooking salt into a mug and filled it with hot water from the kettle. Giving it a brisk stir, she knocked it all back in one long draught and repeated the dose. Then she dropped the mug into the washing-up bowl and collapsed into the chair again.

Sally came back downstairs and put the thermometer in Lucy's mouth. When she took it out a minute later, it was reading a hundred and two.

'Dear heaven, child, you *are* sickly . . . '

At that, Lucy slapped her hand across her mouth and ran upstairs to the bathroom. Quickly pushing a finger down her throat, she brought up the best part of a pint of saline solution, just as Sally hurried into the bathroom.

'You'd best get straight to bed I think,' she said. 'You must have a bug, or a touch of food poisenen, or somethen.'

Lucy undressed and got into bed. Sally gently probed her abdomen.

'Whear does it hurt, dear?'

'All round the appendix,' said Lucy ingenuously.

'Appendix . . . ?' Now Sally was even more worried. Only the previous week a girl from St Just had nearly died of peritonitis because no one had taken any notice of her when she was in pain. 'Perhaps I'd best give Doctor Jamieson a ring then . . .'

She went downstairs and telephoned the doctor. He said he would try and be there within an hour. Within an *hour*? Sally looked glumly at the clock and reluctantly called Tremorna Hall to warn Lord Fred that she might be late.

At that moment Arthur Pascoe, unaware of Lucy's sudden illness, was driving out of St Clare on the Porthcurno road in his new red estate car, intending to branch off inland and take the back lanes to the north-coast village of Zennor, where he knew damn well that Sally Tremayne was planning a top-secret assignation with that bastard, Hoskin . . .

. . . Who, by coincidence, was just then chugging out of St Clare along the *Mousehole* road, in Ben Curnow's clapped-out Minivan.

Working out to Zennor on a Sunday, eh? Hah! Just how daft did she think he was? Obviously she'd got her hands on Lord Fred's keys and was going out to the cottage for a clandestine rendezvous with that fat turd, Pascoe.

At Two-Mile-Cross he turned off and headed inland towards the north coast . . .

*   *   *

Doctor Jamieson drew the bedclothes back over Lucy and put away his stethoscope.

'Well, I don't think it's your appendix,' he said. 'And your temperature's back to normal. But I can't be sure . . . it might just be a touch of food poisoning.'

Downstairs, he said to Sally, 'You'd better not leave her alone for a while, in case the abdominal pains get any worse. I don't think they will, but you should keep an eye on her.'

Sally glanced at the clock.

When the doctor had gone she telephoned Tremorna Hall. Her hand was trembling. She swallowed hard.

'Oh hello, Lòrd St Clare,' she began, as if she didn't have a care in the world. 'Tes Sally Tremayne.' Her courage wilted. 'Oh dear, I dunno how to tell you this . . .'

But his lordship, the perfect gentleman as ever, took it like a lamb, bless him . . .

Freddie was in the filthiest bloody mood he'd been in since Christmas, when he'd heard that his latest ex-wife had inherited a brace of Rembrandts. He'd gone to *so* much trouble. He'd borrowed twenty quid off Miranda to put some petrol in the Alvis. He'd driven all the way to Zennor and back to secrete a bottle of Bollinger in the fridge. He'd spent hours ironing his best underwear. And after all that, bloody little Lucy had had the damnable effrontery to catch food poisoning in her appendix. It really was too, *too* inconsiderate . . .

Reports of Lucy's mysterious illness had already begun to filter through to that esteemed forum of medical science, the public bar of the Proud Pinnace. And just before closing time, Charlie Penrose arrived hotfoot from the Fouled Anchor with news of Mervyn Sharkley, who was still busy in bed being dreadfully ill, even after eighteen hours of relentless vomiting.

'Tes the curse, you!' Ned Gummoe proclaimed fearfully.

'The dreadied curse! I saw they both prancen about on the Hag's Ring juss day 'fore yessdey. I knawed they be strick down be the Druids. I knawed un. They'm ill-wished, you. Tes bess I gaw fetch the pellar djrectly.'

'Well, I'm goan to have one last pint,' said Ben Curnow, totally unmoved. 'Juss to get me digestion en proper shape for dinner.'

'Aw, ais, proper job,' said Ned, eagerly holding out his tankard. 'Juss a small pint an, Benjy . . . seean as you won't take naw for answer.'

'I thought you was off to fetch the pellar djrectly?' said Ben.

'Aw, I am, I am, Benjy,' Ned assured him. 'Djrectly. Djrectly after the next pint.'

Lord Fred's little granite cottage stood alone in an isolated plot of garden to seaward of the peaceful country road between Zennor and Porthmeor, and was partly screened from view by a dry-stone wall, clumps of bracken and bushes, and high hedgerows. It could, however, be discreetly observed from the ruins of various tin-mine buildings round about.

So, guessing that Sally and that foxy sod, Hoskin, would approach the cottage from the Porthmeor side — that being the most direct route from St Clare — Pascoe cunningly concealed his car in the entrance to a field on the *Zennor* side, disguised himself in a blue army beret, sun-glasses, and NATO camouflage jacket, and crept over the fields to one of the mine ruins, whence he had a commanding view of the cottage and all approaches to it.

Once safely ensconced, he took out his telescope and focused it on the windows of the cottage . . .

Confident that Sally and that bastard, Pascoe, would arrive at the cottage from the direction of Porthmeor, Tom Hoskin had cleverly decided to conceal the Minivan in a field entrance on the *Zennor* side, and to creep over the fields to a ruined mine, whence he could watch the cottage unobserved.

But the only suitable parking spot had already been occupied by a gleaming new red Vauxhall estate.

An old biddy was passing by. She stopped and said to Tom, 'Do ee want to drive in thear, an, my dear?'

'Naw. I was juss admiren ees nice new car,' said Tom.

'Well, thear's queer goan's-on 'ere today, you,' she warned him. 'I seen this wan leave ees car 'ere and creep ovver the fields like 'e was hiden from somewan. He's en th'awld scat bal* thear now.' She pointed to the ruined mine building. 'Been thear a while. Geeken round the walls, he es.'

'What's 'e look like, an?'

'Aw . . . 'bout your size, I 'ould say. Wearen a liddel blue hat. And black glassies. And a soldier's coat.'

'Soldier . . . ?'

'Mebbee tes the army on exycisies,' said the biddy. 'But thear's queer goans-on, I can tell ee.'

'I'll keep an eye out for un,' Tom assured her. 'Thanks for the information, my dear.'

She shook her head. 'Well, you can't be too careful these days. Thear's folk from up the country about, and furriners they say, and all sorts.'

She waddled slowly away down the lane.

Tom quickly removed the tyre valves from all four wheels of Pascoe's car . . . So that was *him* stranded, for a start. Then he parked Ben's Minivan in a field entrance a little way away and well out of sight. Disguising himself in a floppy jungle hat and US Marines' battle jacket, he crept across the fields to a *different* mine ruin, whence he had an excellent view of Pascoe's ruin, *and* the cottage, *and* all the approaches.

One thing still puzzled him, however. If Pascoe had a top-secret assignation with Sally at Lord Fred's cottage, what was he doing hiding in a ruined mine?

---

* disused, worked-out mine.

Only time would tell. So Tom settled down to watch and wait.

Meanwhile, many miles away across St Clare's Bay, the motor yacht *Musetta* was cruising lazily through the Atlantic Ocean with her self-steering gear newly restored to full working order.

Stretched out on deck, surrounded by empty wine bottles and dozy groupies from Penzance, the Honourable Miranda Jago lay stark naked to the bright afternoon sun, blissfully content and totally shagged out.

After his wife had finished burning the Sunday lunch, and he'd finished dropping a lot of it onto the carpet, and they'd both finished smashing some of the washing up, the Reverend Owen Borage went upstairs to his study to type out a couple of letters, before Danny Curnow arrived to reclaim his wallet.

He wrote first to the widow Tremayne.

> *'Dear Mrs Tremayne,*
>
> *'It is my pleasure to inform you that my wife found Daniel Curnow's wallet yesterday on Porthcurno Hill and that you need concern yourself no longer, therefore, that it may yet be lying in your back garden.*
>
> *'It is, however, my painful duty to advise you, albeit with great reluctance, that I found in Daniel's wallet the matter I enclose herewith. Further comment, I am sure you will agree, would be superfluous. I leave it in your capable and understanding hands.*
>
> *'Sincerely yours,'*

He signed it, typed out an envelope, inserted the letter and put it to one side. He would add the photographs of Lucy and the contraceptive sheaths after he had spoken to Daniel.

He then wrote a letter to the bishop. It was not a very interesting letter. But then he was not a very interesting bishop. When he had finished it, signed it and typed out an envelope, Constance came stumbling into the room, spilling his after-lunch cup of coffee over everything, and reminded him about the letter in the *Western Morning News* that he had intended sending to the bishop.

'Letter?' said the vicar, never sure from one day to the next what complex web of lies he had recently fabricated to get himself out of a jam.

Constance, being a good wife, obligingly removed the newspaper from his wastepaper basket and cut out the letter in question.

'Ah, but of course,' he said, remembering now. 'The dwindling Methodist congregations. Well done, Connie.' It would make excellent padding to brighten up an otherwise dreary little note.

At that point, there was a sharp jangle on the door-bell downstairs.

'That will be Master Curnow,' said the vicar. 'Kindly show him up here to my study.'

Constance obediently went downstairs, let the lad in, brought him up and abandoned him outside her husband's study door.

Danny opened it and looked in. ' 'Allo?'

'I did not hear anyone knock,' said the vicar, peering over his spectacles. 'Shut that door and knock.'

Danny closed the door, knocked, and opened it. ' 'Allo?'

'I did not hear anyone say "enter",' said the vicar. 'Wait until you are told to come in.'

Danny closed the door and knocked and waited.

'Come in,' called the vicar.

Danny opened the door. ' 'Allo.'

'Ah, Daniel,' said the vicar, rising. 'Here you are. Enter and stand up straight.'

Danny shuffled into the holy presence and stood before it like a wilting dandelion.

The vicar returned to his desk. 'I shall come quickly to the point,' he said, knocking his cup of coffee over a pile of final warnings from the South-Western Electricity Board, British Telecom, and a host of other famous names. He picked up the wallet, opened it and showed it to Danny. 'Can you explain to me what these filthy, disgusting things are doing in your possession?'

'They ent disgusten, sir,' said Danny meekly. 'That's Lucy Tremayne.'

'I am referring,' the vicar replied testily, 'to the contraceptives.'

'Aw. I found they. On the beach.'

'On the beach, indeed?' said the vicar, with a humourless laugh.

'Tes true, sir. Honest.'

'And these pornographic photographs?'

'They ent pornographic, sir. They was took down Whitesand Bay. Cost I a pound each.'

'And what have you and Lucy been doing together?'

'Doen?' Danny was mystified.

'I know. So don't lie. I know all there is to know already. So you might as well tell me again, in even greater detail.'

'Dunnaw what you mean, sir,' said Danny, genuinely bewildered.

'But *God* knows, Daniel. God sees. You can't hide your shame from Him.'

'I avven done nothen bad, sir.'

'Have you had carnal knowledge of this girl?'

Danny didn't have much sort of knowledge of anything, let alone of Lucy. 'What's that mean an, sir?'

'Do you . . . have you . . . *done* it with her?' the vicar gasped excitedly. 'You wicked boy . . . '

'Done what, sir?'

Clearly, the vicar decided, this lad was in a bad way. He was either genuinely ignorant of the facts of life, or else he was lying. So he warned Danny that sex was a very serious thing and not to be trifled with. It was a mechanical act to propagate the species and it involved nasty, messy parts of the anatomy. Which was why *normal* people seldom discussed it, did not do it very often, got it over with as fast as possible, and then only at night, in the dark, whilst hiding under the bedclothes.

'I'm only thinking of you, Daniel,' he concluded,

selflessly. 'I don't like to see young people confused about sex.'

'Aw, thank you, sir,' said Danny, wondering what *propagate* meant.

'You may have your wallet back,' said the vicar generously. 'But for your own good I am going to send these distasteful photographs and prophylactics to Lucy Tremayne's mother. And I shall tell her precisely how I came by them.'

Danny began to panic. 'Aw, please, sir,' he begged, 'you don't have to do that . . . '

'I am motivated solely by a desire to act in your own best interests, Daniel.'

'It edden your property to take, sir. You'm juss goan to make un all look worse than it really es . . . '

'Then let Mrs Tremayne be the judge of that,' said the vicar, putting the photographs and condoms on his desk and handing Danny back his wallet. 'I shall pray for you, Daniel. As always. Now you may go.'

Danny took the wallet, tight-lipped and angry, and shuffled to the study door.

'Aren't we forgetting our manners?' said the vicar. 'Aren't we going to thank me for returning our wallet? And for showing such kindness and understanding in your hour of wickedness?'

'Thank you, sir,' mumbled Danny, head hung low.

He walked out of the study, shut the door behind him, and hurried downstairs and out of the vicarage.

The vicar thought he had handled that rather well. And basking in self-satisfaction, he set about finishing off his mail. He had merely to add a brief postscript to the bishop.

'*P.S.*,' he typed, '*I thought your lordship might be more than a little diverted by the enclosed.*'

He removed the letter from his typewriter, folded it and placed it in the envelope. As he was doing so, Constance returned.

'How did it go with Master Curnow, Owen dear?'

'Oh, I handled it all with consummate tact, even if I do say so myself,' he replied, searching for the letter that

Connie had just cut out of the *Western Morning News* for him.

He was so engrossed for the next few minutes in telling her how tactfully he had dealt with the matter, that he failed to concentrate properly on what he was doing.

And later that afternoon he strolled down to the postbox and dispatched to the widow Tremayne a newspaper cutting on the subject of declining Methodist congregations . . . And to the bishop, for his diversion, three pictures of a fifteen-year-old schoolgirl in a bikini, plus two Black Stallion contraceptive sheaths.

Arthur Pascoe was very puzzled. He'd been lying in a pile of rubble for the past half hour, surrounded by wasps' nests and a colony of sunbathing reptiles — all of which looked suspiciously like butcher-killing adders; and there was still no sign of Sally or Tom Hoskin.

Something had gone wrong somewhere. Either they were not coming after all, or else they were already here and had somehow sneaked through his lines of observation and into the cottage without being spotted. Hoskin was spiteful enough to try and do a cowardly thing like that.

So Pascoe decided to break cover and make a wide flanking manoeuvre, stealing up on the cottage from the Zennor side . . .

Tom Hoskin was watching this from his own nearby pile of viper-infested rubble, and could not for the life of him imagine what Pascoe was up to. If Sally had been in the ruined mine with him all this time, why was he now scampering across the fields, crouching down behind a dry-stone wall, like a retreating trooper under fire? On the other hand, if Sally was *not* in the ruins with him, then what had he been doing in there on his own all this time?

He pondered on this for a while before it dawned on him that Sally was very probably in the cottage already, waiting for Pascoe. But Pascoe had seen Tom approaching and — coward that he was — had hidden in the mine ruins. And now, thinking that the coast was clear at last, he was creeping over to the cottage by some furtive, roundabout route.

Time passed. Pascoe had disappeared completely from view. Tom lay there in the rubble a while longer, wondering what to do next. Finally, convinced that by now the shameless pair would be tearing each other's clothes off in their eagerness to plunge into their hot bed of depravity, he decided to break cover and creep over to a better observation post, nearer the cottage, on the west side.

Pascoe was stealthily approaching the cottage by a devious route, in search of a good observation post on the east side, when he came across Ben Curnow's Minivan, parked in the entrance to a field.

So ho! *That* was their game. Was there no limit to the depths to which the guilty pair would stoop? They had clattered here in Ben's vile van and parked it in a cowardly gateway to conceal their presence, and had then walked furtively to the cottage . . . probably skulking behind walls and hedgerows all the way.

He could just picture them tee-heeing smugly all the way to their torrid bed of lust. And possessed by a sudden fit of uncontrollable jealousy, he tore the valves out of Ben's tyres and chuckled jubilantly as the van sunk onto its wheelrims, in four quick gasps of rushing air . . .

The old biddy had been watching Pascoe's antics for some time and was not at all sure that he was up to much good. So on her way home she stopped at the phone box.

'Thear's queer goans-on, my dear,' she informed the St Ives police. 'I dunnaw who tes, but he do look like wan o' they terryrists you do see on the telly. In dark glassies and a liddel blue hat. And thear's furriners about, and folk down from Camborne, and all sorts . . .'

* * *

Some twenty-four hours after his first and last ever encounter with tasty but distinctly tame keg cider, Mervyn
Sharkley was beginning to feel vaguely like a human being
again. He no longer felt sick. His pounding headache was
responding to paracetamol at last. And he thought he might
be able to tackle a few breaths of ozone and a small cup of
weak tea at Ye Olde Cornishe Lugger hamburger bar on
West Quay.

Back in Chapel Lane, it had taken Ned so long to hasten
djrectly from the Proud Pinnace to Blakey's Ridge with the
urgent news that Lucy had been stricken down by the curse
of the Hag's Ring, that it was almost five o'clock by the time
Granny Polkinghorne arrived at the Tremayne's cottage.

She found Lucy lying in bed looking as healthy as ever.
Sally left them alone and went downstairs to finish her
tea.

'I do hear you've been taken sick, dear,' said the old
pellar, easing herself into a chair by Lucy's bed. She took the
girl's hand and squeezed it in her own arthritic claw. 'Well
now, edden that the strangest thing? And I never seen ee
looken better. And Doccor Jamieson dunnaw what tes
either. I wonder what could have come on so sudden soon,
and so awful bad, that your mother coulden go out to
Zennor weth Lord St Clare like her was plannen?'

Lucy shook her head. 'Strange, isn't it?'

Granny P. smiled. 'I do think you knaw exactly what tes.
And now you've made sure your mother coulden go out to
Zennor thes affernoon, I do think you'm goan to make a
mirac'lous recovery, ready for the feasten tomorrow and
the crownen of the queen. Now edden that so, Lucy
vean?'

Lucy bit her lip and looked away.

'Ais, I thoft 'twas so,' said the old woman. 'Well, I'll tell
ee this, my dear, you'm doan wrong. You'm bein' selfish. If
you do love your mother, as I knaw you do, you'll want her
to be happy. And her edden goan to be happy if her's alone
all her life long, ezzer now? And I'll tell ee somethen else

181

. . . you can't come ovver all mysterious sick *every* Sunday, now can ee?'

Lucy closed her eyes and shook her head.

Granny P. squeezed her hand. 'Well, thear edden much sickness here, so I'll be off home, you. I do think you'm getten better every minute. I'll see ee at the feasten I 'spect. And you all dressed up to be the maiden queen.'

She got up and walked slowly to the bedroom door. Lucy said, 'You won't say nothen, will you, Gran?'

'Promise me you ent goan to do nothen like this again?'

'Promise.'

'Right an.' Granny P. nodded. 'You mind you keep your promise to the pellar, child.'

And she went back downstairs. Sally was waiting for her in the kitchen.

'How es she looken, Rebecca?'

'Aw, I shoulden worry,' Granny P. replied confidently. 'She'll be her normal self be tomorrow, sure enough.'

Sally nodded and said no more. There were certain things you just didn't ask a pellar.

Ned Gummoe had been lurking in Chapel Lane for the last twenty minutes, doing up his boot-laces. At long last Granny P. emerged from Sally Tremayne's cottage.

'Aw, allo thear, Mizzus Polkinghorne!' he exclaimed, as if it was a remarkable coincidence, their meeting like this. 'How es young Lucy, an?'

'Her es getten better very minute, Ned,' she assured him. 'The curse'll be gone be sundown.'

'Proper job,' said Ned, delighted but not surprised. 'I knawed ee could fix un. Doccor Jamieson dedden knaw what 'twas, see. But I *said* the pellar could fix un.'

'Well, I must be goan, Ned. I'll see ee tomorrow.'

Ned doffed his grubby old hat. 'Us'll see ee at the feasten an, Mizzus Polkinghorne. Have a care now.'

Granny P. walked away up the lane and Ned set off in the other direction, towards the sea-front. The pubs were not yet open, being Sunday, but there were plenty of cafés where he could scrounge a cup of tea. He took out a few medals from the collection he kept permanently on stand-by in his pocket throughout the tourist season, and pinned them to the lapel of his old suit jacket. According to this afternoon's selection, he had seen long and distinguished service with Rommel's Afrika Korps, the Australian Girl Guides, and London Transport.

At the sea-front he encountered Mervyn Sharkley, who had just consumed an entire cup of tea without assistance or further medical attention, and was now tottering towards the sands, learning how to walk again.

'Aw, allo an, Mizzer Sheikh Lee,' Ned greeted him. 'Ow be doan?'

'Much better thank you, Mr Gummoe,' said Sharkley. 'Very much better. Funny . . . it's just come over me, how much better I feel.'

'I knawed ee would,' said Ned, beside himself with delight. 'Tes the pellar's work. Don't ee worry, my 'andsome. Mizzus Polkinghorne's juss lifted the curse. You ent ill-wished no more!'

Gratified to hear that, but at a loss to know what the old rustic was prattling on about this time, Sharkley offered to stand him a pot of tea and a cake.

'Well, sence you'm insisten,' Ned replied. 'A drop o' tea and a stecky bun would juss go down a trate, you.'

From his excellent new observation point, behind a black-berry thicket on the west side of the cottage, Tom had been watching the windows very carefully for the past hour and a quarter and listening for tell-tale moans of pleasure. In all that time he had neither seen nor heard a living soul . . . Which was proof that the miserable skulking pair were in there, too ashamed to show their faces, and probably waiting till dark before attempting their getaway.

Well, he could wait too. He could wait all night if he had to . . .

*　　*　　*

And from his excellent new observation point, behind a hawthorn hedge on the *east* side of the cottage, Arthur Pascoe had also been keeping the place under close surveillance for the past hour and a quarter, listening all the while for squeals of delight and the thrustful groan of bedsprings. And it was no surprise to him that there had been neither sight nor sound of the wanton couple in all that time. On the contrary, it was final proof positive that they were in there, too frightened and ashamed to show themselves in the light of day . . . doubtless waiting for nightfall to make good their escape.

Well, he was in no hurry either . . . Three could play at this.

A short distance away, in the lane across the fields, officers from St Ives police were just loading a battered grey Minivan onto a trailer.

'Tes they buggers down from up-country,' the farmer was grumbling. 'They'm al'us blocken my gates. Tes a pretty pass us come to when a man can't get ees tractor in and out of ees awn fields, you.'

'But tes a local registration,' a sympathetic sergeant pointed out. 'They should know better round 'ere.'

'Same as this bugger and all,' said the farmer, as another police Land Rover trundled past, towing a new red Vauxhall estate on its trailer.

'Well, whoever tes,' said the sergeant, 'they'm goan to have a bloody long walk to St Ives to get thear cars back.'

The sun slipped gently down into the Atlantic, and the day died in a blush of bronze and purple in the west.

Far out in St Clare's Bay, on the deck of the *Musetta*, Miranda was watching the sunset and trying to cram half a kilo of marijuana into her bedtime joint. From below came the aroma of frying bacon, the popping of champagne corks and the sighs of delirious groupies.

'Why do I feel as if we're not moving?' Miranda wondered dreamily.

'Because,' Ramon replied, 'I fink za boat is going round and round in 'uge circules . . . '

Darkness descended over Zennor. A full moon spilt its milky light across the fields round Lord Fred's cottage.

Tom Hoskin yawned and shivered behind his blackberry thicket. Not much longer now . . .

Not far away, behind a hawthorn bush, Arthur Pascoe studied the luminous hands of his wristwatch. Any minute now the guilty couple would be out . . .

PART FOUR

THE FEAST OF ST CLARE

FEAST DAY dawned grey and misty. Colonel Hermann H. Hermann (82nd Airborne Divison, ret'd) arose at six, took a cold bath, shaved, did fifty push-ups, and went down to the lobby to see if his *International Herald Tribune* had arrived yet.

But nothing had arrived yet. Not even people. So he strolled down to the harbour at a leisurely march to advise the local mariners about their business.

There was only one local mariner to be seen — a broad, swarthy fellow in oily overalls, just casting off in an old fishing boat that looked as if it had been used for target practice by the US Navy.

'A fresh morning, my good fellow,' Colonel Hermann greeted him.

'Mornen,' Ben Curnow replied, freeing his stern line from the quayside.

Hermann looked down at a row of plastic buckets, full of sea water and gizzards and bits of old fish.

'This be shark bait, be it?' he enquired, confident that he had an adequate grasp of the local patois.

Ben blinked. 'Well, if you say it be, so be it, my awld maate. Some do call un rubby-dubby, but tes all wan to I.'

'Are ye going shark fishing now?' Hermann asked, apparently oblivious of the fact that Ben's battered tosher was about as powerful as a geriatric pilchard.

'No,' said Ben, throwing his stern line aboard and clambering into the boat. 'I'm goan to lift me pots. Thear won't be no shark boats out today. Tes feast day.'

189

'Mind if I ride along?' Hermann waved his wallet. 'I'll pay ye for thy trouble.'

'Well, if all you do want es a turn round the bay, my handsome, step aboard,' said Ben. 'But I ent goan out for long. Us es all getten set for the hurlen out to Addle bridge, the stroke of noon.'

The colonel jumped aboard, and the *Eudoria Lynn* shug-shug-shugged her way slowly out of the harbour and across St Clare's Bay.

They had been out for an hour or so, and while instructing Ben how to pull in his crab pots, the colonel had been observing a curious maritime phenomenon. A large private yacht, some distance out in the bay, was sailing round and round in enormous circles. He passed the glasses to Ben.

'What in the hell you make of that, skip?'

Ben trained the glasses on her. She was a good mile or more away. Flying the French tricolour. And she looked remarkably like . . .

'Well, bless my soul,' said Ben. 'Us best juss make sure her edden en distress, you.'

He opened up the *Eudoria Lynn*'s throttle and made for the distant yacht.

When they were close enough, the colonel read the name on her stern. '*Musetta* . . . '

'Well, I'll be damned,' said Ben, delighted.

'Know her?'

'Aw, no. Never come across 'er en me life.'

After another ten minutes they were close enough to call over to her. Her master waved and came to the starboard rail. Ben pulled his hat down over his eyes and remained in the wheelhouse.

'OK, skipper,' said the colonel. 'Let me handle this.'

'Ais, you do that,' said Ben willingly.

The colonel stood on the prow of the *Eudoria Lynn* and bawled out in his best Midwest accent:

'*Bonjour! Etes-vous* OK?'

'No!' Ramon yelled back. 'Our steerink af jam! We must voyage all zis time in 'uge circules! You may assist, yes?'

'Dear, oh dear,' said Ben sympathetically. 'Us can't let they poor Frenchies go round in *'uge circules* all day. Tell maatey I'll get a boat sent out djrectly from St Clare to take un in tow.'

'Help is on its way!' bawled the colonel. 'Conserve your water! . . . Do not panic! . . . And do not leave this zone!'

'*Qu'est-ce qu'il a dit?*' asked a crewman.

'I think he said,' Ramon replied in French, 'don't have a wee-wee, don't have a picnic, and don't go away.'

'*Il est fou?*'

'*Americain, je crois.*'

'*Ahh . . . Ça s'explique tout.*'

'Reckon we oughta call out the coastguard?' Hermann wondered, as they shug-shug-shugged back across the bay.

'Why, bless your life, no,' Ben replied. 'Tes like a mill pond out thear and the weather's set fair. I know juss the fellow to give Mr Frenchie a tow. Real nice bloke, he es. Name of Norman Strait . . . '

As soon as they got back to harbour, Ben telephoned the police in Penzance. A lone Detective Constable Tuckey was taking all calls for Operation Snowhawk.

'Behaven very suspicious, her es,' Ben told him. 'Goan slowly round en *'uge circules*, like her was looken for somethen en the water . . . or signallen secretly to shore. Tes best you do let Mr Strait knaw about un djrectly.'

' *'Uge circules*, eh?' said Detective Constable Tuckey, solemnly recording every word of this in his finest block capitals. 'And your name es . . . ?'

'Pascoe,' said Ben. 'Arthur Pascoe.'

Ormskirk arrived in St Clare that morning and kicked Sharkley out of bed at the ungodly hour of ten to nine, because he wanted to be shown around the Jago estates before all the hurling and anarchy broke out.

Sharkley was not amused. And he said that if Ormskirk had spent all weekend honking up on rough cider and being rudely awoken at six a.m. by a loony Yank doing push-ups, running baths and singing *The Leaving of Liverpool* at the top of his voice, *he* wouldn't be any too amused either. It was only ten to nine for heaven's sake.

Ormskirk said it was now *five* to nine, to be precise. And if he carried on dithering and blathering at this rate it would very soon be five to *ten*. This was work after all, not a bloody holiday.

Ormskirk secretly resented having to be there, anyway. He'd have much preferred to have been at home for the weekend with his wife and children, concreting over their new back garden, or going for a tour of the local traffic jams. But Sir Wilfrid had insisted . . . After all, *some*body had to be on hand to be sacked if anything went wrong, and Sharkley was nowhere near important enough. So Ormskirk had been flown down to St Mawgan in the Pirana House executive jet on Sunday evening and had elected to stay at a hotel in Penzance rather than St Clare, because there was less countryside in evidence and more cars and tarmac and comforting things like that.

Anyway, he told Sharkley, he too had been awoken at the crack of dawn . . . by great flocks of dangerous, wild seagulls, squealing and screeching outside his bedroom window.

Sharkley said he liked seagulls. Very much. Indeed. And he was going to have a very large fried breakfast before he did anything else. And it wasn't really five to nine, the clock was fast.

Ormskirk said the clock was not fast, it was slow, and he'd thought up hundreds of ways to kill and maim seagulls on the drive over from Penzance that morning, and there was no time for breakfast.

So they went down to the hotel restaurant and Sharkley ordered bacon, eggs, sausages, fried bread, tomatoes, a double portion of hog's pudding, baked beans, and bubble-and-squeak.

Ormskirk was disgusted, and said so.

When it finally arrived, the waitress asked Ormskirk if *he* would like anything. Ormskirk said yes, and ordered everything that Sharkley had ordered. He then knocked back half a bottle of digitalis tablets and took some papers out of his attaché case.

Ormskirk went everywhere with an attaché case. He had lots of them. They were always full of papers. The papers were not always very important, or confidential, or even remotely relevant to anything, but he always liked people to see him taking papers out of a nice full attaché case. It helped him convince himself that he might be doing something useful in life.

He said, quoting from his papers, that Sir Wilf's party would be landing at St Mawgan at one-zero-five-five hours.

Sharkley wondered aloud why they couldn't just say five to eleven, these admin people; or better still round it up to good old eleven o'clock.

Ormskirk felt slighted and held his papers so that Sharkley couldn't see them. He said the party would be met by two official, long-wheel-base, luxury Fujokawa limousines, courtesy of the Japanese embassy in London, and driven to the Imperial Grand Hotel in Penzance, where an entire floor had been reserved for them.

Sharkley asked what for.

So that they could freshen up and titivate themselves, Ormskirk explained. And pray, or whatever Buddhists did before lunch.

Sharkley said they didn't pray, they meditated. And chanted. And they probably weren't Buddhists, anyway.

Well, whatever they were, Ormskirk went on, they would be in St Clare in time for the hurling and would return to Penzance for lunch, at which Lord Fred would be guest of honour. Then they would all be back in St Clare in time for the coronation of the feast queen and the grand parade.

Sharkley asked what was happening about the hot-air balloon and the public relations marquee.

Ormskirk confessed that he was worried about the balloon and the public relations marquee. Bert and his team had set off from Birmingham on Thursday with the expressed intention of spending the weekend with Bert's cousin, who lived in the village of Goonbell, near St Agnes. But nothing had been heard of them since.

Sharkley asked who Bert was.

Bert, said Ormskirk, was in charge of the marquee and the balloon. Hairy fellow from sporting events section. Drank real ale.

Sharkley said that everyone in sporting events was hairy and drank real ale.

Except the women, said Ormskirk.

Especially the women, said Sharkley.

Then Ormskirk's next thrombosis arrived, piled up on a plate the size of a tractor wheel, and as soon as he'd wolfed that lot down and said it was time to go, the hairy Bert arrived with two anthropoid beards called Richie and Nige, and their marquee and ballooning gear. Ormskirk said bravo, they should make all haste to the Fields and get the public relations tent pitched forthwith. But the hairy Bert said bugger that, he was famished, and so were Richie and Nige. And the three of them sat down and ordered everything that Ormskirk and Sharkley had had.

Ormskirk was disgusted, and said so, and ordered a fresh loaf of toast for himself, since nobody it seemed had the least intention of doing a stroke of bloody work.

By the time everyone had finished stuffing themselves, it was getting on for half past ten and Ormskirk decided to retire to the lavatory for a while with somebody's *International Herald Tribune*. He had no idea whose. He'd purloined it from the lobby.

When he finally emerged some time later, Sharkley took him for a short walk across the quay, pointing out the fishermen's cottages on East Cliff, the Proud Pinnace tavern, the shops on West Quay, and concluding that that *was* the estate . . . except for West Meadows and Tremorna Hall, of course.

Ormskirk was exhausted after all that exercise and wanted to stop for a coffee break. Sharkley said there was no time for coffee. If they wanted to pitch the Pirana House marquee and see the start of the hurling, they would have to be off to the Fields pretty sharpish.

Ormskirk wondered whether they could get a taxi.

Sharkley said it was barely four hundred yards.

Ormskirk asked if there was a bus, in that case.

Sharkley said he'd have to walk.

Ormskirk asked the hairy Bert if he could cadge a lift in the balloon team's truck. Bert said no, not unless they ditched the balloon and the marquee to make room for him.

So Ormskirk swallowed his pride and another fistful of digitalis and wobbled away up Middle Street on foot.

'Any minute now,' he said to Sharkley, as they stopped for a rest a few yards further on, 'they'll be stepping off that plane . . . '

Forty miles away, near the north-coast resort of Newquay, a thirty-seat turbojet of Pirana Commercial Airways was just touching down at RAF St Mawgan.

As it did so, two shining black Fujokawa limousines, pride of the Japanese motor industry, drew up on the civil aviation parking lot, and a press photographer from *The Cornishman* woke up and crowded round.

The turbojet crept to a halt by the terminal building. An Air Pirana stairway was wheeled into position and the main passenger door swung open. First to emerge was Sir Wilfrid's head of public relations and his dreary wife, followed by Akiro Toshimoto's senior bodyguard, then Akiro Toshimoto IV himself, his wife Kyoko, her maid-in-waiting, chief adviser Takeo Subishi and his wife, the assistant bodyguard, the valet, a commercial attaché from the Japanese embassy in London, Sir Wilf's personal private secretary, and finally, to a spontaneous outburst of applause from the head of PR and his dreary wife, Their Overwhelming Importances, Sir Wilfrid and Lady Macclesfield.

The head chauffeur held open the doors of the leading Fujokawa limousine. The president and his wife, and Sir Wilf and her ladyship, entered and sank into the multi-thousand-pound luxury of the new Japanese technological miracle. The senior bodyguard climbed into the front, alongside the chauffeur. Everybody else had to squash into the second limo.

It was now eleven o'clock and they were forty miles from St Clare.

The chauffeur started off in the direction of Newquay. Sir Wilf said, hold hard, hold hard, where did he think he was going to? He had studied the maps and knew Cornwall like the back of his hand, and what were they going to Newquay for? The chauffeur would have replied but Sir Wilf told him not to bally well argue, and to go east to St Columb Major and across country to pick up the main A30 trunk road.

The chauffeur respectfully pointed out that he did not wish to land them all in Bodmin or anywhere like that, for it was a good twenty miles in the wrong direction . . . though he admitted he was a mere Londoner.

'Well, I'm from Birmingham,' said Sir Wilf proudly, 'so don't argue. St Columb's nowhere near Bodmin.'

And thirty minutes later, they rolled into Bodmin, where they were promptly diverted onto back roads and lanes because of a burst water-main.

'Fancy leaving a burst water-main on a public holiday,' Sir Wilf raged. 'Doesn't *any*one work on their day off any more?'

Three miles further on they arrived at the village of Helland. They were now fifty-five miles from St Clare, and it was twenty minutes to twelve.

'Give me the bloody map,' Sir Wilf said to the chauffeur. 'Incompetent clot . . . '

'No map, Sir Wilfrid,' said the chauffeur, not lacking courage. 'We learnt the correct route before we left, you see.'

Sir Wilf muttered something that did not translate easily from Anglo-Saxon to Japanese. Akiro and Kyoko Toshimoto smiled happily at Sir Wilf. Sir Wilf beamed back.

The bodyguard enquired, 'We . . . on . . . correct . . . highway?'

'Well, pretty close,' Sir Wilf replied hopefully. 'Assure the president that we're just making a short cut to avoid a burst water-main.'

The bodyguard translated that for Toshimoto. Toshimoto smiled benignly at Sir Wilf. He knew perfectly well that they were lost. He, too, had had a look at the map beforehand.

An elderly local was passing by. 'Stop and ask this shabby-looking serf,' Sir Wilf instructed the chauffeur.

The chauffeur did as he was told.

'St Cleer?' said the local. 'You'm looken for St Cleer, are ee?'

'St Clare, yes, St Clare!' stormed Sir Wilf.

'Aw, well, you aren't too far away,' said the local, amiably. 'You do want to cut across country to the A30 . . . and carry on ovver toward Cardinham . . . and east through Mount to St Neot. Then you'll see St Cleer signposted. No more'n ten miles, tes . . . '

'Excellent!' roared Sir Wilf. 'Drive on, chauffeur! We'll make the hurling, and with time to spare. They wouldn't dream of starting without us anyway.'

It was almost noon. The early-morning mist had evaporated, grey skies had cleared and the sun was blazing down on the crowds that lined the route all the way from the Addle bridge to the village Cross.

St Clare was packed to bursting. Soozie Smiles of BBC TV South-West took her roving microphone around the multitude to canvass estimates of the numbers. PC Hawkins put the figure at about five thousand. Arthur Pascoe thought rather fewer, and Tom Hoskin rather more. And Ned Gummoe, who had maimed and ruptured scores of innocent bystanders to get his face in front of the camera, was confident there were at least twenty thousand there (which was more than the entire population of Penzance), with hundreds more arriving every minute.

The car parks were jammed solid — which was a heart-warming sight for Ormskirk — and the meadows opposite Tremorna Hall had been generously opened by his lordship as an overspill parking area, at a token fee of five pounds per car.

The Fields, picturesquely littered with stalls, marquees and bunting, like a medieval fairground, were practically deserted as the noonday *hove-a* approached.

The players — perhaps a hundred of them, no one was quite sure (except Ned Gummoe, who reckoned there were thousands) — were all in position. Some thirty or so were waiting on Addle bridge in two loose packs . . . Amongst them the captains, Arthur Pascoe and Tom Hoskin, both worn out and footsore after the previous night's fiasco out at Zennor. The remainder of the players were scattered along the route to the village Cross, where the packs of heavy-weights were waiting to stonewall any breakaway runners from the bridge, and to rush a crafty pass to their fly young sprinters, lurking in the lanes for a speedy dash to goal.

The clock of St Clare-by-Addle parish church showed one minute to twelve. Lord Fred, sweating buckets beneath his baronial robes, called for the silver ball, which was being passed from hand to hand amongst the crowds in the time-honoured belief that it would grant each person's dearest wish. It was solemnly passed to his lordship. And his lordship solemnly wiped all the sweat, chocolate and ice-cream off it, and held it aloft.

The minute hand of the church clock swung to the noon mark, and the crowds fell silent as the hour began to stroke. Freddie declaimed the motto *Be bold and fair* in his clearest Eton-Cornish:

'*Bethoh . . . dur ha wheag!*'

The crowds around the bridge roared their approval.

As the cheering died down Freddie cried out, '*Ho-ho-va! Ho-ho-va! Ho-ohhh-va!*' And with the final cry he hurled the ball high into the air above the heads of the players on the bridge and got himself smartly out of the way.

As the ball came down, a dozen pairs of meaty hands went up to grab it. Lofty Len Dunstan took possession for West Village but failed to get it cleanly away from the pack. A loose maul formed around him, the ball disappeared from view entirely, and everyone collapsed in a heap on the road.

'What are they doing?' enquired Ormskirk, tucking into his third ice-cream cornet in fifteen minutes.

'Looking for the ball,' said Sharkley.

All the spectators round the bridge were yelling their advice. At last the ball reappeared, rolling out of the ruck and down the other side of the little humpback bridge, where it was quickly seized by Colly Carlyon for East Village and borne south towards Middle Street at a steady trot.

'You know, Mervyn,' said Ormskirk, 'we could really make something of this opening number. Think of it from the telly point of view. Imagine these crowds all seething with bitter hatred . . . like Celtic-v-Rangers. Imagine the captain calling Lord Fred a dirty lying cheat, like the top stars do at Wimbledon. Imagine camera close-ups of burning viciousness in the eyes of the players, all longing to injure each other, like you get in the World Cup . . . '

'It's not quite the spirit through, Geoff.'

'To hell with the goddam spirit,' said an American tourist, one Hermann H. Hermann of Des Moines, Iowa. 'What is this anyhow? A Sunday school softball trial for pansies?'

The teams were now jogging gently down the lane towards Middle Street, chucking the ball to each other and occasionally stopping to play what looked like piggy-in-the-middle.

'For Chrissakes!' Colonel Hermann protested. 'Nobody's getting hurt!'

'We do need a better prospect of injury, Mervyn,' Ormskirk confessed. 'There's far too much good feeling and pleasantness about it all. We'll never sell this to *World of Sport* and the networks.'

'An ambulance following along behind might help,' said Sharkley. 'Like you get on the racecourse.'

'Not a bad idea,' Ormskirk replied. 'And get that TV camera right in close for something really sickening like a broken leg or a gashed artery.'

The crowds were now pursuing the action along the road towards Middle Street, where the bulk of the heavyweights were waiting to tussle for possession. A great multitude of spectators had already assembled at the village Cross and on the quays for a good view of the finale.

But Colonel Hermann couldn't believe his eyes. 'I've never seen anything so pathetic in my entire life,' he screamed at Ormskirk. 'Whadda they keep stopping to play pat-a-cake for?'

'This bit is like touch-rugby, you see,' Sharkley explained. 'Until they reach Middle Street they have to stop and pass the ball as soon as they're touched.'

'And what happens when they hit Middle Street?' Hermann enquired scathingly. 'They play ring-a-roses?'

'I'm not sure,' Sharkley confessed. 'The rules are a bit vague.'

'They are, huh?' said Hermann, sickened to see so many grown men skipping around in this faggot-livered fashion. 'Well, let's just goddam well liven this fairy-assed, pussy-fingered nursery game up a little and find out.' So saying, he broke away from the crowd, ran down the road and grabbed the ball out of the hands of an astonished Colly Carlyon.

' 'Ere . . . you can't do that, my handsome!' bellowed Tom Hoskin. 'You ent allowed!'

'And who's got the damn guts to try and stop me?' retorted Hermann. And he set off towards the Cross at a brisk pace, snarling, 'Now come get it, sisters!'

The crowd, always game for a bit of impromptu anarchy to hot things up a little, roared their approval.

'That's against the rules!' yelled Arthur Pascoe, puffing along in pursuit.

Spurred on by the cheers of the crowd, Colonel Hermann held the silver ball aloft in contemptuous defiance of the players as he ran on towards the Cross.

Ben Curnow, who was amongst the pack of heavyweights waiting in Middle Street just ahead of him, cupped his hands and shouted, 'Drop un, awld mate! Drop the ball, for Loord's sake, drop un!'

But Colonel Hermann ran on exultantly, yelling, 'Geronimo!' and 'Let's hear it one time for Uncle Sam!'

What happened then he would never know. But he hit

something that appeared out of nowhere. And whatever it was, it was as solid and unshakeable as a rock. As it happened, it was called Charlie Penrose, fruit and vegetable merchant; but Colonel Hermann was not to know that. In fact, he didn't know if it was lunchtime, Christmas or downtown Saigon. He was suddenly all ends up in a wrestler's hitch and flat out on Middle Street with not a breath of wind left in his body. Whilst above him, around him, across him and all over him there raged a ferocious ruction.

An awesome tonnage of men were fighting for the ball that Hermann was now lying on. For East Village there was Ben Curnow, Special Constable Dennis Nancarrow, Jack Penna from the Proud Pinnace, Frank and Barry Pengelly — who between them weighed nearly five hundredweight, Nick Jenkins the ex-Cornwall and England second row rugby international, and every fisherman under pensionable age. But West Village had the combined enormity of Charlie Penrose, Dick Champion, Caleb Trevaskis, the Reverend Micah Dredge, Roger Holman from the off-licence, and Farmer Rosewarne's three big sons, Tristan, Luke and Joshua.

By the time Tom Hoskin and Arthur Pascoe arrived on the scene, there was nothing to be seen of Colonel Hermann. He had disappeared totally beneath the pile of flailing limbs and sprawling bodies. On the fringes of this tangled ruck were the stand-offs, Lightning Bill Lanyon for Westers and Buster Tonkin for East, and their flying sprinters, Samson Trevaskis and Danny Curnow, respectively.

Danny was scared witless. Whatever he did, the future was none too rosy. If he hadn't turned up in the first place, his mother would have bashed him. If he were to sneak off now for a quick wee-wee for the next two hours, his *dad* would bash him. But if he stayed and someone passed him the ball, the *Westers* would bash him. And if the ball went out to Sam Trevaskis, Danny would have to tackle him and then *Sam* would bash him. Life was like that. It was rotten being Danny.

But for the time being the ball wasn't going anywhere. It hadn't even been *seen* for five minutes . . . The problem being that Colonel Hermann was lying on it. And everybody else was lying on *him*. So all that terrifying tonnage of manpower was heeling and groping and shoving to no purpose whatsoever. And within a very short space of time, tempers were beginning to fray and fists to fly, and a hundred and one ancient scores and grievances that had nothing to do with the hurling were being settled in the time-honoured St Clarian manner.

'Now this is more like it,' Ormskirk enthused. 'The commercial channels will go for this all right. The basic ingredients of popular family entertainment: lawlessness, filthy language and mindless violence.'

'We could have live action replays of the really crunchy bits,' said Sharkley, infected with Ormskirk's enthusiasm. 'Get make-up girls to splash on some blood . . . Get some extras in police uniform looking weary and despairing, clutching cans of CS gas . . . '

'No, that's being silly,' said Ormskirk, not convinced that Sharkley was taking this entirely seriously. 'But I *have* got a mate on the *Sunday Mirror* who could run a story headlined: *In God's name, the Mirror pleads . . . Stop this brutal horror they call sport . . . '*

'Dynamite!' said Sharkley.

'That would bring crowds flocking here by the million.'

'Like they do at air crashes.'

'Air crash!' yelled Ormskirk, tucking into his fifth ice-cream. 'Supposing . . . ? Here, Mervyn, you know all those dangerous microlights we bought, that we want written off for the insurance . . . ?'

Not far away, on a peaceful, furze-covered cliff top, a number of extremely serious people were watching a luxury yacht sailing slowly round and round in *'uge circules* in St Clare's Bay.

'She's a Frenchie all right,' observed Norman Strait, focusing his binoculars on her tricolour. 'But what do you make of those other flags she's flying?' He passed the binoculars to Detective Constable Tuckey.

Tuckey studied the boat. A number of curious, coloured pendants were dangling from a line that had been strung between her two masts.

'Looks like a lady's bra,' muttered Tuckey thoughtfully. 'And a pair of socks . . . and a vest . . . '

'Cunning,' said Strait. 'Very cunning. Obviously means something to their contacts on shore.'

Tuckey nodded. They both had a good think about that.

'On the other hand,' said Tuckey, upon reflection, 'it could mean they've just done some washing.'

'Hardly likely, when they're in the middle of a drug smuggling operation,' said Strait derisively.

'But how do we know they *are* smuggling drugs?' said Tuckey.

'Well, who *else* would want to make secret signals to shore with their vests and socks?' Strait reasoned.

Tuckey had another think. 'Good point.'

'Right then,' said Strait decisively, not having a clue what to do next. As it was bank holiday, his superiors would all be out mowing their lawns and washing their Toyotas.

'Well? Are you going to bring her in or not?' the coastguard asked irascibly.

Straight realised that this was no time to vacillate.

'Probably,' he replied, and turned to Tuckey. 'Get on to Detective Sergeant Pearce and tell him I think we ought to intercept.'

'Righto,' said Tuckey.

'We'll take the cutter from Penzance then,' said the coast-guard.

Nobody aboard the *Musetta* was in the least concerned about anything. Partly because it was a beautiful day, and cruising slowly round and round in *'uge circules* was a rather pleasant way of passing the time . . . And partly because they were all stoned out of their minds on Miranda's finest, home-grown marijuana.

Miranda herself, serenely lost on a cloud of oblivion, was just faintly conscious of something she should have been

203

doing, sometime, somewhere, with Ramon and a knight in shining armour.

Sixty-five miles away, on a desolate country road in the middle of Bodmin Moor, two shining black Fujokawa limousines, pride of the Japanese motor industry, were purring around in search of a signpost . . . or a human being . . . or even a trace of life.

A public call box came into view. 'Eureka!' cheered the chauffeur, as if he'd just found a pub in the desert.

'Bet it's vandalised,' growled Sir Wilf, ever the optimist. 'First of all, ring the emergency services and tell them to get us out of this God-forsaken no-man's-land. Then call the Fouled Anchor and tell Ormskirk to hold the start of the hurling for another hour. We might be late . . . '

Colonel Hermann was a gibbering idiot by this time. The ruck had broken up and he'd been rescued from a death worse than fate by a squad of old biddies under the direction of Alice and Dora Uglow, who had dragged him to the nearest available gutter to recover in safety.

The silver ball had now disappeared into the warren of narrow lanes, and it was none too clear to anyone — least of all the players — what had happened to it.

What *had* happened, in fact, was that the Rosewarne brothers — Tristan, Josh and Luke — had secured possession for West Village and had kept it for just long enough to allow Arthur Pascoe to divide the rest of his team into half a dozen scattered groups. At which point, the Rosewarnes had dummied a pass to each of these groups in turn, and each group had run off into the lanes in all directions with the East villagers in pursuit. This had effectively dispersed the entire East Village team whilst leaving the Rosewarnes still in possession of the ball. And they were now setting off together down a quiet lane, unseen, unsuspected and unchallenged, making for their goal, the Fouled Anchor, at a brisk trot.

Back amongst the crowds on Middle Street, Ormskirk was buying another ice-cream cornet. 'It gets complicated, this game, doesn't it?' he said to Sharkley. 'There's more to it than I thought. If we're going to flog this to *World of Sport* we'll need skilled commentators and a lot of cameras to keep up the tension.'

He was approached at that moment by 'onest Eli Tonkin, grave-digger, traffic warden and bookmaker, who was rapidly shortening the odds on West Village.

'Five to four on, Westers,' he told Ormskirk, holding out an expectant palm. 'Easters are threes.'

'How about a tenner each way on Easters?' said Ormskirk.

Eli's eyes narrowed. 'Smart bugger, aren't ee?'

The Easters were now scattered all over St Clare, chasing isolated groups of Westers — none of whom had even *seen* the ball for the past ten minutes let alone taken possession of it — whilst the Rosewarnes were making steady progress towards the Fouled Anchor.

Danny Curnow, meantime, had found to his horror that he was one of half a dozen Easters who were chasing a group of Westers led by Sam Trevaskis. Desperate to be nowhere in the vicinity when his group finally caught up with Sam, Danny announced to his comrades:

'I'm juss goan to duck down thes alley, boys, and cut they Westers off from t'other djrection, see!'

And he abruptly disappeared down a quiet, cobbled passage called Blowinghouse Alley, where nobody was in sight and he could reasonably hope to do up his shoelaces for the next hour or so undisturbed.

But unbeknownst to him, only a couple of lanes away, his father Ben had just spotted the elusive silver ball in the hands of Tristan Rosewarne, who with his brothers Luke and Joshua was now only a hundred yards from goal.

'Git they Rosewarnes!' Ben thundered. 'Ball-ho! Ball-ho!'

And this war-cry was taken up everywhere by the Easters and their supporters, and at last the chase was on.

Now, the Rosewarnes were farmers, as solid as bulls, each and every one — including mother and both sisters. But they were no athletes. And knowing that their team mates were now scattered far and wide, and that they didn't have a hope of outrunning the opposition over a one-hundred-yard spring to goal, they decided to scoot up the nearest convenient alley . . .

And it was here that they found the way ahead blocked by one Daniel P. Curnow, poet and romantic, who was busy having a cigarette and trying to think of a word to rhyme with *Dynothrust*.

Danny couldn't believe what fate was doing to him. He felt like a man trapped in a one-track railway tunnel with a freight train bearing down on him. Instinct told him to do something intelligent . . . like run. But he was paralysed by the sight of Tristan Rosewarne, all seventeen stone and six feet three of him, steaming down the alley towards him at full throttle, with his brothers close behind. And he stood there watching, spellbound, like a rabbit in the headlights of a car at night.

Tristan, however, for all his might and prowess at the noble sport of Cornish wrestling, was a gentle fellow and not widely renowned for the sharpness of his wits. And as the entire Rosewarne train crashed to an abrupt halt in a puddle of sweat, Tristan beamed down at the cowering Danny and gasped, 'Damnee, Dan Curnow, you'm juss in the nick o' time. Us'll block they Easters off right 'ere. You run on, my 'andsome.' And he plopped the sweaty silver ball into Danny's trembling hands.

But Danny was a sportsman to the end, and there was such a thing as cheating, even in the hurling. 'Aw, no, Triss,' he protested. 'I can't. You'm maken a terrible mistake, see . . .'

'Go, go, go!' panted Tristan. 'Us can hold back they Easters, don't ee fret now.'

And at that moment half a dozen Easters, led by Danny's father, came storming up the alley in hot pursuit.

If only to get well away from the dreadful fracas which was about to develop, Danny turned and fled back down the alley and out into the relative safety of the open lanes, where there was not a soul in sight.

Clearly he now had a perfect opportunity to whip through the lanes to the quay, shut his eyes and make a mad dash for the Proud Pinnace. But Danny had a very refined sense of fair play, and poor old Triss had obviously made a simple mistake in the heat of the moment. To that extent Danny felt he had taken the ball under false pretences. So he decided to go and find Lord St Clare and refer the matter to him, in his official capacity as neutral arbiter and greatest living authority on cheating.

By this time all hell was breaking loose in Blowinghouse Alley. The passage had been totally blocked by the unmovable Rosewarne brothers, and as fast as more Easters were arriving from one end, more reinforcements were arriving for the Rosewarnes at the other. Within a matter of minutes some thirty men were jammed into the alley, fighting for a ball that was nowhere in the vicinity.

News of the battle spread quickly, and a large number of spectators began to converge on the area to enjoy the accumulated chaos. But a sizeable majority of the crowd hadn't got a clue what was going on. And those who were packed around the Cross, where East Quay met West, were even more confused when they saw a worried-looking youth emerge from the lanes, holding the silver ball and searching for Lord St Clare.

'*Now* what's going on?' Ormskirk demanded. 'What is that ragamuffin doing, dawdling around like Christmas in Skegness?'

'Perhaps there's been a nasty accident,' said Sharkley.

Ormskirk brightened up. 'Do you reckon?'

The crowds were yelling at Danny now, screaming, 'Run, boy, *run*!' But Danny refused to be deflected from his righteous course. He walked solemnly up to the Cross, and presented himself to an astonished Lord St Clare.

'I'm sorry to trouble ee, your grace,' he began, wondering if he ought to kneel. 'But I got thes problem, see.'

Freddie was sweating to death in his baronial robes and in no mood to be accosted by the village idiot. 'For Christ's sake, lad,' he said, 'there's hurling going on here . . .

207

Somewhere. Can't you see I'm up to my eyes, waiting for something to happen?' And now he perceived that this wretched impersonation of a scarecrow had the silver ball in his grubby hands.

'But see,' Danny pleaded, 'I do think I did get this by false pretences, your worship. I was juss doan up me lacies down Blowinghouse Alley, when dear old Triss Rosewarne comes along . . .'

But at that moment Arthur Pascoe was lumbering across Middle Street on his way to join the battle of Blowinghouse Alley. He took one look at Danny, roared 'Ball-ho! Ball-ho!' and set off at the nearest thing to a run that his vast beer-belly would permit, bawling for reinforcements on the way.

Danny was still trying to make Lord Fred understand what he was wittering on about, when he saw Pascoe bearing down on him like a rhino in full charge. 'Aw, this edden fair!' he protested. 'You juss wait wan moment, Mr Pascoe . . .'

But Pascoe — backed up by Charlie Penrose and Roger Holman — crashed headlong into the group around Lord Fred and brought everyone to the ground . . . including Freddie, who disappeared in a flurry of ermine and a storm of disgusting language. Danny was somewhere at the bottom of the lot, and the ball ran free into the centre of Middle Street.

Players were converging on the Cross from all directions now, spurred on by the cheering of the crowds and the sight of a loose ball at last. Barry Pengelly was the first to pick it up, was set upon by the Reverend Micah Dredge, and promptly told the minister to bugger off. Then he realised who he was speaking to and said, 'Sorry, Rev'ran. Didden see ee comen up thear . . . Crafty sod.'

'The Lord forgiveth and the Lord taketh away,' gasped Micah Dredge, snatching the ball off him and charging straight into the unyielding mass of Dennis Nancarrow.

Back at the Cross, Lord Fred was being helped to his feet and invited to say a few words for BBC Television. But he could think of nothing longer than four letters. And Danny — who thought the whole business was dreadfully unfair but was amazed to have been dug out alive — was limping away to the first-aid post on East Quay, in search of sympathy and a head-to-toe chest X-ray.

The blockage in Blowinghouse Alley had now been cleared and the survivors were making all speed for West Quay, where the Reverend Micah Dredge was making a valiant effort to fend off Ben Curnow and half a dozen others. Hopelessly overwhelmed by sheer weight of bad language, Micah threw a wild pass to Len Dunstan. But it was intercepted by Lightning Bill Lanyon, the chemist's son, who made a clean break across open ground to East Quay, closely pursued by Samson Trevaskis.

Back at the first-aid post, Danny suddenly realised that the whole ghastly business was heading his way again and hurriedly began telling everyone that he thought he'd just sprained both ankles.

Lightning Bill Lanyon was only fifty yards from the Proud Pinnace when Trevaskis caught him up. Aware that Tom Hoskin was not far behind, Lightning threw a wild pass back over his head just as Sam leapt on him. The ball eluded Tom by a long way and rolled harmlessly into the crowd, where it was picked up by Lucy Tremayne. Now, according to the unwritten, unspoken and unheard of laws of hurling, Lucy was obliged to throw the ball straight back to the nearest player to hand. And the nearest player to hand at that moment happened to be Daniel P. Curnow, romantic, sonneteer and proud possessor of a full set of sprained ankles. So she chucked the ball at him.

Danny was stunned. How could Fate do this to one man? He stared at Lucy. Then he stared at the ball. And then he stared at Samson Trevaskis who was hurtling towards him with malice aforethought.

'Well, run, Danny!' Lucy screamed. 'Don't just stand there, *run*!'

Danny needed no further encouragement. He was off like a whippet. By any standards it was fine running, but for a lad suffering from two sprained ankles it was nothing short of miraculous. In fact, he ran so fast that nobody could get near him. But it was not until he had covered well over a hundred yards of ground that he realised he was running in entirely the wrong direction. So he wheeled round in as tight a half-circle as G-forces would allow, and set off back towards the Proud Pinnace again.

By now the crowd (over fifty thousand strong, by Ned Gummoe's reckoning) were cheering him on in a tumult of excitement, and Danny's mind was wonderfully concentrated. He knew that between him and the Proud Pinnace lay a wide stretch of tarmac occupied by dozens of extremely large men, most of whom were purposed solely to flatten him. And there were very few options open to him, it seemed. He could simply drop the ball, fall over and pretend that he'd had a heart attack. Or he could make for the harbour's edge, jump in and pretend that he'd slipped. Or he could keep on going, into the midst of those extremely large men, and suffer a tragically early death before an audience of millions.

He was still considering the harbour option — for it was high tide and he could swim several yards or more in calm water — when he realised that he was already half way across East Quay. Bodies were tumbling all around him, as tackle after tackle narrowly missed his weaving, swerving body. This weaving and swerving was not intentional; but Danny was so flat-footed and knock-kneed that he could no more run in a straight line than he could walk, write or even think in one. So he was careering wildly across the quay, like a drunken meteorite, and proving totally unstoppable. And by the time he was passing the first-aid post once more, and only forty yards from goal, there was only one Wester who had any chance of catching him . . . And that was Sam Trevaskis.

Trevaskis, being a wily sort of thug, saw that the only way of stopping Danny now was to charge into him, broadside on, and trample him down. Which he now attempted to do. But he failed to make allowances for Danny's free arm, which was flailing about all over the place with a life of its own, and by pure chance caught Trevaskis full in the face, sending him tumbling in a heap on the tarmac with blood streaming from his nose.

Danny had no idea what he'd done. If he had, he would have fled Cornwall immediately and sought asylum in another county. But he had other things on his mind at this moment; for he was only twenty yards from goal, and there was absolutely nothing now between him and the Proud Pinnace. The crowds were beginning to close in around him and the cheering was deafening. The BBC camera was rolling. Soozie Smiles was screaming excitedly into her microphone. Lord Fred was poised to declare goal. Ormskirk wasn't even thinking about ice-creams. And just five yards from the Proud Pinnace, Danny tripped over his feet, fell sprawling on the ground, and watched in mortified disbelief as the ball slipped out of his hands and rolled gently to a standstill just two feet away from the doorstep of the public bar.

Butcher Pascoe, fighting to the bitter end, summoned up one last gasp of breath to try and kick it back across the quay. But as he reached the ball, Tom Hoskin, wheezing along a few yards behind, stretched out and grabbed him by the waistband of his trousers.

Pascoe lashed out desperately with his foot to kick the ball away, but Hoskin tugged him backwards with a vice-like grip. Caught between the irresistible force and the unstoppable momentum, Pascoe's trousers burst open at the seams, his foot missed the ball by a mere whisker, and he and Hoskin fell in a heap where they had fallen in heaps many a time before . . . at the entrance to the public bar.

Momentarily blinded by dust and sweat, Pascoe groped for the ball, got his fingertips to it, and in a desperate attempt to grab it and pitch it clear, nudged it gently forwards.

To roars of approval from the crowd, the ball trickled slowly but relentlessly towards the doorstep of the public bar, and came at last to rest for another year against that well-trodden block of granite.

And for the first time in recorded history, the captain of West Village was proclaimed scorer of the winning goal for *East* Village, and Arthur Pascoe staggered to his feet, with his trousers round his ankles, to acknowledge the tumultuous applause.

Meantime, tremendously serious things were happening out at sea.

Her Majesty's coastguard cutter *Atalanta*, with a party of police and preventive officers aboard, was closing fast on the motor yacht *Musetta*. But believing them to be day-trippers, taking a turn round the bay, everyone aboard the *Musetta* had gathered along the starboard rail to wave.

'Good God . . . Those girls are stark naked,' gasped Strait, trying to focus the binoculars.

'Is there no end to their depravity?' said Detective Sergeant Pearce, snatching the glasses off him with unnecessary force.

Strait picked up the loud-hailer and called across the water: 'We are the Customs and Excise! We are boarding your vessel! Do not attempt to leave!'

Whereupon everyone aboard the *Musetta* burst out laughing. Which Strait thought was rather unkind.

Miranda Jago called back: 'Don't panic, Mr Christian! We left the getaway car in Penzance!'

The *Atalanta* drew alongside and the customs officers climbed aboard.

Ramon Grenoux introduced himself. 'Our steering af broke,' he explained. 'So we are oblige to voyage in zis 'uge circules.'

The coastguard examined the steering gear and pronounced it *kaput*.

'In that case we'll search the passengers and crew,' Pearce said to Strait. 'Then we'll put them aboard the *Atalanta*, take this boat in tow and return to the nearest harbour to search her.'

So everyone on board the *Musetta* was searched, told to get dressed and board the *Atalanta*. Which they all did . . . with the exception of Miranda who could not get dressed, because she'd fallen into the sea that morning and all her clothes were dripping wet. All she could find to wear was the bottom half of someone else's bikini (none of the other girls had a top half that would fit her), and a grubby white raincoat that she found lying about on the coastguard boat. Thus accoutred, she said 'Hello, sailor' to the coastguard's mate, and the *Atalanta* chuntered away across the bay with the *Musetta* in tow, making for the nearest convenient harbour. Which happened to be St Clare . . .

Back in the village, thousands were packed into the Proud Pinnace, celebrating the Easters' great victory. The ancient tavern was bulging to the very eaves, and happy patrons were spilling out all over the place . . . onto the pavement, across East Quay, down each other's trousers . . .

Over at the Fouled Anchor, Ormskirk was attempting in vain to find out what had happened to the most important person in the world, and his distinguished guests from Tokyo.

Freddie was furious by this time. It had been a disastrous weekend from the start. He'd spent all Saturday ironing his best underpants. All Sunday not getting his end away with the widow Tremayne. And now all Monday not getting his free slap-up luncheon at the Grand Imperial Hotel, Penzance, with the president of Japan and Sir Walter Ecclesthorpe.

Ormskirk was trying to mollify him with a slap-up luncheon at the Fouled Anchor instead. He handed him the menu and told him to go mad. So Freddie ordered the most expensive thing on it. Which was plaice and chips. Sharkley ordered sausage, egg and chips, to be different. So did Ormskirk . . . but with an extra portion of chips, two more sausages and a double helping of eggs.

'I just can't make head or tail of it,' he said apologetically to Lord Fred. 'They landed on time. The limos were there. They all set off for Penzance according to schedule.'

He looked at the telephone message again: '*Sir Wilfrid rang. Don't start hurling. May be few minutes late.*'

'I wonder where they were ringing from?' said Sharkley.

*   *   *

Seventy miles away, on a desolate track in the middle of Bodmin Moor, two brand new, shining black Fujokawa limousines, pride of the Japanese motor industry, were drawn up line-astern before a drab green Land Rover, pride of the British army.

'This is a firing range,' said a belligerent corporal. 'There's no A30 round 'ere.'

'Then where the hell is it?' demanded Sir Wilf, as if the army could have hidden it out of spite.

'Don't ask me,' said the corporal.

'Well, *some*body must know.'

'Try the nearest village.'

'Which is?'

'St Cleer.'

'But that's precisely where we're trying to get to.'

'So much the better,' said the corporal. 'Kill two birds with one stone.'

'Well, where *is* it?' Sir Wilf demanded.

'Don't ask me. I'm in Signals. And there's shooting going on.'

'Then take me to your commanding officer.'

'He's in Brighton. There's a bank holiday going on.'

'Then ask your driver!' Sir Wilf exploded.

'He's from Dorset. He *never* knows what's going on.'

Akiro Toshimoto and Takeo Subishi, meanwhile, were standing on the moor gazing at the distant white mountains of China-clay waste with nostalgic memories of their homeland.

'Mystery, Takeo-san,' said Toshimoto. 'Why snow on volcanoes in summer?'

Takeo Subishi began thumbing through his *AA Guide to Britain*. 'Mystery . . . ,' he agreed.

Back at the Land Rover, things were looking up for Sir Wilf.

'St Cleer?' said the driver. 'Yeah . . . of course. Ten minutes. Follow your nose. Can't go wrong. A doddle . . . '

It was well after time at the Proud Pinnace and no one was

214

taking a blind bit of notice. Heart-warming scenes of reconciliation had been taking place between Easters and Westers. All rivalry and ancient grudge had been swept away in a torrent of ale, and eternal friendships that would endure for many days had been lovingly pledged under many a table.

This spirit of good will had even imbued the two arch-rivals, Tom Hoskin and Arthur Pascoe, who had sworn solemn and incomprehensible oaths never again to be divided by feminine guile. And to demonstrate their newly pledged solidarity, they had agreed to break with centuries of tradition and to choose the Queen of the Feast together.

Out on East Quay, some seventy-five thousand people — by Ned Gummoe's reckoning — were assembling to watch the grand coronation ceremony. But few had noticed the coastguard boat *Atalanta*, that was just putting in to harbour, for everyone along the harbour wall was facing the wrong way. Or was blind drunk. Or both.

In the middle of the quay, all thirty-two pretenders to this year's crown were gathering sheepishly in a large circle, dressed in brilliant white creations of satin and lace, posing for the press, and making last-minute adjustments to hair, make-up and bra straps.

'Onest Eli Tonkin had stopped taking bets on Lucy Tremayne by this time. Her nearest rival, Lorna Pengelly, was five to one. And the rest of the girls were thirty-three to one . . . With the exception of Brenda Trevaskis, younger sister of Samson, who was a hundred to one; for she was built like an all-in westler, and distinguishable from Sam only by the LOVE and HATE tattoos on her knuckles, and the fact that she had not yet started shaving. But then, she was still only fifteen.

On the north-west corner of the quay, at the village Cross, Farmer Rosewarne was waiting at the reins of his brightly painted gypsy cart to convey the new queen to her coronation.

Close by, arrayed once more in his baronial robes, Lord Fred was waiting to place the official tin crown upon the royal head.

And beside him, sweating profusely in his vast white colonial governor's outfit, Ormskirk was waiting anxiously for news of Sir Wilf and the arrival of an ice-cream van.

And down below, by Ormskirk's elbows, little Sharkley was anxiously awaiting the arrival of St Clare and her knights in shining armour.

'Where the hell can they have got to?' he asked Freddie.

But Freddie was sulking because he still hadn't had his free, slap-up banquet with the emperor of Japan and Lord Ecclesfield of Birmingham. He told Sharkley he didn't know, he didn't care, and he hadn't seen Miranda all weekend.

Meanwhile, the enemy was hard at work. The Reverend Owen Borage and a random representative sample of retired wing commanders and Volvo owners were parading under the banners of the St Clare's Bay Preservation Front, collecting signatures for their petition, and distributing leaflets that were riddled with scurrilous truths about Pirana House Investments.

But all eyes were now turned to the public bar of the Proud Pinnace, where Tom Hoskin and Arthur Pascoe were just lurching out into the daylight to begin the ritual ceremony of choosing the Queen of the Feast.

Out on the quay, the massed bands of the West Penwith Brass Ensemble and the Salvation Army struck up with that celebrated opus, known and loved throughout the far corners of the Proud Pinnace, 'The Grand Jig of St Clare' . . . Which was uncannily reminiscent of a sordid little ditty, called 'Barnacle Bill the Sailor'.

Tom and Arthur now linked arms and pranced out across the quay, vaguely in time to the music, followed by every other hurler who was capable of remaining on his feet. They then jigged their way through the ring of girls, singing that boring old refrain, '*Whear es our queen this saint's day feast? Our chaste and beauteous maiden* . . . ' And the other hurlers followed on in one long, stumbling disorderly snake, singing the same refrain . . . or whatever variation came into their heads at the time.

With all this going on, nobody had noticed the *Atalanta* tying up in the harbour . . .

An argument was now breaking out between the principal forces of law and order.

'You can't just let these people go *free*,' Norman Strait was protesting. 'They could be guilty of *anything*.'

'But I can't arrest them,' said Detective Sergeant Pearce, 'unless they're guilty of *something*.'

'But, Christ, man . . . They've been sailing round in circles all morning, flying their vests and socks from the mast!'

'That may be eccentric,' Pearce conceded, 'but it's not illegal.'

'When you two boys have done arguing,' the coastguard interrupted, 'I want this lot off my boat so I can put back to Penzance. There's a storm forecast and the glass is falling.'

'Oh, very well,' said Strait petulantly. 'But the French skipper stays here while we search his boat.'

Pearce agreed. So one by one, everyone else was helped ashore and told they were free to go, pending a search of the *Musetta* . . . Everyone, that is, except Miranda, who was grabbed by Strait as she tried to disembark.

'*That*,' he said indignantly, seizing her by the sleeve of his grubby white mac, 'is my raincoat, young lady.'

'Then it's high time you sent it to the cleaners,' she said, slipping it off and bundling it into his arms. 'It really is *too* disgusting. I dread to think what you've been doing in it.'

And so saying, she climbed off the *Atalanta*, clad in nothing but a tiny bikini bottom, and walked along the quay to find out what all the singing and dancing was about, and why she wasn't the centre of attention for once.

Pushing her way through the throng, she emerged right out in the middle of East Quay to tremendous applause from the crowd, who were delighted that some fine figure of a streaker had had the decency to disrupt proceedings at last.

Tom and Arthur took one look at that familiar bosom and came to an abrupt halt. And gradually the entire train of dancers ground to a standstill behind them, and the brass band faded away, one by one, like a succession of elephants breaking wind.

For a moment the whole of St Clare fell silent.

'Well, don't stop for *me*!' Miranda cried, running up to Tom with her arms open wide. 'Mindy wants to dance too!'

So, loath to deny a fair damsel this modest request, Tom and Arthur took her by the hand and began jigging round the ring of beauty contestants again, as the band struck up and all the hurlers joined in the new refrain, '*We've found our queen this saint's day feast. Our chaste and beauteous maiden . . .* '

At this, Farmer Rosewarne shook the reins and urged Lysander, his faithful old Clydesdale, out across the quay, pulling the brightly painted gypsy cart, to collect the new queen and bear her to her coronation at the Cross.

As the cart drew to a halt in the middle of East Quay, Tom and Arthur swept Miranda aloft and dumped her unceremoniously on the back seat. And when Danny Curnow protested, 'Aw, that edden fair, Uncle Tom. Her's too awld to be Queen of the Feast . . . ' he too was swept aloft and dumped in the cart beside her; whereupon he took one look at her bosom and almost died of fright.

Farmer Rosewarne then shook the reins, and Lysander trotted gently back across the quay to where Lord Fred was waiting with the coronation crown.

Nobody in St Clare had ever witnessed anything like this before. Tutting loudly in disapproval, they struggled in their thousands to get a better view. The cheering and wolf whistling was deafening.

Back at the Cross, Freddie was hunting feverishly for his spectacles, muttering, 'Naked girl? Naked girl? Disgusting . . . '

'Who . . . is . . . *that*?' gasped Ormskirk, frog-eyed at the sight.

'That is our St Clare,' said Sharkley.

'Looks familiar,' murmured Freddie, gazing myopically at the approaching face.

'They are phe*nomenal*!' said Ormskirk.

218

'Christ almighty,' said Freddie. 'That's my daughter.'

'Are they really?' said Ormskirk. 'You must be very proud.'

The cart drew to a halt at the Cross, and hundreds of willing arms reached up to help Miranda down, whilst Danny fell out of the other side in shock.

'She's drunk,' Freddie raged. 'Get her out of here, somebody . . .'

PC Hawkins was beside him with a blanket. 'Tes all right, my lord. I do have me panda car close by. I'll have her back at Tremorna in two shakes.'

'Thank God you're here, Percy,' said Freddie, reaching under his robes for his house keys. 'I'll send someone along with you.'

'Aw, naw, that won't be necessary,' said Percy.

'Essential,' said Sharkley, snatching Freddie's keys.

'Thank you, Mervyn,' said Freddie. 'Get her straight to bed . . .'

'I will, I will,' Sharkley promised.

Miranda came bouncing up to her father to be crowned.

'Papa! Guess who's Queen of the Feast? Mindy! The boys have chosen *me* out of all those other dreary tarts!'

Percy Hawkins wrapped the blanket round her. Freddie pushed her away, hissing: 'Out of my sight, you brainless little trollop . . .'

'Little *trollop*?' said Miranda indignantly. 'How dare you! I'm perfectly tall for my height . . .'

Percy led her away and pushed her into the back seat of the panda car. Sharkley climbed in beside her.

'Not on the back seat of a *police* car, surely?' she protested. 'Constable Hawkins . . . I'm being molested! Help him or something.'

'You curb your language, ma'am,' said Percy, starting up the car. 'No wan es goan to lay a finger on ee while *I'm* around.'

'Then I shall telephone the chief constable immediately in writing and complain.'

'You'm goan straight back home to bed,' Percy retorted firmly.

'Ooh, goody,' said Miranda, placing her hot little hand in Sharkley's.

'We can't go through all the singing and dancing *again*,' said Freddie, turning to the Reverend Micah Dredge for guidance. 'What are we going to do for a queen? We can't start the coronation without a queen . . . '

'Pick the nearest girl to hand,' said Micah. 'It doesn't matter who.'

Freddie turned to Danny Curnow. 'Danny, *you* nearly won the hurling. *You* do it.'

'Aw, not me, your 'ighness,' Danny replied apologetically. 'I'm a boy, see. I can't . . . '

'Not asking you to *be* queen, you silly tit, I'm asking you to *pick* one.'

'Aw, righto,' said Danny, obligingly. 'Who shall I pick?'

'Anyone, anyone,' said Freddie, exasperated. 'The whole village is waiting. Pick the nearest girl to hand.'

'Aw, righto.'

Danny looked around for Lucy. But she was nowhere in sight.

'Oh, *do* get a move on, lad,' said Micah Dredge. 'Everyone's waiting. Choose anyone. All girls are equal in the sight of God. Any Methodist will do.'

Danny scanned the quay in desperation. Where was Lucy? Where *could* she be . . . ? Where were *any* of the other contestants? The only one close at hand was Brenda Trevaskis.

'She'll do,' said Freddie, his patience exhausted. 'The one with the hairy legs.'

Danny tried to pretend this was not happening. He went up to Brenda and said miserably, 'Allo, Brenda. I juss been told I got to choose ee as Queen of the Feast.'

'Aw, proper job!' chuckled Brenda, belting him in the kidneys with delight. She barged her way up to Lord Fred. 'I'm the queen,' she informed him, displaying what teeth she had left after a hard winter beating up Hell's Angels on the streets of Penzance.

220

'I hereby crown thee Queen of the Feast, Maid of St Clare and Grand Virgin of the vernal equinox,' gabbled Freddie.

He slammed the tin crown on her head, but her skull was so large that she had to hold the thing in place.

Now Soozie Smiles crept up and pushed her microphone towards Ormskirk's mouth.

'It is my very great pleasure,' began Ormskirk, stunned by Brenda's unloveliness, 'on behalf of Pirana House Investments, to award this cheque for one hundred pounds to the one who has been adjudged the most beautiful girl in St Clare.'

He took an envelope out of his sweaty jacket pocket and handed it to Brenda, who grabbed it and ripped it open.

'We give you the *real* thing later,' Ormskirk murmured. 'When we know whose name to put on the cheque.'

'How about cash instead?' Brenda suggested, not without menace.

'How about you just jump up into Tucker Rosewarne's cart, you ungracious whelp,' Freddie replied tersely. 'The parade is waiting to begin.'

So Brenda elbowed her way back to the cart and clambered into it, swinging her great beefy legs over the side like a *routier* climbing into the cab of a forty-ton truck.

The grand coronation parade set off at last up Middle Street towards the Fields, led by Lysander and Tucker Rosewarne's cart, with Good Queen Brenda happily waving to everyone and picking her nose. They were followed by teams of Cornish and Breton wrestlers, street tumblers, and gaily painted clowns from Dizzie Lubin's Travelling Circus. Behind them skipped the merry Morris dancers of Mousehole, a Cornish bagpiper, and Rachel Trefusis with her performing tortoises. After them came the massed bands of the West Penwith Brass Ensemble, the Salvation Army, and two trumpeters from the Royal Marines. Followed by the sombre-faced Reverend Owen Borage and his wife and fan club, under the banners of the 'St Clare's Bay Preservation Front'. Then the Latin American singers, Trio Los Bravos, from Helston; Mad Jack the Fingers with his puppets and conjuring tricks; the bronzed and brawny men of the St Clare's Bay Surf Life-Saving Club, marching under the state flags of New South Wales and Queensland; Nobby Visick, driving his amazing petrol-engined Bavarian steam organ; all the notables, worthies and dignitaries of West Cornwall, including Ned Gummoe; the veterans association of the Duke of Cornwall's Light Infantry, also including Ned Gummoe; the Royal National Lifeboat Institution's acrobatic team; and two ice-cream vans pursued hotly by Geoffrey Ormskirk . . .

PC Hawkins drew up outside the front door of Tremorna Hall.

'Now are you sure you can manage on your own?' he asked Sharkley. 'She's more than a handful for any man.'

'I've got everything firmly under control,' said Sharkley, pushing Miranda out of the car with unseemly haste.

'All right an,' said Percy. 'I'd bess get back the Fields. We'll see ee back thear djrectly.'

'If not sooner,' said Sharkley, scrambling out of the car and slamming the door.

Percy drove away down the gravel drive towards the lane.

'Sharklet, petal,' purred Miranda, coiling her arms round his neck. 'Why don't you pop down to Papa's wine cellar and pinch a bottle of Bollinger for afters?'

Sharkley nodded and was going to ask what Bollinger was. But Miranda had just plunged her tongue into his mouth and was already lashing furiously at his tonsils.

Percy reached the end of the drive and turned into the lane. And there he was confronted by an inelegant heap of imitation chain mail, astride a grey mare.

Unaccustomed as he was to bumping into incompetent-looking medieval knights trotting through the Cornish countryside in broad daylight, Percy leapt out of his car, fearlessly brandishing his peaked cap.

222

'Stop right thear!' he shouted. 'This es the police!'

'I'd never have guessed,' Alf replied.

Percy thought he recognised the voice inside that ill-fitting coal scoop. 'Who the devil's that, an?'

'King Arthur,' said Alf, taking off her helmet. 'Who do you think it is, Percy, you loon? Ambushing me in this ridiculous fashion . . .'

'That sword is an offensive weapon, Alfreda,' he said, as if there was nothing otherwise remarkable about her appearance. 'Whatever are ee doan with un?'

'I'm a Pirana House knight in shining string mail. And I'm supposed to be escorting Miranda. Where is she, the dozy doxy?'

'Her's juss arrived back at Tremorna.'

'What on earth is she doing there?'

'Goan to bed.'

'Ask a stupid question . . .'

'Her's been drinken.'

'Haven't we all, dear. Where's little Sharkley?'

'In thear. Putten Miranda to bed.'

'Have they no self-control? We're supposed to be working. Where's the Frenchman? In there too, I suppose.'

'Frenchman?' Percy looked round suspiciously. 'What Frenchman?'

'You know . . . the other knight.'

'Naw . . . What night was that, an?'

'A tall French sailor. I can't find him anywhere.'

'Want to file a missen persons report, do ee?'

'Don't be daft, Percy. He's only been missing since half past two. It's now barely twenty past three.'

'Well, how am I supposed to know that?'

'Got a watch, haven't you?'

'Course I have . . . I'm a police officer.'

'Then don't ask stupid questions.'

Alf turned her horse round and started back towards the stables.

'Damnee . . . look 'ere, Alfreda!' Percy shouted angrily. 'I want to know juss what's goan on round 'ere!'

'And *I* want my fifty quid appearance money,' Alf grumbled, trotting away.

Sharkley had found the wine-cellar door at last. Trembling with anticipation, he lifted the latch, pulled open the heavy oak door, and stepped down into the dark cold depths. The door crashed shut behind him.

He fumbled about in the dark for a light switch. No light switch. He tried to open the door, but the latch had dropped home. He tried to lift the latch. But the latch had dropped to the floor. He trod on something metallic. The latch. He tried to put it back where it belonged. It didn't want to go back. It didn't seem to belong. He pushed the door. It was firmly shut.

This was ridiculous. He put his shoulder to the door and rammed it. That merely hurt his shoulder. He tried kicking it. And that merely hurt his foot.

Bang on the door, that was the obvious answer. Shout and bang on the door. Before very long, Miranda would begin to wonder where he'd got to and would come looking . . .

Upstairs in her bedroom in the east wing — about as far away from the wine cellar as it was possible to get, without actually sitting on the roof — Miranda threw herself down on her enormous four-poster bed to wait for all that beautiful bubbly Bollinger to arrive . . .

. . . And fell fast asleep.

At half past three that afternoon, two shining black Fujokawa limousines, pride of the Japanese motor industry, glided into the village of St Cleer, on the southern edge of Bodmin Moor.

'Thank God one of us knows how to navigate,' said Sir Wilf modestly. 'Now we can let them start the hurling.'

But the village was almost deserted.

224

'Ask this peasant where the harbour is,' Sir Wilf instructed the driver.

The driver braked to a halt and summoned a gnarled old rustic across the road with an imperious snap of the fingers.

' 'Arbour?' the old man replied, mystified. 'Thear edden no 'arbour round 'ere, my dear.'

'What do you mean, no harbour?' said Sir Wilf. 'This is St Clare, isn't it?'

'Aw, ais. This es St Cleer all right. But the sea don't come within ten mile of 'ere, my awld cock.'

The village of St Cleer was eleven miles inland from the nearest harbour at Looe, and sixty miles from the ancient fishing village of St *Clare* in Penwith . . .

By Ned Gummoe's reckoning, there were well over a hundred thousand people packed onto the Fields for the grand spring fair that afternoon, all eating, drinking, singing, dancing, playing, making merry, being sick and generally having a whale of a time . . . All, that is, except Danny Curnow, who was sitting alone by the river, composing a heart-searing threnody for his own tragically premature funeral.

Lucy crept up and sat down beside him. 'Hello, cheerful. What are you looking so happy about?'

He couldn't even pluck up the courage to look at her. 'You know what tes, Lucy,' he mumbled. *I* didn't want Brenda to be queen. Her's the ugliest sow for miles around.'

'Now, Danny, that's unkind,' she said. 'True. But unkind.'

'And you'm far and away the loveliest girl around.'

'I know. But who cares about being Queen of the Feast? All I wanted was the money. And what you've never had, you don't miss, do you?'

Danny saw a glimmer of hope in her words. 'You mean . . . you ent mad with I an, Lucy?'

'Of course not. Why should I be? It wasn't your fault. 'Twas Miranda who messed everything up.'

225

'Aw, thank heaven for that,' said Danny. 'I thought you'd never talk to I again.'

'Don't be silly, Danny. I don't care about being a beauty queen. I'm sick to death of being told how beautiful I am. I want people to tell me I've got a *mind*.'

'Aw, I knaw you've got a mind all right,' Danny assured her. 'I knawed that when us was liddel kids, and you was signen your own name in proper slopey writen by the age of twelve.'

But the mention of writing reminded him of the Reverend Owen Borage and the contraceptives, elevating his spirits to fresh heights of depression. For being Danny was such a rotten thing to be, that every time he burrowed his way out of one steaming heap of misfortune, fate immediately dumped another lot on top of him.

'But I do have somethen awful to tell ee, Lucy,' he said woefully. 'I dunnaw how to begin.'

'Dear heaven, Danny,' she said, smiling, 'Doesn't anythen ever go right in your life?'

Danny shook his head. 'Tes the vicar's wife. Her's gone found me wallet. On Porthcurno Hill.'

'Well, that's *good* news. Where was it?'

'Juss where I left me bike. En a clump of nettles. So she gave un to the vicar. And he's sending they to your mum.'

'What . . . the nettles?'

'Naw. The thingies her found en me wallet. And the photos.'

'What photos?'

'Photos of you. En a liddel bikini. What I bought off Buster Tonkin.'

'Bought my bikini off *Buster*?'

'Naw, your pictures. Cost I a quid each.'

'Never?' Lucy was shocked. 'That's disgusten. You shouldn't have, Danny . . . '

'Aw, Lucy, I juss wanted somethen to remind I . . . '

'Shameful, Buster charging you a pound each. You should have asked me. I've got hundreds at home like that — in colour too — you could have had for nothing. Is that all you're grumbling about?'

Danny shook his head and looked up to heaven. *Aw, Loord*, he thought, *tes so rotten being I*. He closed his eyes. 'Thear's the thingies too. En me wallet. What the vicar's senden to your mum.'

'What thingies?'

'Fancy wans. Black jobs.'

'Fancy *what*?'

Danny took a deep breath. 'Contraceptives.'

'Oh, wellies, you mean,' said Lucy. 'What do you call *fancy*?'

'Black Stallions.'

'Oh, good'uns, eh?' said Lucy, impressed. 'They're pricey, they are.'

Danny was taken aback. 'How would *you* know?'

'I seen 'em in Boots in Penzance, t'other day.'

'But your mum's goan to murder I! The vicar's goan to send her they photos and thingies and make it look like you and me been . . . ' Danny wished he could just disappear into a hole in the ground. 'Well, you know . . . '

'Don't be daft, Danny,' Lucy scoffed. 'My mum's not *that* stupid.'

'But her'll think I'm a maniac or something!'

'Of course she won't. She's used to people going crazy over me. Thousands of boys are in love with me, after all.'

Thousands, thought Danny, despondently. *Thousands*. Why couldn't he fall in love with someone that nobody else wanted? Like Brenda Trevaskis . . .

Sally Tremayne had more important things to worry about at that moment, in any case. She'd been searching for Tom Hoskin and Arthur Pascoe for the past hour; but they had very wisely disappeared into the teeming multitude and lost themselves amongst the ten acres of stalls, sideshows and marquees.

She finally caught up with Tom, stuffing his face at Mary Tonkin's pie stall.

'So *thear* you are!' she said triumphantly.

Tom was unmoved. 'Ais. 'Ere I am,' he agreed.

'You woulden be hiden from me, would ee, Tom Hoskin?'

'Well, does et look like I'm hiden from anywan?' he reasoned. 'Standen 'ere in front of all Cornwall, eaten a brave old piece of Meary Tonkin's starry-gazey pie?'

'Well, you *ought* to be hiden!' Sally retorted. 'Hiden your shame!'

'Aw, ais? Why's that an, my dear?'

'I never seen anythen so disgusten in all my life! You dancen on East Quay with Miranda Jago was bad enough. But to go putten her up on Tucker's cart as feast queen, embarrassen Lord Fred in front of all the village, the visitors, the television . . . Why, tes downright shameful, Tom Hoskin! Shameful!'

'Shameful, ezzer?' said Tom calmly, spitting crumbs of starry-gazey pie everywhere. 'Then you ent upset wi' I because your Lucy edden Queen of the Feast?'

'The thought never even crossed my mind,' said Sally.

'Well, that's all right an,' said Tom, wiping his mouth with the back of his hand. 'I thoft you might be mad wi' I because her didden win the hunnerd pound, see . . . '

'How can you stand there and even suggest such a thing?' said Sally, outraged by this blatantly correct reading of the situation.

'Still, you say you ent mad wi' I,' Tom continued, 'so that's all right an, edden un?' He turned to Mary Tonkin. 'Handsome piece of pie thear, mizzus.' He smiled at Sally. 'Well, I'll be strollen on. See ee later, my dear.' And he walked away into the crowd.

Speechless with rage, Sally watched him go and then stormed off to find Arthur Pascoe.

Pascoe was quietly observing the Pirana House balloon team, who were trampling all over the Hag's Ring trying to get the balloon inflated, under the personal supervision of Colonel Hermann H. Hermann of Des Moines, Iowa, who knew all about such things. On hearing from Len Dunstan that Sally was out looking for him, Pascoe did the decent, gentlemanly thing and hid behind a clump of hawthorn bushes in West Meadows.

Nearby, Lord Fred and Ormskirk were posing for photographs and giving interviews to the press and wondering what had happened to Sharkley.

Back at Tremorna Hall, Sharkley was still entombed in the cold, dark wine cellar, wearing only his Otello Bocci feather-light suit and Monsieur Trend gossamer-fine shirt, and was slowly succumbing to hypothermia.

Upstairs in the east wing, beneath the benevolent gaze of the Lady in Grey, Miranda was snoring like a trooper.

Thirty miles away, near the village of Blackwater on the A30 trunk road to Penzance, one shining black Fujokawa limousine, pride of the Japanese motor industry, was standing in a lay-by with its bonnet raised and a dozen perplexed faces staring down at the complex technological contents within.

'Beyond me,' said an AA engineer. 'You need a computer programmer, not a mechanic.'

Immediately behind them, Akiro Toshimoto stood smiling in shame and embarrassment. And Takeo Subishi began mentally composing a telex to Tokyo demanding the immediate resignation or ritual disembowelment of the chief engineer of the Fujokawa Corporation.

'We'll take the other limousine,' Sir Wilf told Toshimoto, through his chief bodyguard. 'Everyone else can wait for a hire car.'

'No possible,' the chief bodyguard explained. 'President Toshimoto never travel without chief adviser, Subishi-san, and madame's maid-in-waiting. *They* go on in rimousine. You and Mrs Maccersfield wait for taxi with others.'

Outraged, Sir Wilf turned to his personal private secretary.

'Phone the public relations director of British Leyland, right now . . . on his home number. Tell him I want a

Daimler limousine here *immediately*. Or Pirana House buys Ford fleet cars from now on!'

Stabbed to the heart by this ultimate humiliation of being rescued by British Leyland, Akiro Toshimoto and Takeo Subishi burst out laughing.

From the pellar's tent, close to the boundary with West Meadows, Granny Polkinghorne was observing the efforts of the Pirana House hot-air balloon team to get off the ground. And she was repeating — at fifty pence a time — the dire prognostications of her wise ancestor, Yseult Polkinghorne, the Penwith witch . . .

'When the devils do come and make fire and sacrilege upon the Ring, the heavens shall split. A great light shall bright the night. The wild beasts will rage. And the ghost of awld Matthew Jago shall be seen gallopen across West Headland once again.' And having paid careful attention to the weather forecast that morning, she now added, 'And thear will be a great crashen boomen noise come from heaven, you. And a flood of water. And a strong awld wind, force five to six, veeren west. Wi' temp'tures droppen to seven or eight centigrade on higher ground . . .'

But the balloon team were getting nowhere and were all hard at work scratching their beards.

Nige said the wind was to blame, it was shifting easterly. Bert said it wasn't, it was veering westerly. Richie said it was still blowing from the south. And Hermann H. Hermann of Des Moines, Iowa, said it was coming from the north. Nige asked Hermann not to interfere. Hermann said he knew everything about balloons. Nige said no he didn't, please to keep quiet. Hermann said he'd escaped death by the skin of his teeth thousands of times, parachuting with 82nd Airborne. Nige told him to shut up before his luck changed. Hermann said they just needed a few more willing guys to help get the balloon up off all those goddam heaps of old rock. And he shouted across to the man hiding behind the hawthorn hedge.

The man hiding behind the hawthorn hedge was Arthur

Pascoe. The woman pulling him out into the open was Sally Tremayne.

'Son of a lousy bitch has run out on us,' sneered Hermann.

Arthur hadn't run anywhere. He'd been violently abducted.

Sally rounded on him furiously. 'Skulken behind bushes then, Arthur? Too ashamed to show your face? Or still drunk, are ee? Like you were on East Quay? Dancen with Miranda Jago, stark naked!'

'I never danced stark naked in all me life,' he protested. 'Anyhow, what's all the fuss about? She had a little pair of what's-its on.'

'You disgust me, Arthur. You've shamed me and shamed the village.'

'Now just because Lucy didden win the hundred pound . . .'

'You too?' said Sally, pained to find that an old friend could look her straight in the eye and tell her the bare-faced truth. 'What a nasty pair of minds you and Tom do have.'

'And after *all* I've done for you since Kenwyn passed on,' said Arthur resentfully . . . as if he'd been fiddling with her tap washers all year out of anything more than pure lust.

'And what es that supposed to mean?' Sally demanded.

'You do know perfectly well what I mean. Messen me and Tom around all this time. Playen us off, one against t'other. We're not stupid, my dear. We do know what your game es. And the way you'm goan you'll end up a lonely, frustrated, old bag like Alice Uglow.'

Which was indeed a thought that had begun to haunt Sally of late. 'Still drunk, I see,' she retorted. 'Drunk out of your wits.'

'Not so,' Arthur replied. 'I had to get drunk to find me senses and see things clear for once. Now you'll have to find yourself another clown. Because you'm not the only woman en these parts, you know. Thear's hundreds of lovely young

231

ladies out thear right now, just waiten for an eligible fellow like me to come along.'

And so saying he stomped off to prove his point, and walked straight into the hairy arms of Brenda Trevaskis, who was demanding money with menaces at the rate of one pound per kiss (eight for a fiver) in aid of some charity she was refusing to name, to protect the innocent.

The press corps had finished photographing Lord Fred and Ormskirk by this time, and were gathering by the Addle bridge where the Reverend Owen Borage and assorted activists of the St Clare's Bay Preservation Front were busy daubing protest slogans all over the stone walls with white paint.

This had brought a swift response from PC Hawkins, who had driven the full forty yards from where his panda car was parked, right up to the Addle bridge, with his blue lamp flashing.

'What es a-goan on 'ere an, vicar?' Percy demanded angrily. 'You can't paint this bridge white! Tes the property of the county council.'

'This is a protest in the name of the preservation front,' the vicar replied defiantly. 'We shall not be moved!'

Percy pointed to where someone was painting *Pirana House Go Home* on the granite parapet. 'You can't vandalise the Addle bridge en the name of preservation!'

'This is a democracy, Mr Hawkins, not Germany in the 1930s!' the vicar proclaimed, in the direction of the television camera. 'Every Englishman is free to paint his mind.'

'Not on the Addle bridge, he edden. Not without plannen permission from County Hall.'

'It's only distemper, Mr Hawkins. It'll wash off in a trice.'

'Aw, and will it so?' said Percy. 'Then you'd better go off right now en that trice of yours and fetch a scrubben brush and give me a demonstration.'

'But you already *have* a demonstration,' said the vicar proudly. And he indicated with one sweep of his arm as fine a body of god-fearing reactionaries as Attila the Hun could have wished to meet.

'You'll get these walls scrubbed clean right now, Mr Borage,' Percy warned him, 'or I'll order up Special Constable Nancarrow and have un clear the bridge.'

'Hark! The jackboot!' the vicar cried. 'We shall defend democracy to the very last drop of paint!' And he clutched the nearest placard to hand and waved it defiantly in the direction of the press corps.

Unfortunately for the vicar, the placard too had been vandalised. Some wily saboteur had stolen a dollop of white paint and obliterated two essential parts of the letter *B*. So that much to the delight of the press and television cameras it now read:

I'VE JOINED
ST. CLARE'S GAY
PRESERVATION
FRONT

All was now clear. Ormskirk had paid Danny Curnow the princely sum of one pound sterling to leg it back to the Fouled Anchor to see if there had been any further communication from Sir Wilf and his party. And Danny had returned with the good news that Sir Wilf was alive and well, and had broken down on the A30 near Blackwater. British Leyland were sending a relief limousine, and Sir Wilf had generously suggested that Lord Fred might as well start the hurling now, before darkness descended. The party would arrive in plenty of time for the evening barbecue.

Thus reassured, Ormskirk jubilantly conveyed these tidings to Lord Fred, and wobbled off to West Meadows to help the balloon team get airborne, pulling ineffectually at all the wrong ropes and being of no assistance whatsoever, but having tremendous fun. It was only now that he began to wonder what could have happened to Sharkley.

Sharkley was still locked in the cellar in his Otello Bucci feather-light summer suit and Monsieur Trend gossamer-fine shirt. But being a man of resource and ingenuity, he had stumbled around in the pitch dark for an hour or so, tripping over the rats, and had finally discovered daylight.

The light was leaking in around the edges of a manhole cover in the cellar roof. The manhole led up to the garden terrace outside. It was a very rusty, narrow hole. But with effort and determination he just managed to squeeze through it and pull himself up onto the terrace above.

He now had a very rusty Otello Bocci summer suit, and a Monsieur Trend shirt in dozens of gossamer-fine pieces. But then the shipwrecked look was all the rage up Solihull way.

Frozen to the marrow of his bones, he let himself into the house with his lordship's door keys and hurried upstairs to the east wing, as fast as his teeth could chatter. There he found Miranda fast asleep with her legs wide open. Unable to resist the impulse, he tore off his rusty suit and shredded shirt, and plunged hungrily into all the thick woolly sweaters he could find, and huddled up in front of the electric fire to thaw out.

On board the good ship *Musetta* meantime, an air of triumph prevailed. After many hours of painstaking endeavour, Norman Strait had unmasked what looked like a cunning conspiracy to smuggle into the UK well over several grams or less of a highly suspicious substance, disguised as the contents of a polythene bag and openly secreted in a lady's handbag.

'Yours?' Strait asked Ramon Grenoux, pointing to the handbag. Ramon looked down at the lipstick, nail lacquer, mascara, earrings, eye shadows, cheek blusher and three tampons.

'Mine?' he said incredulously. '*Vous vous moquez de moi?*'

'Now don't come the foreigner with me,' Strait warned him.

'But I *am* a foreigner.'

234

'Precisely,' said Strait, as if that proved his worst suspicions. 'So whose handbag is this?'

Detective Sergeant Pearce found a driving licence in a separate compartment of the bag. He read aloud: '*Miranda Jane Louise Jago. Tremorna Hall.*'

'So . . . a woman, eh?' said Strait darkly, proud of that remarkable piece of deduction. He picked up the polythene bag and said to Ramon, 'This is going for analysis.'

'*Je ne comprends pas,*' shrugged Ramon, pretending he'd never seen stuff like that in his life.

'*Voici une substance suspicieuse,*' Strait replied gravely. '*Pour fumer, je pense.*'

'*Nom de Dieu!*' Ramon crossed himself. '*Le vice? Ici? Pas possible . . .*'

'You're not very convincing, are you?' Strait observed, unimpressed.

Thirty miles away, on the A30 near Blackwater, a shining black Daimler limousine, pride of Albert Merryman and Sons, Car Hire Limited ('*YOUR funeral, OUR speciality*'), was just drawing into a lay-by.

'About bloody time too,' Sir Wilf greeted the driver. 'When do you think we'll arrive in St Clare?'

'That depends,' said the driver.

'On what?'

'How long it takes.'

'Just as I feared,' Sir Wilf replied. 'Well, just put your foot down. They can't start that barbecue without us . . . '

It was a sultry, sticky night. The wind had dropped, and storm clouds were already gathering in the west and threatening to swallow up the last of the sun. But nobody was taking any notice. The bonfires were now alight. The evening air was heady with the aroma of freshly burnt sausages. And the valley echoed to the vibrant Latin American rhythms of Trio Los Bravos from Helston.

Over by the Addle bridge, the Reverend Owen Borage

235

and his fan club were staging a sit-down demonstration in the middle of the road. They were being entertained by Rachel Trefusis and her performing tortoises, and Nobby Visick, playing a medley of gypsy dances on his amazing Bavarian steam organ.

On the other side of the Fields, Ben Curnow was just tucking into a steaming hot pastie, when he thought he saw a vaguely familiar face in the crowd . . . Several familiar faces, in fact. French faces. And if he was not very much mistaken they belonged to the crew of the *Musetta*. And if he was not even more mistaken, the skipper himself was already busy chatting up Sally Tremayne.

Loyal Englishman that he was, and unable in all conscience to resist any opportunity to precipitate a speedy deterioration in Anglo-French relations, Ben decided to bring this to the immediate attention of Tom Hoskin.

Sally had had a miserable day so far. All her plans had come crashing down in ruins. She had no Lord Fred. She'd lost Tom. She'd lost Arthur. And Lucy had lost the crown and the one hundred pounds.

But every dark cloud (and there were plenty gathering above) had a silver lining. And out of the gloom and bonfire smoke, a tall, strong, handsome Breton sailor had suddenly appeared at her side.

'Our steerink af broke,' Ramon explained, pouring another half pint of five-star cognac into her beer glass. 'I could be maroon 'ere many nights.'

'Oh dear, that *es* bad luck,' said Sally enthusiatically. 'Perhaps we could go for a picnic one evenen . . . '

Over in West Meadows, the Pirana House hot-air balloon had been inflated at last and had just risen a hundred feet into the atmosphere with the hairy Bert in the wicker basket. Whilst down below, Ormskirk had requisitioned the public address system and was telling everyone how kind Pirana House had been to lay on all the free beer and pasties. Then the balloon came down again and Ormskirk said *he* wanted to go up next, with Lord Fred, for publicity photos. Hairy Bert said he couldn't because he was too heavy. Colonel Hermann also said that Ormskirk was too heavy . . . but went on to say that *he* was not too heavy — he was just the right weight, in fact — and *he* ought to go up next because he'd done this sort of thing in Vietnam and knew everything there was to know about it.

Ormskirk told Hermann H. Hermann to bugger off.

Bert said Ormskirk was *not* going up in the balloon, and that was final. So Ormskirk threatened him with the sack. So Bert said he was disclaiming all further responsibility for what happened and went off to get himself a hamburger. Ormskirk called him a cowardy custard and told Richie and Nige to send him and Lord Fred aloft immediately or else *they*'d get the sack.

So Richie sent them aloft and Nige went with them. And the press corps took lots of photos, and the television camera wasted lots of film, and the wind started blowing again from all directions . . . And carried the balloon straight into the outspread, waiting branches of a one-hundred-and-twenty-foot beech tree . . . Where the rigging got hopelessly entangled and they remained suspended, swinging gently in the wind. Ormskirk went white and Nige said cripes.

Down below, Colonel Hermann told everyone not to panic . . . He'd handled this kind of crisis millions of times before whilst parachuting into Cambodian rain forests. And he started to climb the tree.

Meantime, several public-spirited citizens hurried across the Fields to report the accident to PC Hawkins, who was sitting in his panda car, tucking into his third free Pirana House pastie. Springing to action, he immediately switched on his flashing blue light and radioed for the fire brigade.

Some miles away, in the general environs of Penzance, dozens of police officers were busy having the day off. Which left Detective Sergeant Pearce to make a critical decision all on his own.

To raid or not to raid, that was the problem. For every raid attracted publicity and warned other smugglers, and, more importantly, cost a fortune in petrol and overtime.

But Norman Strait of Her Majesty's Customs and Excise had no doubts. For the Honourable Miranda Jane Louise Jago had a long criminal record already. She had been convicted of reckless driving, dangerous driving, extremely dangerous driving, and lethal driving. And with a record like that, no woman could be trusted. Even on foot. At that very moment, Strait argued, she and persons unknown were probably stashing away staggering quantities of suspicious substances, into holes in the ground, holes in the wall, holes *any*where, before the law could descend on Tremorna Hall in strength.

Pearce was finally persuaded. Working on the pathetically daft assumption that Norman Strait knew what he was talking about, he decided to swoop at once, with his full operational strength of several officers.

At that very moment, two shining black limousines, packed with incredibly important people, were purring gracefully out of Penzance along the winding country road to St Clare.

Sharkley was having a horrendous time. Miranda had woken up at last, and finding the poor little fellow swathed in her thickest skiing sweaters and trying to thaw out in front of the electric fire, had leapt upon him without the slightest provocation and pitched him into her soft warm bed, moaning 'Baby, baby . . . ' and plunging her tongue down his earhole.

Sharkley was petrified. Despite his passionate lust for Miranda, he was not used to this barbaric sort of behaviour. Before his disastrous marriage to a respectable virgin of thirty-two, he'd been a paragon of moral probity. It had taken him at least three dates at the Solihull Essoldo even to get round to holding hands in the two-and-nines.

So now, with his genitals scarcely recovered from three hours of frostbite in the wine cellar, this sudden traumatic attack proved too much, and he felt himself shrivelling up like a dying slug.

Miranda tried every trick in the book . . . And many believe she wrote the book in the first place. But hard as she tried, she could not arouse the slightest twitch of tumescence.

And outside, it was getting ever warmer and stickier, like a tropical night before the monsoon.

Sally and Ramon were strolling arm in arm down Chapel Lane towards her cottage. Some fifty yards behind them, two figures were creeping along in the shadows of the hedgerow.

'The blackguard,' Tom hissed. 'The dirty foreign bastard. Arm en arm, in broad daylight!'

'Who es he?' whispered Arthur.

'The Frenchie who took Ben to court for tryen to ram un amidships out en the bay.'

'Never? The swine,' muttered Arthur. 'They'll go to court for anythen, those Frenchies.'

'Arm en arm . . . ' Tom shook his head, disgusted. 'And Kenwyn not nine months en ees grave.'

'Some folk have no shame,' said Arthur bitterly.

Ormskirk, Freddie and Nige were now marooned in their little basket, dangling ninety feet above the ground, with the rigging entangled in the branches of the beech, and the balloon, deflated, lying across the top of the tree like a heap of laundry that had been chucked out of a passing aeroplane.

Colonel Hermann, however, was climbing speedily to the rescue . . . to do *what* exactly, no one dared hazard a guess. But the question was immaterial, because he got to within ten feet of the basket and then chanced his weight on a bough that took exception to the liberty. And it abruptly cracked and gave way, and pitched him twenty feet back down the tree, sending a deluge of timber cascading onto the spectators below.

The shock waves of this travelled all the way up through the venerable beech and released some of the tangled rigging. Whereupon the basket plummeted some fifteen feet in a couple of seconds, before being arrested once more by another tangle in the branches above.

'Don't *do* that!' Ormskirk screamed, sick with terror. 'I've got a wife . . . children . . . heart condition . . . Don't even *move*!'

But Colonel Hermann couldn't move, even if he'd wished to. He too was now completely marooned, half way up the tree and clinging for dear life to a creaking bough.

Down on the ground, the hairy Bert was doing unhelpful things like sulking triumphantly and telling the BBC he'd said something like this would happen all along.

In the meantime, the fire engine had arrived from Penzance but could not get across the Addle bridge, which had now been blocked by the Reverend Owen Borage and his preservation front who were adamantly refusing to budge. PC Hawkins and Special Constable Dennis Nancarrow had hastened to the scene to prevent the leading fireman from tossing the vicar into the river.

'Damnee, Rev'ran, this es an emergency!' Percy exclaimed hotly. 'You can't sit en the way of the fire brigade! Thear's human life at risk!'

'Don't be dramatic,' said the vicar contemptuously.

'Are you goan to clear this bridge voluntarily? Or am I goan to have to shift ee be force?'

'I defy you to assault a holy man of God,' said the vicar. And, turning to the crowd of onlookers, he called, 'Send for the press. Send for the BBC.'

'Then if you won't move voluntarily I shall have to arrest the lot of you.'

'For what?'

'For not volunteering.'

'The Lord is watching,' the vicar warned him.

'I don't doubt He es,' conceded Percy. 'But He edden tryen to get across Addle bridge. So move or be moved.'

'We shall never surrender,' cried Constance Borage.

'Never!' cheered the others.

'Right an,' said Percy resolutely. 'Special Constable Nancarrow . . . whear's the panda to?'

'T'other side o' the bridge,' said Dennis.

'Right. Drive un ovver 'ere, my 'andsome.'

'I can't,' said Dennis. 'Thear's a fire engine en the way.'

'Well, damnee . . . ' Percy looked around despairingly. 'Commandeer transport en the name of the Queen.'

'Righto, Skip,' said Dennis, and lumbered off to collar Charlie Penrose, the fruit and veg merchant, and requisition his pick-up truck.

Following a highly enervating encounter with an overtaking fire appliance, hurtling through the narrow lanes at seventy miles per hour, a shining black Fujokawa limousine, pride of the Japanese motor industry, was purring gracefully in a ditch, surrounded by sweating, grunting minions.

'Well, push, you lazy blighters!' Sir Wilf bawled from the back seat. 'Put some *beef* into it!'

PC Hawkins seized the vicar by the feet, and Dennis Nancarrow took him by the armpits.

'Right an,' said Percy. 'Heave-ho. One . . . two . . . three . . . heeeeeeeave!'

And they swung the Reverend Owen Borage over the side of Charlie Penrose's pick-up truck and dumped him in the back, like a sack of potatoes.

'Lord forgive them,' the vicar intoned solemnly. 'For they know not what they do.'

His good wife Constance stood up and protested that she wanted to go wherever her husband was going. So Percy and Dennis obligingly helped her into the truck too. And then Nancy Curnow loyally vowed to go as well. As did the other six demonstrators sitting in the road. So they all got up and

241

climbed into the back of Charlie Penrose's truck. And Dennis drove them away, into the village and back out again, three miles down the road and almost into Mousehole . . . Where he helped them all to disembark.

'Now what?' the vicar demanded. 'Are you going to charge us, Special Constable Nancarrow?'

'Aw no, vicar,' said Dennis amicably. ' 'Twas only a few mile. Have this ride on the county police, with our compliments.'

So saying, he got back into the truck and returned to St Clare, leaving them all to find their own way back to the village on foot.

The fire engine had crossed the Addle bridge by this time and had driven over the Fields to West Meadows, where Ormskirk, Lord Fred and Nige were still swinging about in the breeze, some seventy-five feet above the ground. But the vehicle was too wide to get through the gateway into the meadows. So the firemen had to drive back across the Addle bridge, out onto the Land's End road, and down the bridle path, past Alf's stables, through her main paddock, across two of Tucker Rosewarne's fields, past Socrates the bull — who had never seen so much red in his life — and finally into West Meadows through a wider gateway.

One fireman now began climbing up the tree to rescue Colonel Hermann, whilst the turntable escape ladder was elevated towards the swaying basket.

But in the heat of the moment no one had seen fit to bother closing all the field gates behind the fire engine. And Socrates — whose quiet ruminations had been wonderfully diverted by the sight of this enormous red rag on wheels — thought that life looked much more fun next door; and one of Alf's more skittish yearlings decided he rather liked the look of the bridle path and the distant open spaces on West Headland.

The fireman who had climbed up the tree had now safely reached Colonel Hermann . . . but he could not get down again. Nor could he go up. Or sideways. Or anywhere. So there were now *two* men marooned half way up the beech tree.

Above them, another fireman was perched atop the escape ladder, trying to coax Ormskirk into forsaking the insecurity of his laundry basket for the greater insecurity of the ladder. But Ormskirk was not easily fooled, and he was adamantly refusing to budge.

Over in the adjacent field, a French mariner from the *Musetta* was trying to persuade Brenda Trevaskis to dance to the Bohemian gypsy music of Nobby Visick's amazing Bavarian steam organ. And using the only sign language in which she was fluent, Brenda was intimating — by belting him in the solar plexus — that she didn't wish to.

Seeing this, Ben Curnow — public-spirited citizen that he was — hastily intervened and used his best endeavours to make matters worse. Whereupon the other Breton mariners began to gather round, hurling abuse at Ben in French. To which Ben responded by hurling some of Arthur Pascoe's best pasties at them in English — which, given the tensile strength of Arthur's pastry, was no mean response.

A bystander immediately hurried off to find PC Hawkins or Special Constable Nancarrow, before serious violence could develop. But Percy was over by the Addle bridge, where Rachel Trefusis was in hysterics because her performing tortoises had escaped. And Dennis Nancarrow was speeding to the riding stables in the panda car with Alfreda Mitchell, in pursuit of her escaped yearling. At the junction with the Penzance-Land's End road, however, they were almost in terminal collision with three police cars and a Transit van, hurtling towards Tremorna Hall . . .

It had been one of the most harrowing hours of Sharkley's entire life, lying there engulfed and hopelessly outnumbered beneath the torridly passionate Miranda. But perseverance and determination had finally won the day, and the little chap had come good at last.

With a groan of relief, Miranda lay back as Sharkley slithered about on top of her, poised, like a sardine at the mouth of the Bosporus, to enter that vast mysterious darkness that he had been panting for for so long . . . When the door flew open and Detective Sergeant Pearce crashed headlong into the room, followed by Norman Strait and two uniformed PCs.

'Police!' screamed Pearce, waving his Barclaycard in lieu of more authentic bona fides. 'Nobody move!'

'Good God almighty!' said Strait. 'They're on the job!'

'In the middle of a raid?' said Pearce, aghast. 'Have they no respect for the law?'

'Are you Miranda Jane Louise Jago?' Strait demanded.

'No,' said Sharkley.

'Not you, tit-head,' snarled Pearce. 'Get him out.'

The two constables dragged Sharkley out of bed and down the stairs.

Another constable came into the room. 'No one else in the house, Sarge, except a young lady in grey upstairs. But she's acting stone deaf, dumb and blind.'

'Bring her down for questioning,' said Pearce.

'She won't take any notice of us, Sarge.'

'Then arrest her.'

'You can't arrest her,' said Miranda. 'She's a ghost.'

'I can arrest anyone I want,' retorted Pearce. 'No one is above the law!' He turned to the constable. 'If anyone pretends to be a ghost, don't be fooled. Arrest them immediately for being suspicious.'

'Right, Sarge.' The constable hurried back upstairs.

Detective Constable Tuckey rushed in.

'How many are you?' Pearce demanded.

'Just me, Sarge.'

'Then surround the house.'

'Right, Sarge.' And Tuckey ran back downstairs.

'Miranda Jane Louise Jago,' Strait said, incredibly seriously. 'I am ordering a search of these premises and everyone in them.'

'Oh, Christ, all right,' said Miranda, spreading her legs. 'Where's your warrant?'

'I don't need a warrant,' said Strait proudly. 'I'm a Customs and Excise officer. It's enough that I suspect you on suspicion of being suspected of possessing a suspicious substance.'

'I take it you'll come quietly,' said Pearce, looking her straight in the bosom.

'Chance would be a fine thing,' Miranda sighed.

Following a highly enervating encounter with two police cars and a Transit van, overtaking on a blind bend at breakneck speed with their eyes shut, two shining black limousines full of terribly important people were resting quietly in a ditch, with an elevated and commanding view of Tremorna Hall, the Fields, and the distant West Meadows. A delicious aroma of barbecued meat was drifting across the Addle valley.

' 'Struth, I'd sell my bloody wife for a hamburger right now,' grumbled Sir Wilf to Lady Macclesfield, as the first drops of rain splattered onto the windshield . . .

. . . And onto the stable roof, as Alfreda saddled up her grey stallion, Achilles, buttoned a waterproof cape around her shoulders, and cantered away up the bridle path to catch her escaped yearling.

Freddie had climbed out of the laundry basket by this time, and was back down on Mother Earth, where he was urgently telling Soozie Smiles of the BBC about his narrow escape from the jaws of death, and trying to persuade her to return to Tremorna Hall for an all-night in-depth interview in the privacy of his own four-poster.

Nige was also back on Mother Earth. But not Ormskirk, who was still in the basket and yet to be persuaded that stepping out of it was perfectly simple, straightforward, and as easy as falling off an eighty-foot ladder. One fireman was in the basket with him and another was standing on top of the ladder to assist. But nothing — not even the first drops of rain and rumbles of thunder — would induce him to move. Colonel Hermann, who was still stuck in the tree just below the basket, was bellowing all sorts of unhelpful advice, telling him not to worry . . . hundreds of guys fell eighty feet each day, and only *some* of them were completely killed.

Down below, large crowds of spectators had deserted the bonfires, their attention divided between the high drama in the beech tree and the ructions that were breaking out nearby on the Fields, where Ben Curnow was being set upon by the entire crew of the *Musetta*.

Seeing that this was four to one, Brenda Travaskis — still in her queenly dress of white satin and lace — promptly came to Ben's aid. This made it the equivalent of about four to half a dozen. But perceiving that their fellow villagers were outmanned, the brothers Frank and Barry Pengelly quickly weighed in to even up the numbers. Seeing that Brenda Trevaskis was involved in the action, the Penzance chapter of the Hell's Angels then pitched in on the side of the French. This brought a swift response from the Sam Trevaskis gang, who rushed to the defence of the St Clarians.

All of this was too much for Socrates the bull, who was a convivial and sociable sort of beast and wanted to join in the fun. So he wandered out of his field, and into West Meadows to see what all the commotion was about.

Half a mile away, in the peace and security of their own ditch, with an elevated and commanding view of the entire proceedings, two limousine loads of important people were giving their instructions to Sir Wilf's personal private secretary, who had agreed to proceed on foot to the nearest barbecue.

'And for President Toshimoto,' said Takeo Subishi, 'two cheeseburger, with no onion. French fries and green salad.'

'And make mine a double portion of chips,' Sir Wilf added. 'With lots of brown sauce . . .'

Tom Hoskin and Arthur Pascoe had now joined in the

ructions, which were spilling right down to the banks of the Addle and into the river itself. And they were quickly assisted by Dick Champion, Charlie Penrose, Caleb Trevaskis, and the three Rosewarne brothers . . . All of whom were abruptly set upon by a coachload of postgraduate engineering students from the Camborne School of Mines, a team of visiting Breton wrestlers, and the two off-duty trumpeters from the Royal Marines, Plymouth.

In the midst of it all, Special Constable Dennis Nancarrow was bawling into PC Hawkins' ear. 'Penzance says they can't send us no reinforcements, Percy! Every spare man has been sent on a drugs raid!'

'Tell 'em I got a riot goan on!' Percy screamed back. 'And it's getten out of all control!'

'Lend us five p. then,' yelled Dennis. 'I'm right out of change.'

'Dial 999, you daft bugger!' Percy shouted.

'Aw, ais. Righto,' said Dennis, trotting away to the phone box.

Nearby, Rachel Trefusis was rounding up a search party to hunt for her escaped tortoises, and a little girl was saying, 'Look, Mummy . . . nice moo-cow,' and patting Socrates affectionately in the eye.

At that point there was a vivid flash of lightning and a great crash of thunder. People began to run for their cars. And nice moo-cow Socrates thought this was all part of the fun, and to show that he was no spoilsport, obligingly lowered his horns and took off after them at ramming speed.

As soon as PC Hawkins saw this he whipped out his radio transceiver and yelled into it, 'This es Percy Hawkins at St Clare . . . Callen Mousehole! Porthcurno! Any bugger who's listenen! Thear's mass insurrection breaken out here, and Socrates the bull has juss got loose . . . '

The words *bull loose* spread like a forest fire through the crowds, and panic stricken people began to run in all directions. Socrates could hardly believe his luck.

All this was being observed with some bewilderment by His

Inscrutable Watchfulness, Akiro Toshimoto IV, from his elevated and commanding position on the roof of a shining black Fujokawa limousine.

'Mystery, Takeo-san,' he said to Subishi. 'Do Druids have to kill bull? Or does bull kill Druids?'

'Mystery,' agreed Subishi, thumbing through his *AA Guide to Cornwall*.

The two distinguished-looking Orientals, hiding on top of an expensive limousine concealed in a ditch on the Penzance road, were being observed from a window high up in the east wing of Tremorna Hall.

'My God,' muttered Strait. 'The Chinese connection . . .'

Ignoring a young lady in grey who passed him in the passageway outside, he ran all the way downstairs, shouting, 'The limo on the hill! Arrest those bloody Chinks for Christ's sake . . . !'

And a Transit van full of Detective Constable Tuckey hurtled out of the driveway.

Alfreda was thundering along the bridle path on her fleet-foot stallion, Achilles, in pursuit of her errant yearling, when a second flash of lightning arced across the darkening sky. And another clap of thunder crashed overhead, even louder than the first.

Achilles' eyes rolled fearfully in their sockets.

'Only a storm, you silly arse!' Alf shouted at him.

Which merely confirmed what Achilles had been suspecting all along. He immediately broke into a frenzied gallop, and with the next flash of lightning pinned back his ears and bolted away up the track to the wide open headland, out of all control . . .

The thunder and lightning had put a spring into Socrates' stride as well, and thousands were now fleeing for their lives in a state of accumulating terror.

From his vantage point, sixty feet up a beech tree in West Meadows, Colonel Hermann was bawling ineffectually at everyone below, telling them not to panic like soppy pansies. It was only a cattle stampede, and as soon as he was out of that goddam, fairy, faggot tree he'd get the situation under control in no time.

A few feet above him, the imminent prospect of being fried alive had finally induced Ormskirk to step out of the laundry basket. Which he did with all the elegance of an elephant on a high wire.

This left him standing on a narrow ledge on the outer perimeter of the basket, clinging for dear life to the rigging above, only inches from the outstretched arms of the fireman on the escape ladder.

The sudden displacement, however, of all that weight from the middle of the basket to the outer edge had upset the delicate balance of tangled ropes and branches above. And with much creaking and groaning, the venerable beech slowly yielded to the superior forces of gravity, freeing long coils of entangled rigging as it did so.

Ormskirk could see exactly what was going to happen next. The fabric of the balloon itself was impaled securely on the top of the tree, one hundred and twenty feet above the ground. And everything beneath it was now free to swing back to earth like a trapeze. And that was precisely what it did.

Hanging on to the rigging with white-tipped knuckles, and squealing like a sow in labour, Ormskirk plunged down towards the ground in a smooth and curiously graceful arc. The basket cleared *terra firma* by a few feet, at an air speed of twenty knots, and continued to swing back up into the air on the other side under its own tremendous momentum. In this curiously hypnotic fashion, Ormskirk went on swinging to and fro, screaming like Tarzan, for some considerable time.

Few were there to appreciate the spectacle, however. For there was total uproar on the Fields by this time, where hundreds were embroiled in the mass brawl on the banks of the Addle, and thousands more were fleeing for the shelter of their cars as the rainstorm broke. Socrates was charging madly through the terrified tumult, having the time of his life.

'Callen Mousehole! Callen Porthcurno!' Percy Hawkins screamed into his radio. 'Everyone's on the rampage 'ere! Men . . . cattle . . . tortoises . . .'

But at that moment there was a flicker of lightning and a deafening crash of thunder that shook the Addle valley from one end to the other. It brought everyone to a standstill. Then another brilliant flash of lightning lit up the whole West Headland . . . Where Achilles was galloping frenetically along the cliff path, out of all control, and Alfreda was clinging on like grim death. The terrified stallion now skidded to an abrupt halt and reared up in panic at the brilliance of the lightning.

Down on the Fields, thousands stared wide-eyed at the distant rider on the headland, silhouetted against the lightning, cape billowing out in the wind, as the horse reared high on his hind legs.

'The ghost of Matty Jago!' Ned Gummoe cried. 'The pellar prophesied!'

'Loord be praised . . .' gasped Dick Champion. 'The pellar's very words!'

'The wild beasts will rage,' the Reverend Micah Dredge recalled aloud, 'and the ghost of Matthew Jago shall be seen galloping across West Headland once again . . .'

Snug in her cottage, high on Blakey's Ridge, Granny Polkinghorne smiled modestly to herself and gazed down with quiet satisfaction upon West Meadows, where the mighty, sacrilegious Ormskirk was still swinging gently, like a huge pendulum, above the gaunt grey rocks of the Hag's Ring.

PART FIVE

JUNE

IT WAS a wet summer's day in the heart of Birmingham, and at the offices of the Department of Employment two former executives of Pirana House Investments plc were queueing up to sign on for their unemployment benefit.

'Here, listen to this,' said Sharkley, reading an advert in the *Birmingham Post*. *'Central heating company urgently requires agents for new franchise in Libya.'*

'Oh, go on,' Ormskirk pleaded. 'Lend us fifty p. for a doughnut.'

That very same summer rain was even then leaking through the skylight window in Penwith magistrates court, and dripping into a little puddle at the feet of Benjamin Michael Curnow, forty-one-year-old fisherman of St Clare, paddling in the dock in his Sunday best.

'Mr Curnow,' said Mrs Felicity Hope-Bolitho, JP, 'why, oh *why*, do you persist in bearing this irrational grudge against the French?'

Mr Nathan Gouldmann, defending, arose.

'With respect, your worship, I should like to call a totally independent, expert witness who will testify that my client was the innocent victim of an unprovoked attack by Breton mariners in possession of stolen pasties.'

'Very well, Mr Gouldmann,' sighed Mrs Hope-Bolitho. 'Call your independent expert.'

'I call Thomas Hoskin,' said Nathan Gouldmann.

'Your go, Tom!' said a voice in the corridor outside.

Not many streets away, in a quiet cobbled lane, the proprietor of Sindy's Boutique (mags, tapes, fun-wear and marital aids) was arguing with two highly dissatisfied customers.

'I've sold dozens of these and I haven't had one single complaint yet,' he grumbled, reassembling the same defective vibrator that he'd been trying to fob off on unsuspecting customers for the past six months. 'What's wrong with it?'

'It doesn't vibrate,' said Sally Tremayne, pushing her sunglasses further up the bridge of her nose.

'It af broke,' added Ramon.

'Well, it rumbles,' the proprietor said hopefully.

Six miles away, at Tremorna Hall, Freddie St Clare was in the library industriously writing '*GONE AWAY*' and '*NOT KNOWN HERE*' on all the brown envelopes that had arrived in the morning post, when the telephone rang and a vaguely familiar American voice asked for him by name.

'Never heard of the man,' said Freddie unhesitatingly. 'Does he owe you money?'

'This is Hermann H. Hermann of Des Moines, Iowa,' said the voice. 'I'm calling from America, concerning your estate — which I believe may still be up for sale.'

'A decision you'll never regret, my dear colonel,' said Freddie. 'My chauffeuse, Miranda, will meet you at Heathrow in the Alvis with her overnight bag . . .'

High up on Blakey's Ridge, Ned Gummoe sat puffing his pipe in Granny Polkinghorne's kitchen, reflecting on the great days of their youth.

'Ais, feast day juss edden like her was when us was young, ezzer now?' he croaked nostalgically.

'My dear life, no,' said Granny P., drafting that week's

press copy for her new '*Pellar's Prophecy*' column in *The Cornishman*. 'Us did knaw how to enjoy ourselves in they days, and no mistake.'

'Ais, us did that,' sighed Ned. 'Damnee, feast day was *fun* when us was childern . . . '

'*My Lord*,' the Reverend Owen Borage typed, addressing the Bishop of Truro with two fingers, '*You will be delighted to hear that my campaign against the rape of St Clare has been an unqualified success and that Pirana House Investments have withdrawn from all negotiations to purchase the Jago estate. I believe I can modestly claim to have saved this village from unthinkable depredations, and now I feel confident that we can look forward to a peaceful, never-changing future once more . . . *'

A very long way away, in Washington DC, a committee of highly distinguished officers of the United States Defence Intelligence Agency, weighed down with medals and dripping in scrambled egg, were in session on the second floor of the Pentagon, rearranging their golf schedules and listening to evidence for the proposed siting of new Pershing-14 intercontinental ballistic missiles, to be deployed in the United Kingdom.

'Cornwall,' explained Colonel Hermann H. Hermann 82nd Airborne Divn., ret'd), 'is a rugged, narrow leg of land, about eighty miles long on a clear day . . . '